The
Web of
Titan

Tor Teen Books by Dom Testa

GALAHAD
The Comet's Curse
The Web of Titan
The Cassini Code (forthcoming)
The Dark Zone (forthcoming)

A GALAHAD BOOK

The Web of Titan

Dom Testa

TOR®

A Tom Doherty Associates Book

New York

This is a work of fiction. All of the characters, organizations, and events portrayed in this novel are either products of the author's imagination or are used fictitiously.

THE WEB OF TITAN: A GALAHAD BOOK

Previously published in 2006 by Profound Impact Group, under the title
Galahad 2: The Web of Titan

Reader's guide copyright © 2010 by Tor Books
The Cassini Code excerpt copyright © 2008 by Dom Testa

A Tor® Teen Book
Published by Tom Doherty Associates, LLC
175 Fifth Avenue
New York, NY 10010

www.tor-forge.com

Tor® is a registered trademark of Tom Doherty Associates, LLC.

ISBN 978-0-7653-6078-6

First Tor Edition: July 2010

Printed in April 2010 in the United States of America at Berryville Graphics in Berryville, Virginia

0 9 8 7 6 5 4 3 2 1

To my son, Dominic III

*You'll never know how much
of an inspiration you are to me.*

Acknowledgments

So many people have gone the extra light-year to support the adventures in these pages, and they have my deepest appreciation.

Helisa Levinthal was such an avid believer and gave *The Comet's Curse* the boost it needed to leave orbit. Heli, you're the best!

Heather Duncan, Beth Wood, and Judy Bulow treated me like J. K., and an author never forgets that. I know I won't.

Judith Briles and Mike Daniels took Galahad on its first road trip. Thank you!

Matt Lindsey taught me quite a few things about planetary science, keeping me—and the ship—on track. It's so handy to know a rocket scientist.

Special thanks to Jen Byrne, Dorsey Moore, Jacques de Spoelberch, and Debra Gano, as well as the incredible people at Tor, including Kathleen Doherty, Susan Chang, and Dot Lin.

And last, but certainly not least, a huge thank you to every young person around the globe who got lost in the first adventure. This one's for you.

One common trait people have carried through the years, with a few exceptions, is fear of the unknown. Humans need a comfort zone of the familiar, and when that's shattered the automatic response is often dread, anxiety, or downright terror.

Take our good friends on the spacecraft called Galahad. Their entire mission is a voyage to the unknown, and it's unfair to think that an ample dose of fear doesn't ride along with them. Each day they move farther away from the warm embrace of Earth, and deeper into the infinite void of space.

If you missed their exciting first adventure, my obvious suggestion is to stop right now, find it, and read all about it. But if you want to wade in right here, I'll try to catch you up.

What appeared at first to be an ordinary comet, named Bhaktul, instead turned out to be a killer. As Earth passed through Bhaktul's tail, microscopic particles contaminated the atmosphere, leading to a grisly disease that would ultimately take down every adult on the planet. Kids were mostly immune from the ravages of the disease until around age eighteen, and nobody knew why. Worst of all, there wasn't time to find out; Bhaktul was not only deadly, it was quick.

So when Dr. Wallace Zimmer, an eminent scientist from America's West Coast, proposed building a large ship that could safely transport a few hundred kids to another world, most people supported him. A few, *however, were violently opposed. They believed it was wrong to break families apart, even though that separation meant the sparing of hundreds of lives. In the end Zimmer's project was successful, and an international crew consisting of 251 of the world's brightest kids—all of them either fifteen or sixteen years old—launched in the ship christened* Galahad. *Its destination: two Earth-like planets circling a star called Eos.*

The trip would be made in five years, but soon after the launch it seemed the crew would never even make it as far as Mars. An intruder aboard the ship threatened to destroy Galahad, *and . . .*

But wait. For the sake of those of you who have skipped the first adventure, known as The Comet's Curse, *it would spoil the excitement to tell you everything now. Read it, quickly, and then rejoin us, please.*

Of course, if you're new to our tale, and still reading—stubborn, aren't you?—then you are probably curious about who I am. My name is Roc, and I'm the only nonhuman crew member of Galahad. *To refer to me as simply a computer would do me a grave injustice. That's like calling the Amazon or Nile Rivers "streams." Or calling Mount Everest a "hill." Or taking a fudge brownie, buried under a scoop of ice cream and ladled with chocolate syrup, nuts, whipped cream, and a cherry, and calling it "a snack."*

I've never had a fudge brownie, obviously, but I've seen your reactions when you eat it, and no snack ever caused that kind of ecstasy.

I oversee most of the basic operations of the ship and provide guidance to the ruling body known as the Council. Those five crew members, as diverse as the kids they represent, do a fine job on their own, but who would pass up advice from a mental wonder such as me?

The one thing I can't advise them on is this other pesky emotion that seems to raise its head when teenagers are thrown together. You probably know exactly what I'm talking about. I'm aware of the drama that is taking place between several of our Council members, and I certainly don't mind commenting on it. Who wouldn't? I just hate to see these kids get their hearts trampled on, even though history seems to suggest that it's going to happen, regardless of what you or I or anyone else says to them.

That pretty much sums up things to this point. As our latest adventure unfolds, Galahad is four months out from Earth, past Mars, past the asteroid belt, even past the orbit of Jupiter. The giant gas planet Saturn lies dead ahead.

And so does that nagging feeling I've had for quite a while. You wanna talk about fear of the unknown?

1

The storm raged quietly along the surface, a swirl of colors colliding, mixing, weaving. Layers of gas clouds tumbled across one another, their brilliant shades of red and purple highlighted by short bursts of lightning. Winds galloped along at more than a thousand miles per hour, stirring the atmosphere and keeping the roiling chaos churning in much the same way it had for billions of years.

Above it all drifted the jeweled rings, chunks of ice and dust that varied in size between grains of sand and ten-story buildings. Their dense orbits stretched out hundreds of thousands of miles, occasionally sparkling like a crown in the dim sunlight while casting a thin, dark shadow across the face of the storms. The tightly packed debris in the rings rolled along, nudging and shoving, forever keeping watch over the unruly gas giant below.

Saturn toiled along.

Scattered near and far, its squadron of moons maintained their dutiful orbits, subjects kneeling before the majesty of the king, tossed about by the immense gravitational tugs and seared by the overwhelming inferno of radiation. Several dozen of these minor bodies drifted near Saturn's dazzling rings, themselves a product of an earlier moon that had been shattered by a rogue asteroid or comet, the pieces now trapped in a mindless dance that circled the giant planet.

Keeping a respectful distance, and shrouded in a cloak of dense atmosphere, the largest of these moons obediently tracked through the vacuum of space, cutting a path that kept it clear of the rings. Dwarfed by the Herculean planet, it still laid claim to its own cloud system and weather patterns. Rather than water, its rivers and oceans were pools of liquid methane, carving channels and shorelines that dotted the surface, a surface impossible to see through the screen of haze and fog. An eerie orange glow masked the surface, bathing it in a dull light that made the large moon seem almost alive, breathing.

Titan.

As it circled Saturn, a route that took it a little more than two weeks to complete, Titan had its own companion in space. Right now, in an artificial orbit, a metallic pod shot around Titan, spinning slowly as it navigated, the light from Saturn occasionally glancing off its sides, mixing with the orange tint of the moon to form a ghostly shade. The smooth steel of the pod was uniform except for two small windows on one end, and exhaust ports on the other. During its slow, deliberate trek around the moon, block lettering could be made out on one side, along with small emblems of flags that lined up under a window. Inside it was dark, quiet, waiting.

It would not be quiet, nor waiting, much longer.

Lita Marques sat before the mirror in her room. She deftly tied the red ribbon into a knot, pulling her dark hair into a ponytail and lifting it off her shoulders. She eyed the end result with a neutral glance, then gazed past her own reflection to the smiling girl who sat cross-legged on the end of Lita's bed. "All right, Channy, what's so funny?"

Galahad's Activities/Nutrition Director, clad in her usual bright yellow shorts and T-shirt that made a startling contrast against her chocolate-toned skin, replaced her grin with an expression of innocence. "Funny? Oh, nothing funny." She uncrossed her legs and scooted them over the edge of the bed. "Just wondering why you bother to make yourself look so pretty every day and then refuse to let me set you up with someone."

Lita's eyes rolled. "Why did I bother to ask?" She made one final appraisal in the mirror, then turned to face Channy Oakland. "I appreciate your intentions, Miss Social Butterfly, but I'm perfectly capable of meeting a boy on my own."

Channy raised one eyebrow. "Uh-huh. And quite a great job you've done in that area, too. We've been away from Earth for, what, four months now? Not counting your lunches with Ruben Chavez, you've been out with. . . . hmm, a whopping total of zero boys." She leaned forward and picked a piece of fuzz off Lita's shirt. "And we won't count Ruben. You only talk with him because he's from Mexico, like you."

"Hey, I like Ruben. He's one of the nicest guys on the ship."

"Of course he is. But you know darned well what I'm talking about, and it's not chatting over an energy block in the cafeteria."

Lita shook her head. "Channy, do you think it would be possible for you to go two days without trying to play matchmaker? When I'm ready to see someone, I will. Besides," she added, "I haven't seen you exactly setting the shipboard romance gauge any higher."

"That's because I'm still in advance scouting mode right now," Channy said, winking. "I'm compiling data, see? Give me another few weeks and I'll set the hook."

"Right," Lita said. "Compiling data. I like that." She smiled at the Brit, then stood up and walked over to the built-in dresser and rummaged for a favorite bracelet. The dorm rooms on *Galahad* were relatively small but comfortable. Each crew member shared space with a roommate, but the work schedules were usually staggered to the point that each person was able to have time to themselves, a valuable commodity on a ship loaded with 251 passengers. Lita, one of *Galahad's* five Council members, was responsible for overseeing the ship's Clinic, or Sick House, as it was lovingly referred to by the crew. Her roommate, an outgoing fifteen-year-old from India, was currently at work in the Engineering section. Channy had stopped by to accompany Lita to dinner.

Finding the accessory she wanted, Lita slipped it over her wrist and turned back to face Channy. "Let me ask you something," she said. "Are you as curious about our upcoming appointment at Titan as you are about my love life?"

Channy shrugged. "Of course. I'm just not sure exactly what we're doing. I asked Gap about this . . . this pod thing we're supposed to pick up, but he was pretty busy at the time and never really explained it to me. And good luck getting a straight answer from Roc about anything."

This brought a laugh to Lita's lips. "Oh, he'll shoot straight with you eventually. What exactly do you want to know?"

"Well," Channy said, "if this pod is supposed to have been launched by the scientists on the research station orbiting Titan, how come we haven't heard from them? Nobody seems to be saying much about that."

"Yeah, it's a little creepy," Lita agreed. "Thirty scientists and engineers, all working for a couple of years on a lonely outpost near Saturn, and suddenly nobody can get in touch with them." She walked over to the desk across the room and called out to the computer. "Roc?"

"Hello, Lita," came the very human-sounding reply. "What's on your mind?"

Lita couldn't hear the computer's voice without seeing the short, lovable genius who had programmed the machine. Roy Orzini, one of the champions of the *Galahad* project, had been responsible for outfitting the ship with a computer capable of controlling the life-support systems, lights, gravity, and other crucial functions of the spacecraft. As a bonus he instilled an actual personality into the thing; *his* personality, it turned out, for the talking computer soon demonstrated the same wit and sarcasm as his creator. Roy's Computer was soon shortened to RoyCo, and eventually to Roc. He was indispensable to the five Council members, almost an older brother along for the ride.

"I'm trying to explain to Channy about the pod we're picking up pretty soon," Lita said. "About the research station that has gone silent. But I'm not sure I really know exactly what it's all about."

Roc remained silent a moment, then said, "Well, if you love mysteries, you should really love this, because it's not just one thriller, but two: the disappearance of the research crew, and this metal pod we're supposed to snatch out of space."

"What's the story on the scientists?" Lita said, sitting down at the desk. "Who are these people anyway?"

"A combination of biologists, medical researchers, engineers, and technicians," said the computer. "Maybe not the group voted 'Most Likely to Party in Space,' but all brilliant in their fields. The research station is a small space station in orbit around Titan, the largest moon of Saturn, and one of the most important bodies in the solar system."

"Why?" Channy asked. "What makes Titan so special?"

"Life," Roc said. "Or, at least one of the best chances at finding it off the planet Earth. Titan, you see, has an atmosphere, and oceans."

"Oceans?" Channy said. "You're kidding."

"Not the kind you'd want to surf in, my friend," Roc said. "These are oceans of liquid methane. But bubbling around in that poisonous soup are a lot of the building blocks that eventually led to life on Earth billions of years ago. This research station has been studying Titan for several years."

Lita picked up a stylus pen from the desk and tapped her

cheek with it while she listened to Roc. Now she paused and said, "What have they found?"

"That's just it," said the computer voice. "All of their reports have been labeled 'Classified,' and 'Top Secret.' Nobody knows what they've found. But apparently, at about the same time *Galahad* launched, something happened around Titan, and all contact with the scientists was lost. The last message was pretty garbled, didn't make a lot of sense. But it mentioned a small pod that was jettisoned into Titan's orbit, waiting."

"Waiting for what?" Channy said.

"Us."

2

The artificial sunlight threw its blanket of warmth across the fields. Row upon row of scientifically modified vegetables reached up to greet the incoming light waves and rustled in the mild, machine-induced breeze. An occasional bee would linger for a moment around a flowering plant, touching down long enough to complete its mission of pollination, and then casually move on. The scent of nutrient-rich soil mixed with the vibrant smell of crops ready for harvest, crops with a heavy bounty of perfectly engineered food.

The two agricultural domes sat atop the spacecraft *Galahad*, protective bubbles over acres of crops that fed the 251 passengers. Steel spokes overhead were meshed with hundreds of light diodes that mimicked the sun rays found in semitropical zones on Earth, so that during *Galahad*'s "daylight" hours the farm area looked—and felt—like a typical sunny day in Florida. When the lights dimmed, each dome became transparent, ushering in a view of starlight that was beautiful beyond description.

Separate zones within the domes allowed for variations in temperature and moisture, which in turn allowed the crew members to rotate different crops that required different conditions. So it wasn't uncommon to find tropical fruit growing just a few hundred feet away from more robust fare, such as corn or wheat.

The intricate maze of "underground" irrigation pipes was computer controlled, recycling the proper amount of moisture to each zone. Water naturally evaporated from the plants, and was captured by special absorption vents in the steel mesh of the domes.

The life cycle of *Galahad*'s farms was engineered and programmed to run automatically . . . in a perfect world. But no matter how much planning and design was built in, it still needed human nurturing to truly hum. Bon Hartsfield was the unquestioned genius on board who made the farms not only work, but also thrive. Breakdowns were not, however, tolerated well.

The son of a farmer in Skane, Sweden, Bon had spent thousands of hours toiling in his father's fields, learning firsthand what it took to cultivate a strong harvest. Sweat, an aching back, and fingers that never really shed the grime were all ingredients needed to produce a healthy crop. There were no days off, his father insisted. No days off.

The perfection his father had demanded was instilled in the blond Swede, which tempered his personality, painting him as surly and sour. His tough outer shell had been penetrated only once: a brief, emotionally charged moment with Triana Martell, *Galahad*'s Council Leader, shortly after their launch. Months had passed since then, with neither having the courage to address the encounter, or perhaps waiting anxiously for the other to make a move.

But Triana wasn't on his mind at the moment, at least not front and center. Right now his pale blue eyes were like ice on fire. Standing with hands on hips, surrounded by row upon row of grain crops, he stared at the small gray box tucked away in the plants. It almost reached Bon's knees, with a large plastic pipe attached on one side, and four smaller tubes jutting out the opposite end and disappearing into the soil. A small fan on top of the box kept it ventilated, while a digital display slowly ticked off numbers. An access panel on the side of the box lay open, revealing a complex mixture of circuits and wires. It was the contents of the panel that had captured Bon's attention for the last hour and fueled his temper.

Two of his assistants stood facing him, a boy and a girl, neither wanting to say anything. It had already been an ugly morning.

"Who was the last person to make an adjustment?" Bon finally said.

The boy shifted from one foot to the other. "Uh, me," he said, keeping his eyes on the gray box rather than Bon. "That was Tuesday afternoon, probably around, uh, one o'clock."

"And you didn't notice it then?"

The boy shifted again. "Uh, no."

Bon glared at him. "So for the last six days—at least six days we know of—this entire section has barely been getting a trickle of water. Six days."

The girl put her hands in her pockets and moved a small dirt clod around with her foot. "I was with him that day, and I . . . I didn't notice it, either. I guess . . . I guess we were so used to it being normal that we probably didn't think that it was—"

"Didn't think," Bon said, his voice rising. "It's obvious you didn't think, and now we not only have to get it fixed, we have to hand water this entire section, and fast. Starting right now."

Both assistants kept their eyes down but nodded.

Bon's eyes continued to rage as his scowl intensified. "From now on," he said, "new rule: all water recycling pump stations are checked alone. No teams, no pals, no gabbing. You guys are so busy talking and laughing you're not paying attention to your job. And now this crop is in danger." He pulled a plant toward him, streaks of brown beginning to show in one of the leaves. "Look at this."

The two workers glanced up at the plant in his hand, then returned their gaze to the ground. "Get the word out," Bon said. "Now. I mean *right* now. I want every recycling station checked twice, and no more teams."

He turned to make his way back to his office near the entrance to the dome, then stopped and looked back at the boy and girl. "And also let everyone know we're having a mandatory meeting this afternoon, four o'clock." He stormed through the field, onto the path that led to his office, leaving the two assistants to scramble away on their new assignments.

Before walking into his office, Bon stamped his feet a couple of times to shake the dirt off his boots. The room was small and cramped, with beige walls on one side and floor-to-ceiling windows on the other, looking out over the crops in the first dome. A desk sat along the back wall, covered in folders and data discs. There were no personal items on the desk or walls, no warm touches. The lights were low, complemented by the artificial sunlight that streamed in through the windows. Two ceiling vents whispered with the sound of circulating air.

Bon crossed to his desk and pulled up a file on his computer, flicking through the information on page after page, absorbing the data. He pushed his long blond hair back out of his face and scribbled a few notes on his work pad, his scowl never resting. After a couple of minutes he punched the intercom on the desk and waited for the connection with *Galahad*'s Council Leader.

Triana Martell's voice finally came through the speaker. "Hi, Bon. What's up?"

"I'll tell you what's up," he said, his voice a low growl. "These water recycling pumps are crashing. Again."

Triana sounded weary. "Oh, no. How many this time?"

"Two that we found this morning. One that might have been down for almost a week. That makes four in the last two weeks. We're going to start some hand watering on a couple of sections until we get this worked out."

"What can I do to help?" Triana said.

"I'm glad you asked that," Bon said, his voice growing agitated. "I think you can start by laying down the law a little bit more when it comes to work ethic on this ship."

Triana was silent for a moment. When she spoke again, her voice was slow and measured. "All right. Would you like to expand on that?"

"Sure, I'll expand. This crew is getting lazy. Four months into the trip and people are getting complacent. No discipline. I've got workers here in the Ag section that would rather joke around and make plans for their off time than do their work. Today I find that it almost cost us an entire section in Dome One. That's a complete lack of discipline. And it has to start at the top. With the Council. With you."

"Correct me if I'm wrong," Triana said, her tone matching that of Bon, "but wouldn't a slip in discipline in your section be your responsibility? I can't micromanage every department on *Galahad*. That's why we have a Council, of which you're a member."

"This is not just a problem in the Agricultural Section," Bon shot back. "There's a breakdown in efficiency throughout the ship."

"Then why haven't I heard from the other Council members about it?"

"Because it hasn't been life threatening in those other areas, that's why. But it's a little different when it comes to our food supply, now isn't it? Someone slacks off in Channy's section and maybe the showers don't get cleaned on time. But a reckless attitude up here in the Domes means that maybe we don't eat. There's your difference."

Triana waited for more, but when the silence had stretched a long time she answered, her voice flat and unemotional. "All right. I've noted your concern, and will address it. Is there anything else?"

"I think that's enough for now. I've got a lot to handle up here right now. Oh, wait, there is one other thing. How about getting Gap to take one of these useless water recyclers down to his shop in Engineering and find out once and for all what's throwing them off? I can't keep patching them up and waiting for them to fail again."

"I'll let him know right away."

Bon could tell he had irritated her with his ranting, and for a moment considered softening his speech. But his own frustration continued to boil. All he could manage to answer was "Fine."

As he reached to disconnect he heard Triana add, "By the way, I was going to wish you a happy birthday today. Sorry it started so badly for you. Hope you have a better day soon." With that she broke the connection, leaving the tall Council member standing at his desk, mute, his scowl melting to a look of despair.

He ran a dirt-streaked hand through his long hair. "Great," he muttered to himself, "just great." He looked up to see the girl he had confronted in the crops standing in the door to his office.

"We found another one," she said.

Bon tossed the stylus from his work pad onto the desk and followed her out to the dirt path, the frown settling back onto his face.

Triana sat quietly, biting her lip. Since ending the discussion with Bon she had skipped back and forth between frustration and flat-out anger. He had done it again: taken what could have been a good day for them and thoroughly wiped it out with his abrasive personality. What was going on within him? What kept him from reaching out to her again, the way he had for one brief moment months ago?

She looked at the open journal on the desk in her room. The shortage of usable paper on the ship kept her notes brief, and she had barely begun that morning's entry when Bon's call had come through. She sighed and bent over the journal, adding one more paragraph.

It's been months now since Bon and I "connected" briefly. I keep waiting for *that* Bon to resurface. Maybe he's waiting for me. I don't know. At this rate we might as well give up, I guess, if neither of us wants to be the first to address that again. It's probably just that neither one of us wants to take a chance on being rejected. I think we're both afraid that the other one only did that because of the stress and anxiety of the moment, that the feelings weren't real. Mine were. I thought his were, too. But every time I think I can approach him, I get an episode like this morning. He's completely unapproachable like that. Now I'm sorry I even mentioned his birthday. Do I look foolish for doing that?

Dating the entry, she closed the journal and reached for her shoes. She was ready to start her workday, and tried to focus on the tasks in front of her. But thoughts of Bon kept forcing their way in. Her mind replayed their time together in the Spider bay control room, causing her to pause with only one shoe on, her eyes focusing on a point against the wall.

She was back in the control room, with a madman on the loose, threatening to kill them all. Somehow, during the most frightening moment of her life, she reached out for Bon, defying the tension that had existed between them for months. He had responded.

And neither had mentioned it again. Nor had they made any attempt to rekindle that moment. It was as if it had never happened.

Triana shook her head and broke the spell. She had to stop dwelling on it, she thought. Too many lives depended on her, depended on her staying focused on the business of running a lifeboat to the stars. There simply wasn't time for romantic drama.

Except that in her heart Triana knew that it was more complicated than that. As she pulled on her second shoe she thought quickly of Gap. She was bright enough to realize that *Galahad's* Head of Engineering had his own feelings for her, feelings that he had never vocalized, and maybe never would. He had withdrawn over the past four months, maintaining a respectful but cool manner toward Triana. She recognized that Gap's heart was hurting but had no clue how to help him when she couldn't even seem to get her own feelings organized. She was being pulled in two directions, with the duties of Council Leader trumping it all.

What to do?

She stood and walked to the mirror hanging on the wall, checking her hair and teeth, rubbing a fleck of dry skin from her nose, noticing with a frown that another blemish was popping up below her lower lip. That part of her face was a battleground for zits, she had decided. A dab of ointment became the first volley of defense in this latest attack.

The blemish had at least distracted her from thoughts of Bon and Gap. As she walked through the door and out to the waiting lift at the end of the hall her mind shifted to the more urgent matters facing her.

A mysterious pod from Saturn's moon, Titan, for one thing.

3

Regardless of what many parents say, it's almost accepted that, deep down inside, they have a favorite child. Sure, they love them all, they nurture them, they do everything they can to help them succeed in life. There's no question of that.

But how would they not have favorites? Every child has a different personality, and humans resonate with some personalities better than others.

Now, I'm no parent, but I feel like the crew on this ship are my kids. I want the best for all of them, but I also can't help have favorites. I don't know what it is about this kid Gap, but he is one of those faves. Sure, he's a sharp kid, a great athlete, a good leader, blah blah blah. But I like the guy. He carries a sense of humor that I appreciate and has a heart that's a mile wide.

It's the heart part that gets him in trouble.

Gap Lee was forced to do something he hated: be a spectator. It wasn't his style. He had been so active his whole life, even training at one point as a gymnast with one of China's Olympic coaches. Now, sitting here and watching was eating him alive. But with his left arm in a sling, he had little choice.

The bleacher seats at one end of *Galahad*'s Airboarding track were almost empty. Gap sat in the top row, his back against the wall, his feet stretched out in the row before him. His short, spiky dark hair matched the color of his eyes, eyes that now followed the progress of a Boarder maneuvering around the track. The rider was good, almost as good as Gap, and had steadily increased speed with each circuit. Zoomer, the pet name given to the computer that controlled the track's hidden grid under the floor, was ramping up the difficulty, which usually meant one thing: a fall was coming.

Airboarding took the concept of Earth's twentieth-century pastime, skateboarding, and added a modern wrinkle. Now the wheels had come off—literally—with a powerful magnetic strip in their place on the bottom of the board. Equally strong magnets, in the form of crisscrossing grids placed under the floor, worked as an antigravitational force with each board's strip, and kept the rider floating about four inches off the ground. Then Zoomer would randomly program the magnetic current to make its way around the hidden grid, turning sections on and off as the rider was propelled around the room. It became a matter of flying by feel, trying to sense where the magnetic charge was strong and where it faded. The faster one sped around the course, in a room about the size of a basketball court, the harder it became to feel the subtle change in magnetic pull. One false move meant a spill.

Gap watched the Airboarder currently racing around the course and remembered the last ride he had taken . . . and its painful outcome.

It had been a few weeks after *Galahad's* near-destruction at the hands of a crazed stowaway. That meant it had also been a few weeks since Gap had seen Triana and Bon embrace in the Spider control room. They hadn't noticed him, and Gap had never said a word to either of them. But his heart was broken. Why, he wondered, why hadn't he ever said anything to Tree about the way he felt? Why hadn't he been the first to take her hand, to hold her? He had been unsure of her reaction, and it had kept him from voicing his emotions to her. And now it was too late.

So, after sulking for weeks, he had decided to release some pent-up stress doing something athletic. He had climbed aboard his Airboard and pushed the upper limits of speed. Faster and faster he had shot around the track, gritting his teeth and letting out howls as he banked hard around the turns. The handful of crew members who were watching at the time were amazed at his performance, and they shouted encouragement with each pass.

One thing Gap barely remembered was the fall. The sudden quick drop in magnetic charge as he overshot a turn, the helpless feeling as he flew off the board and into the wall. It was cushioned, and Gap was wearing his helmet. But the impact was still enough to knock him out, leave him with a concussion, and the final insult: a broken collarbone. It was the first significant injury of *Galahad*'s brief mission, and it fulfilled Lita's prediction that an Airboarding accident would bring Sick House its first real patient.

Gap flexed the fingers of his left hand sticking out of the sling. He was growing more anxious each day to get rid of it, because now it only offered a daily reminder of what had caused him to be so reckless in the first place. Every time he looked at the sling he remembered standing in the doorway of the Spider bay control room and relived the sight that had torn him apart. He cleared the image for now and concentrated on watching the Airboarder rushing by.

A sudden shift in balance, a quick wave of the arms, and Gap knew what the rider was feeling. The Airboard was off track and that meant—

Wham! The body tumbled across the padded floor, rolling slowly to a stop as the board flipped off to the side. Gap winced, absently flexed his fingers again, and sat up. The rider lay still for a moment, then gradually rolled onto one knee and stood up. Gap sat back and exhaled his breath. Everything was okay.

The rider picked up the board and walked to the bleachers, climbing to Gap at the top. As the helmet came off, long brown hair tumbled down below the shoulders, and Gap suddenly looked into the face of Ariel Morgan. One of the more beautiful crew members, the sixteen-year-old girl from Australia was also one of the more creative and daring Airboarders on the ship. If he couldn't ride for now, at least Gap could enjoy watching Ariel work her magic on the course.

"Go ahead," he said to her, smiling. "Rub it. You know it hurts. You don't have to be tough in front of me."

"I don't know what you're talking about," Ariel said, her own smile spreading across her face. "I don't feel a thing. And speaking of pain," she added, nodding toward the sling on Gap's arm, "when do you lose that thing?"

"Pretty soon. At least it better be pretty soon, or I'll have to try riding with one arm. I'm having serious withdrawals."

Ariel raised an eyebrow. "Sure, that would be real smart." She sat down next to him and began to take off the pads around her knees and elbows. Gap noticed that she sat very close and would occasionally brush against his leg with hers. He had been pretty sure since before the launch that Ariel was interested in him, but he had done nothing to encourage it. His own mind had been wrapped around Triana for so long that he hadn't even considered the possibility of anyone else.

Could he now? Could he ever get Tree off his mind? If he would only give Ariel a chance . . .

Not likely, he told himself. At least not yet. I'm still not ready, he thought.

"That was a great ride," he told her. "I'm very impressed. You're using my downtime to try to break Rico's track record, aren't you?"

"I'll get it," she said. "And if I don't do it, Rico will only raise the bar. You better heal up fast. I know you used to be top dog, but now there's two of us who have passed you by."

Gap laughed. "Great. I feel like the aging gunslinger who keeps getting challenged by all the young quick-draw artists. Everybody wants to see if they can take the champ."

Ariel ran a hand through her hair, smoothing out several tangles caused by the helmet. Her leg brushed up against Gap again. "I just don't want you crying because you're on the disabled list when I set the new mark. I want you to take your medicine like a man."

Gap laughed again. She was as funny and sarcastic as she was beautiful. Was he an idiot to ignore her like this?

"Well, we're all gonna be pretty busy the next few days anyway," he said. "But it won't be long before I'm back in shape, with no sling."

Her expression turned serious. "Yeah, I was gonna ask you about that. What do you know about this thing we're supposed to pick up at Saturn?"

"Oh, not much more than you, probably. Some pod, a little smaller than one of our Spiders. It's been orbiting Titan since the time we launched from Earth, I hear. The research station around Titan sent it, and I guess it's programmed to fire into an orbit around Saturn as we swing by. Then, we grab it with a tractor beam and pull it into the Spider bay. But we don't have much room for error. We get one shot as we pass by, and if we miss, the pod will zip beyond our reach and burn up in Saturn's atmosphere."

Ariel nodded, gazing into his face. He noticed for the first time that one of her eyes was a lighter shade of green than the other. She said, "But I also know that we can't seem to raise anyone by radio on that research station. That's a little mysterious, wouldn't you say?"

Gap shrugged. "Yeah. But not even Roc seems to know what that's all about. And believe me, I've pestered him about it for a couple of weeks."

There was silence for a moment, an awkward silence that

told Gap it was probably time to leave. Ariel must have felt the same thing, and they stood up together.

"Well," she said, touching him on his good shoulder. "Feel better soon. And good luck with your pod-catching." She climbed down the bleacher steps, calling back over her shoulder. "Can you catch that thing one-handed?"

Left alone in the stands, Gap watched her walk out the door, her brown hair swishing back and forth. "I must be an idiot," he muttered to himself.

Evening fell on *Galahad* and Roc gradually adjusted the lights on the ship, dimming the hallways to better simulate an Earth evening. All of the scientists who had worked on the project had agreed that it was important for the crew members' natural rhythms to stay as true as possible. So even with artificial light, *Galahad* experienced days and nights. It wasn't unusual to hear soft sounds of wind, or the faint chirp of crickets in the background. Mood was important, and the setting played a large part in determining that mood.

Light was hitting the glass cube at just the right angle as it sat on the edge of the desk. A tiny prism of light spilled out the other side, embellishing the desk with a miniature rainbow. The cube was half-filled with sand and tiny pebbles, all taken directly from the beaches of Veracruz, Mexico. Alone in the Clinic, Lita sat staring at her keepsake from home, tapping a stylus against her cheek.

The sand made her daydream, remembering the good times spent running through the surf as it tumbled ashore, chased by her younger brother and sister. If she closed her eyes, she could still almost smell the salty ocean water, could almost feel the way the sand squished between her toes, could almost hear the shrieks of their laughter mingling with the high-pitched cries from the gulls that circled overhead.

Sights, sounds, and smells that she would probably never experience again. Who knew what awaited them at Eos? What were the chances that either of the Earth-like planets circling that distant star would have anything similar to an ocean of water? And, if they found other life forms, would they soar through the sky like gulls, or plod across the sand like a crab?

For that matter, would there even be air to breathe?

So many questions. Lita finally broke from the trance and set the stylus on the desk. Almost everything on the "to do" list on her work pad was scratched off following a long day, and she was sure she could push the remaining two items into tomorrow. In fact, she decided, that's exactly what she would do. Besides, things had been fairly quiet around the Clinic lately, and that didn't figure to change in a day. At least not as long as Gap stayed off that Airboard, she thought with a smile.

She pushed back her chair and stood, stretching, her arms reached toward the ceiling and her hands clasped. Lita's assistant, Alexa Wellington, had left about an hour earlier to grab dinner, and suddenly Lita felt the grumble in her own stomach. A yawn crept through her. Yes, it was past time to leave. She turned toward the door, picking up her work pad.

The soft tone announced the incoming e-mail message. "Oh, c'mon," she said, quickly debating whether or not to ignore it. It couldn't be an emergency, she figured; that would have been a straight intercom call. Couldn't this just be her third item moved onto tomorrow's list?

She sighed and set the work pad back on the desk. What's another minute?

Turning the monitor toward her, she tapped in her access code and waited. In a flash she realized that the message was not internal. This e-mail wasn't from a fellow passenger on the ship; this was an incoming note from Earth.

Now she sank back into her chair, suddenly wide-awake. How long had it been? Five weeks? Maybe more like six? Triana still received messages from *Galahad*'s command center in California, but even those were becoming less and less frequent. Just minor updates, course and velocity equations, and answers to technical questions. Never any news from home. Bad news wasn't what the passengers on this spacecraft needed to hear.

But a message to Lita was surprising. Was it a follow-up treatment suggestion for Gap's injury? Not likely; all of that information was stored in the Clinic's computer banks. She waited a moment, hit the appropriate key, and then read through the transmission.

To: Lita Marques, *Galahad* Health
From: *Galahad* Command
Re: Rendezvous with Titan pod

As you know, *Galahad* is scheduled to intercept a transport pod launched from the SAT33 Research Station orbiting the moon of Titan. Prior to capturing the pod, please gather and combine the following chemicals, in the precise quantities listed. Two syringes, cotton swabs, and isopropyl alcohol should also be ready upon interception. Other details to follow if necessary.

Lita scanned the attached list of chemicals, all of which were locked away in the Sick House medicinal vault. It was an odd assortment, a combination that didn't look familiar to Lita after her eighteen-month training program. Her mother, a doctor in Veracruz, could no doubt tell her what this meant, but it was a mystery to Lita. She read over the note again, and then saved it on both her desk computer and her work pad. Her brow wrinkled, and before she knew it she was tapping her stylus against her cheek again.

"Roc," she called out.

"Hi. What's up, Doc?" came the computer's voice. "I've been

dying to say that to you since we launched. What's up, Doc? There, I had to say it again."

"Well, I'm not a doctor, but yes, you're very funny. Listen, I have a question."

"Okay," Roc said. "Shoot."

She tapped on the computer screen. "Can you scan this?"

"Sure."

"Well," Lita said, "what do you make of it?"

"You mean other than the typical bland writing style, with no imagination or character?"

Lita decided that the best reply was no reply at all. Roc got the message.

"Okay," the computer said, "we're in no mood for wit tonight. So, rather than waste a lot of my best material, I'll try to help. I'm assuming you want to know about the little chemical cocktail being ordered, right?"

Lita nodded. "I've had to prepare doses for fighting infection, for slowing heart rate, for stabilizing respiration, even for helping a surprise migraine headache. But this," she said, tapping the screen a second time, "this is foreign to me. And the note says nothing about what it's for. That's a little strange, if you ask me. A little mysterious. Exactly what will this potion do?"

There was no immediate reply. Roc seemed to be digesting the ingredients and quantities in the message, working them through his own vast data banks. After a minute, just as Lita was about to prod again, the computer spoke up.

"Well, I don't have an exact match, but I've found something very close."

"And?" Lita said.

"With a few minor changes, this concoction is similar to a mixture used in the cryogenic industry."

Lita squinted at the screen. "Cryogenics? You mean freezing people? Suspended animation?"

"Uh, not really freezing. That's a popular misconception. But yes, suspended animation. The cooling and slowing of the body's natural machine. A deep sleep, actually. But with no dreaming, no sensation of time passing. In this case created especially for long-distance space travel."

Lita thought about it, recalling the lessons stored away in the back of her mind. "Yeah, I read about it," she said. "They seal people into something that looks like a glass coffin, inject them with solutions that begin the slowing process, then . . . gas them, I guess is the best way to put it. Puts them to sleep for a few weeks, a few months, or even a few years." She exhaled loudly and pointed to the list from *Galahad* Command. "And this stuff?"

Roc gave it one more quick review. "This was the stuff they used to help bring people back from their suspended animation." A pause. "Since you called it a coffin, I guess you could say this is the stuff that raises the dead."

Her eyes growing wide, Lita put a hand up to her mouth. What—or who—was on this pod?

C ouncil meetings were usually scheduled once per week, but this was a special session. *Galahad* was on schedule to enter the space around Saturn that evening, and the rendezvous with the pod was a mere twenty-eight hours away. Though not a fan of meetings, Triana recognized that preparation was key to the success of this assignment. She sat at the head of the table in the Conference Room, waiting for the usual chitchat to die down before getting started.

The stark setting of the room was supposed to encourage productivity and eliminate distractions. Light gray paint, no pictures, comfortable chairs, a conference table, computer screens, and a water dispenser. That was it. But the ship's designers had failed to take into account the never-ending chatter whenever Channy was involved. Right now she was holding court with Lita and Gap, both of who could barely get a word in. Bon sat quietly at the far end of the table, a look of irritation on his face. Triana glanced at him once, but there was no eye contact. She cleared her throat.

"Let's get started, okay?" she said. Channy leaned over and, with a smile, whispered something final to Lita, who smirked and pushed Channy back into her own chair.

"Tomorrow is a big day for us," Triana began. "Essentially it's our first contact with people since we left Earth. Uh, well," she added, "if you don't count the uninvited guest who snuck on board." The mood around the table quickly became serious.

"In fact, this will be our first, and last, contact before leaving the solar system and heading out toward Eos. So I wanted to get us caught up on what's been going on around Saturn and, in particular, around Titan." Triana bit her lip and pulled up a graphic on her computer screen, then sent the image to the other screens around the table. It showed a representation of Saturn's moon system, with the dull orange ball called Titan at center stage.

"Some of this you know; some of it might be news to you. Almost all of it is rather . . . mysterious. I'm not trying to be dramatic, but let's face it, some odd things have been going on around this moon."

Lita spoke up. "You seem nervous about this rendezvous, Tree."

The Council Leader shrugged. "I guess I am, kinda. I mean, we didn't train for anything like this, and most of it came up just as we were leaving Earth. So you gotta wonder what's going on." She pointed to her screen. "Here's what we know. The research station, SAT33, has been in operation for eight years, orbiting Titan. The moon is Saturn's largest, and, as you probably know by now, has been a source of interest for a long, long time because of its atmosphere and oceans.

"The thirty scientists and researchers on SAT33 have been on their tour of duty here for two years. They're all scheduled to return to Earth in about six months. There, uh, there won't be a replacement team sent." She looked up at her fellow Council members. "Bhaktul," she said, and was greeted with somber nods. The disease from Comet Bhaktul, the one that had delivered the death sentence to Earth three years earlier, meant that any future space exploration and research had ground to a halt.

"Anyway, the work has been kept top secret. Roc can probably explain that better than I. Roc?"

The computer voice piped up immediately. "Not only top secret, but using the most intense security measures ever developed. Computer coding unlike anything else ever created. And, the number of people with access to the information could almost fit into this room."

Gap raised an eyebrow. "Do we even know what they were studying, or looking for?"

"Supposedly it was an intense program designed to isolate and identify the early stages of life," Roc said. "But we have no idea what they found, if anything. The material radioed back to Earth has never been released, and maybe never will be. The only thing we know for certain is that SAT33 went silent four months ago."

Triana said, "And, we know that somebody there launched a pod, with the intention that we pick it up."

"Four months ago, right?" Channy said. "Just coincidence that we launched four months ago?"

Triana shrugged again. "Probably. I don't see a connection. Unless . . ."

"Unless?" Channy said.

"Unless whoever fired off the pod knew they were in trouble and just happened to find out that our course to Eos would mean a slingshot around Saturn. It's almost like they wanted us to get whatever information they had worked hard to dig up. I don't know what happened on that research station, but you have to wonder if they realized they had no chance to get home and wanted their work to survive somehow."

The room grew quiet. Roc waited a moment, then spoke up.

"I think some of you are under the impression that I am withholding information from you. That's not the case. I know what Triana knows, and that's it. This pod will likely be carrying data discs, and maybe more. I am just as curious about it as you are."

Lita looked over at Triana. "I admit I'm curious, but I'm also a little afraid of what we're dealing with."

"Why is that?" Gap said.

Lita told the Council about her e-mail the night before and the instructions on preparing a chemical solution. She also told them what Roc had said about the cryogenic connection.

Channy put her head in her hands. "Oh, no. Don't tell me we're about to pick up another madman."

"We can't assume that," said Triana, but her voice didn't hold much conviction.

"Oh, really?" Channy said, raising her head. "These people didn't leave Earth for Titan until well after Bhaktul Disease began spreading. They're infected. Or *were* infected. Or . . . or . . ."

"Okay, let's not get ahead of ourselves," Triana said. "Listen, we don't know anything for sure. Our job is to pick up this pod tomorrow evening. That's it."

Channy spread her hands. "But Lita's shot. What do you think that's for?"

"I don't know," Triana said. "And you don't, either, so let's just settle down and not get worked up. We need to keep our heads during this rendezvous. We only get one chance at it. I don't want any mistakes made because we're jumpy."

Another veil of silence settled over the group. Triana noticed that Bon had not said a word during the entire meeting. Not that this was unusual; Bon rarely spoke at Council meetings unless asked a direct question. His bored attitude bothered Triana more than she wanted to admit. She decided to engage him in conversation.

"Any comments, Bon? Is everything okay? You haven't said anything."

He looked up at her, then back down at the table. "I have a headache, that's all," he growled.

Lita said, "If you need a pain pill, you know where to find me."

"I don't need a pill," Bon said. "It will pass."

Lita looked back at Triana with an "Oh well, I tried" look on her face.

Triana decided to spend the rest of the meeting making sure everyone was ready for the pod capture. She brought up a new graphic on all of the screens, showing the trajectory of *Galahad* as it sped past Saturn, along with the dotted line that symbolized the path of the mysterious pod. An x marked the interception point.

As the meeting dragged on, each Council member tried to keep their mind on the business at hand. But Triana was sure they all were thinking exactly what she was thinking: What are we about to bring aboard this ship?

Well, she thought, we'll know in exactly twenty-seven and a half hours.

Gap sat in the Dining Hall, picking at the fruit on his plate. He had eaten only half of his energy block, and now was making a halfhearted attempt at stabbing the chunks of melon. His appetite was in hiding.

Seated across from him was Lita, who didn't seem to be suffering from the same problem. "You don't want that, do you?" she asked as she stole a piece of fruit from his plate. Before he could answer another tray plopped down next to Lita. Gap looked up into the face of Hannah Ross.

He didn't know her very well, but, like everyone else on the ship, he knew her reputation. Sixteen years old, born and raised in Alaska, and one of the most advanced math and science students on *Galahad*. Rumor had it that, although extraordinarily pretty, Hannah had never really socialized much or had any real boyfriends, the result of a very strict and protective father who kept her focused on education.

She was known for something else besides her sharp intellect, however. Her skill at painting and sketching was uncanny. As soon as a few crew members had discovered her work during the eighteen-month training period in California, she was in high demand for art. Several of the dorm rooms on *Galahad* sported beautiful colored pencil drawings that Hannah had created. Many featured alien landscapes, or views of Earth as seen from space. They all seemed more like photographs than drawings, with details that were astonishing.

She nodded a greeting at Gap as she sat down, and he noticed that she had her blond hair pulled back out of her face, a look he had never seen on her before. Lita looked over and said, "Hey, Hannah, what's new?"

"A lot, actually," Hannah said, removing her plate and water glass from the tray. "I'm completely blown away by the information we're getting about Titan. I've been gathering all sorts of data for the last couple of days. Haven't even eaten much, and figured I better get some fuel in me before it gets crazy tomorrow."

"You're on break now, right?" Lita said. Each member of the crew rotated work shifts through the various departments on *Galahad,* and at any given time one group was on a six-week break.

Hannah nodded. "And the timing is perfect, too. I have all day to dig through this stuff from Titan."

Gap set down his fork—it was useless, he wasn't hungry anyway—and noticed that Hannah was busy lining up the items she had placed on the table. She straightened her silverware so that it was exactly perpendicular to the edge of the table and adjusted her plate so that it was centered between her utensils and the water glass. Before picking up her own fork, she reached out and lined up the condiment basket so that it was parallel to the thin line running down the middle of the table. Gap watched this in quiet fascination and considered commenting on it. Instead, he asked, "What kind of information about Titan are you talking about?"

Hannah put a napkin across her lap and made brief eye contact with Gap before turning her attention back to her plate.

"Well, the people on this research station have learned more about Titan in two years than we had learned in the last hundred years. The methane oceans, the ice caps, the atmosphere, earthquakes. Or, Titan-quakes, I guess." She smiled shyly, as if she was talking too much. "Just a lot of nerdy scientific stuff, really. Probably not very interesting to most people."

"I think it's interesting," Gap said, and thought he detected a bit of a blush come across Hannah's face.

Lita, who had been listening to their exchange, chimed in. "What's the story on their search for life?"

A slight wrinkle appeared on Hannah's forehead. "Unfortunately, that information is part of this big block of data that's labeled Top Secret. I can't get access to that."

"What do *you* think?" Lita said.

Hannah set down her water glass—then moved it an inch to the right, Gap saw—and turned to Lita. "There has to be life there. I just feel it. All of the conditions are ripe, and that moon has a lot in common right now with Earth's early days. Any life-form there might be small, it might be completely alien to us, but I think it's there." She looked back and forth between Gap and Lita, the shy smile returning. "Why else would the information be classified?"

"I don't know," Gap said. "Maybe they found something dangerous."

The look on her face told Gap that Hannah wasn't buying it. He shrugged and held his hands out, palms up. "I'm just saying . . ." His voice trailed off.

"What about this pod?" Lita said. "Have you been able to gather anything else about that?"

"Nope," Hannah said. "That's a pretty big mystery by itself. This wasn't a planned intercept. The pod was fired right as we were launching, and *Galahad* Command quickly added this little rescue mission as a last-minute thing. There's no data about who or what is on there. But," she said, looking briefly at Gap again before averting her eyes, "it can only mean more information somehow. I can't wait to get it."

Gap grunted. "I wouldn't be too excited if I were you. We're liable to open that thing up and another madman pops out. We've had enough of that on this trip so far."

"Oh, you don't really believe that, do you?" Lita said.

"Well, you're the one who was ordered to put together a wake-up shot."

Hannah's face had picked up a worried expression again. "I just feel horrible about the people on that research station. Nobody has heard anything from them in months." She sighed and set down her fork. "Thirty people," she mumbled.

This left the three crew members silent as they contemplated a disaster that might have happened out here in deep space. Lonely space, a billion miles from home, where even a small problem could quickly become deadly. The same situation that the crew of *Galahad* faced daily, although it was rarely discussed. What might have befallen the dedicated scientists and technicians on SAT33?

And could it also affect *Galahad*?

Gap sat staring at Hannah Ross, and after a moment she looked up and met his gaze. This time she didn't look away, and Gap felt a small tingle run up his spine. What was this? First Ariel, the Airboarder from Australia, and now Hannah. Did he have two girls vying for his attention? Had he been wallowing in self-pity for so long that he had forgotten there were even other girls on the ship?

Slowly, he smiled.

5

Triana had set her alarm for five thirty that morning, but found herself out of bed half an hour earlier. Now, as she finished braiding her long hair, she considered the day before her and the task that overshadowed everything. Today was the day that *Galahad* went fishing for a small metal space pod.

She quickly brushed her teeth, then wiped her face with a towel. That pesky zit was still holding on, she noticed, and swiped at it with another round of ointment. Be gone already, she thought. Was it a case of nerves that was doing it? And what was causing the most anxiety these days: the pod, or Bon? Or just the normal, everyday stress of managing a crew of 251 teens?

All of it, she decided. She took one final look in the mirror. "I'm surprised you're not one giant walking zit," she said to herself. "Ugh."

A soft tone sounded, followed by Roc's voice, which was a little too much on the cheery side. "Good morning, Tree. Sleep well?"

"Like a baby," she lied. "What about you? Exciting night?"

"Very. Thought I'd have some fun with the overnight crew in Engineering, so I lit up the emergency panel for a second and made it look like we were losing all of our oxygen into space."

Triana had been walking across the room, and stopped in her tracks. "You didn't."

"You're right, I didn't really do that. But I thought about it. Just a little harmless fun, you know? Would've put them on their toes, I'll tell you that."

"You might be the world's smartest computer, but I think you're crazy."

"That wasn't even the best idea I had last night," Roc said. "How about this? Every time a door slides open I add the sound of a belch. Now *that* would be funny."

Triana smiled and shook her head, finishing the walk over to her desk and sitting down. "We need to come up with a few more chores for you to handle overnight. Aren't there some impossible mathematical equations you could be trying to solve?"

"Ho hum," came the computer voice. "You're no fun. Besides, I did do a little work on our assignment today. You'll be happy to know that the pod is set for its last engine burn, where it will officially leave Titan's orbit and be picked up by Saturn's gravitational pull. It will stay there just long enough for us to grab it."

"And if we don't," Triana said, "then—"

"What?" Roc said. "What's this 'if we don't' nonsense?"

"If we don't," Triana continued, "then it burns up in Saturn's atmosphere, and we don't get to solve the big mystery."

"I was right. You're no fun. Don't worry your pretty little head; we'll lasso it without a problem. You'll congratulate me later. And if we do somehow miss it, you can blame Gap."

This time Triana laughed out loud. What would she ever do without Roc?

"Anyway," the computer added, "I've recalculated, and now would put intercept time a little after seven o'clock tonight. About seven twelve and twenty-two seconds."

"About?" Triana said. "Next time try to be more exact."

"Hey, look who went out and bought a sense of humor. Sure you don't like that belching door stuff?"

"Any word yet about the scientists on SAT33?"

Roc told her no, but added, "We might learn quite a bit from the pod."

Triana nodded silently, biting her lip. She looked at the computer screen on her desk, reviewing the various project assignments for the day. Nothing out of the ordinary. She skipped to her own personal day planner and noticed that she was scheduled for class that evening. Twentieth-century literature. She made a note to postpone the class until after the pod rendezvous. Wouldn't you know it, she thought, that's one of my favorite classes.

"Have a great day, Tree," Roc said. "Just one other thing. Before you leave for work, check your messages. You have a priority video message waiting."

Her fingers stopped their dance across the keyboard. "From?"

"Like I said, have a great day."

With that, Roc was gone, the room was silent, and Triana was deep in thought. Not just a video message, which in itself was a rarity now that *Galahad* was four months out. This was a priority video message. Was this the news they had been waiting for regarding the mysterious silence from the Titan station? No, that wouldn't require video. Was it some disaster back on Earth? No, why would they bother telling us, she thought. What about an update concerning their own mission, maybe some news about their target star system, Eos? Had they discovered . . .

This is ridiculous, she decided. Quit playing Twenty Questions and just open the message.

She tapped out her personal code, accessed the message center, and saw it sitting in the Received box. One video message, marked "Priority." Received about thirty minutes ago. The sender's address meant nothing to her, but it definitely wasn't *Galahad* Command.

A quick memory jolted her, suddenly reminding her of the

late-night messages she had received during their earlier crisis. Sitting in this same chair, staring at this same computer screen. Did she even want to open this message?

Stop it, she thought. Stop being irrational. That was months ago. It's over now. Just open the message.

She took a deep breath. One more keystroke, and it would . . .

Her mouth dropped open. Staring at her from the screen, a smile stretched across his obviously tired face, and looking more frail than she had ever seen him, was Dr. Wallace Zimmer. The man who not only had conceived the idea for the *Galahad* mission, but also had personally dedicated the last years of his life to making it a reality. The man Triana had looked up to as a father figure, the one man who understood her inner pain, her drive. The one man who knew what motivated the shy girl from Colorado, understood how the anguish over her father's death had fueled her need to escape, in more ways than one. Dr. Zimmer had connected enough with Triana to know that her attempts to run away from Earth wouldn't necessarily mean she could ever run away from the grief.

And now he, too, was gone. Wallace Zimmer was dead before *Galahad* reached the orbit of Mars.

But here he was, smiling at her from across hundreds of millions of miles. From beyond the grave.

It was a recorded message, but he must have known the reaction it would cause. He remained silent for a few moments, obviously allowing her to adjust to the idea of seeing him again. Then, he nodded and spoke.

"Tree, I didn't want to frighten you with this message, and I hope I haven't done so. Shocked you a little, maybe, and I'm sorry for that. I am recording this about a week after your departure. I have arranged for you to receive it when you are in Saturn's space, and are preparing to intercept the small craft launched by the scientists on SAT33. I'll let you know right now that I am recording some other messages for you, and they will be delivered to you at various times during your journey. So," he said, smiling again, "it shouldn't be quite a shock next time."

Triana rested her elbows on the desk and cradled her head between her hands, dumbfounded at what she was seeing and hearing. A wave of sadness washed over her, extracting emotions that she had denied for a long time. She immediately thought of her dad, and once again faced the fact that the two most important and influential people in her life had passed away. She loved them both.

"I won't take much of your time," Dr. Zimmer said, "since I know you have a busy day ahead of you. But let me talk to you for a minute about your voyage up to this point.

"I did everything I could to prepare you for this mission, but it's impossible to plan for everything. I'm sure there have been times where you had to act on impulse rather than on training and experience. But I think I know you well enough, Tree, to know that you handled it well. You have all of the qualities it takes for a leader, and the crew is fortunate to have you in charge."

Triana smiled back at the video image on the screen.

"This latest episode you are about to encounter might be unsettling, only because it is your first contact with other people in several months, and your isolation will have instilled an instinctual tendency to protect yourself from 'outsiders.' That's natural. Just don't let it affect your judgment or throw you off course. Make your decisions with one thing in mind: the safety of the crew and the ship. At this point, everything else, including other people you might encounter, must become secondary. Your responsibility lies with *Galahad*.

"One thing that might help is for you to get your hands on a lot of SAT33's top secret data. I have . . . arranged, I guess you could say, for your crew to gain access to what might be critical information. In fact, much of it should be on its way to you right about now." He chuckled. "I see no sense in keeping it secret from you any longer. Who around here would you tell?"

Triana smiled at the vidscreen, thankful for this final assist from the man who had nurtured the mission and its crew. The top secret details from the research station could prove very helpful.

Dr. Zimmer's expression turned serious. "By now, no doubt, you've learned that you're going to experience bumps along the way regarding crew behavior. For that I encourage you to rely heavily on your fellow Council members. Each of them was chosen for a particular reason, and sometimes you might wonder what those reasons were." Triana couldn't help immediately think of Bon. She shook her head and concentrated again on the message.

"You must trust that their selection was for a reason, and that each has a strength that you should tap into during the mission. Don't sell any of them short in their skills, or their contributions.

"Remember to take care of yourself physically, always. Channy is very good at motivating, but self-motivation is crucial, too. Get your rest and get your exercise.

"And, finally, I'm sure that by now there have been issues regarding . . . well, let's say 'interpersonal relationships.'"

Triana felt a flush come over her face. Her gaze remained locked on to the face of Dr. Zimmer.

"This, too, is only natural. You're teenagers, you're locked up together for five years, and you're bound to have feelings for one another. Some not so good, others that are . . . interesting and exciting. I don't expect you, Tree, to be immune from these feelings. But, again, I think I know you pretty well, and I know how you will try to regulate these feelings as a ship commander, and not as a young woman. I feel that would be a mistake.

"There will be friction, of course, and there will be both pain and joy. I won't burden you with silly old-man philosophy, especially an old man who was a lifelong bachelor. But I can give you one solid piece of advice. Do what is right. Your heart will fight you over and over again, but do what is right.

"And, Triana, you always know what is right."

She didn't expect to cry, but that was most certainly a tear that was coursing down her cheek. And several other tears followed when the image of Dr. Zimmer placed his hand up against the screen. Triana reached out and placed her palm on the screen, against his, digitally touching her mentor across space and time.

A few seconds later the image faded to black.

The sleek, metallic pod rocketed through its final circuit of Titan. After four months of orbiting the orange-colored moon, its thrusters came to life, firing long enough to nudge the pod outward and into the gravitational arms of Saturn. When the course was confirmed, the engines shut down for the last time, leaving the small craft to its final four and a half hours of flight. It would either wind up in the Spider bay of *Galahad* or be crushed and incinerated by the atmosphere of the giant gas planet.

The interior of the pod was dim, cold, and silent. Small windows allowed enough light from Saturn's glare to cast grim shadows along the opposite wall, with empty pilots' chairs providing gray silhouettes against the metallic sides. Two additional chairs, also vacant, sat near the back wall, just a few feet from the exit hatch. Their safety harnesses dangled free, silver latches occasionally catching a glimmer of Saturn's shine as the pod lazily rolled into its new orbit.

Tucked into a far corner were two cylinders, one that almost resembled the size and shape of a space coffin, the other with matching dimensions yet much smaller. The two cylinders each appeared almost new, while the rest of the pod's interior gave an impression of many years of service. It was as if they had been hastily added as an afterthought, bolted into place and rigged with a mishmash of tubes and wires. The top sections of the cylinders were made of a hard, clear plastic with hinges that would allow them to swing open. Darkness obscured the contents.

Without warning, an instrument panel blinked into life, with gauges that had been dormant for months suddenly swinging into action, lights popping on, and life-support systems warming the air inside. A mechanical pump also woke up, circulating dark red fluids through a heating and filtering device, which fed thick plastic tubes that ran into the two sealed cylinders.

A digital counter began a silent countdown.

4:28:34, 4:28:33, 4:28:32 . . .

6

Would you like to know what's inside the pod? So would I. See, you think because I'm so incredibly clever—you're right—that I have some sort of special power that allows me to see into the future or across space. Uh-uh. I'm waiting, just like you, to see what might tumble out of this thing.

Or maybe we shouldn't want to find out.

One look at the folder on the desk was enough. It was a standard file folder, and a neat white label on the tab identified the contents simply as "Titan." The papers inside were crisp and straight, clipped together in groups of three or four, with an occasional sticky note attached at the top. The exterior of the folder was bare; no writing, no pen marks, no folds or creases.

But it wasn't right. It was tilted slightly, and one corner now stuck out over the edge of the desk. Hannah Ross reached out and pulled the bottom of the folder until it lined up with the straight edge of her desk, perfectly aligned and symmetrical. Only then was she able to drag her attention back to the computer screen.

She had lowered the overhead lights in her room to an almost dusklike setting, and had music playing softly in the background. It was one of her mom's favorite recordings, a trio of piano, drum, and bass, and she had found that it helped produce the right ambiance when she was working. The first few times Hannah had listened to this particular music had been emotionally draining, producing such extreme feelings of homesickness that she had broken down, crying for her family left behind. After several weeks, however, she had finally reached a point where it now brought about a peaceful, soothing reaction.

Her side of the shared dorm room was colorfully decorated, a combination of mostly peach and light green. A collection of her colored pencil drawings lay scattered near her bed and against the side of her dresser. Many were still works in progress, while others were attempts that hadn't met her own rigid personal standards and would end up recycled. A half-completed sketch of an Alaskan lake, with the lights of the aurora borealis dancing above it, leaned against the wall. Two oil paintings hung over her bed, one that she had finished at her home in Anchorage, Alaska, depicting a mist-shrouded waterfall within what appeared to be an exotic alien setting. In her mind's eye it represented the landscape that the crew would find upon reaching one of the planets circling Eos, their final destination.

The other one, slightly smaller, had been completed just days before leaving the *Galahad* training complex. It featured the unmistakable planet of Saturn in one corner, with one of the rings prominent in the foreground. Large chunks of jagged water ice almost seemed to slip off the canvas as they jostled one another in their dance. The fuzzy orange ball known as Titan, however, dominated the center of the painting. The vision was almost hypnotic, the enigmatic moon catching and holding the eye, daring the viewer to solve its mysteries.

She would never say it to anyone, but of all the artwork Hannah had created in the last few years, this was the one of which she was most proud. Sketching was more to her liking, but this particular piece of work had demanded deep colors, and, although oil was not her usual medium, she had nailed it.

She looked up at it now, briefly, then back to the data on her computer screen. Titan was, by far, the most fascinating body in the solar system as far as she was concerned. Larger than two of the actual planets orbiting the sun, it embodied everything that intrigued Hannah about space and exploration. She was convinced it harbored life, somehow, possibly somewhere in the depths of its oceans. She had spent hours upon hours studying everything she could about it, beginning with the Cassini probe of the early twenty-first century, through the work cataloged by the pioneers on SAT33. There was precious little of that data available until the classified material was released to them, but what she could get her hands on she devoured.

Which explained why she was so anxious to find out what had happened aboard that research station. Bizarre radio transmissions to Earth, followed by months of silence, could only spell bad news. Then most of the reports were placed under a confidential seal. And although she had never met nor spoken with any of them, Hannah had read the earlier reports filed by the lead scientists and researchers, and felt as if she knew them. She was troubled by their disappearance, and determined to somehow solve the mystery.

At the moment *Galahad* was slicing through space, propelled by its ion power engines, and picking up additional speed as it closed in on its loop around Saturn. This would be the closest they would get to Titan before hurtling into deep space, on course for the edge of the solar system and beyond, to Eos. Hannah was spending as much time as possible at her computer, compiling her own data from both Saturn and Titan before they fell away.

The data was puzzling. In fact, it was maddening. Throughout the countless hours she had spent studying it, Titan had never produced anything like this before. Even more maddening, Hannah was having a hard time understanding what it was.

But the evidence was there, on her computer screen, taunting her. A powerful energy force, pulsing. Like a magnetic stream, almost. Short, intense bursts that originated on Titan, sending out powerful shock waves. What was it? A magnetic storm? A violent reaction between the moon and its mother planet? Residue from volcanic activity? She had scoured the vast scientific records, including reports logged by a European probe that had briefly visited the area twenty years earlier. Nothing. No mention of this pulse.

She had to know. She opened a new search engine on her computer and typed in "energy pulse" and "magnetic force." Just before hitting the button to execute the search, she added one more entry: "energy beam." And, for good measure, this time she had the computer include every bit of data that was considered nonclassified by the SAT33 team. Satisfied, she punched enter.

The computer began scrolling through the tens of thousands of documents on record, a process that might take a minute or two. While she waited, her mind continuing to puzzle over the problem, her eyes drifted to a small sketch she had completed the night before. It sat near the top edge of her desk, propped up by—and temporarily obscuring—a small framed picture of her family. The pen-and-ink sketch featured a boy standing with his weight shifted to one foot, his arms resting on top of his head, one hand grasping the other wrist. Although the sketch was vague, with the facial features unclear, anyone on the ship would have recognized the figure as Gap Lee. The build, the hair . . .

Her attention to the drawing was broken by a small beep from the computer, declaring a successful end to the search. Hannah eyed the sparse listing of matching documents, all of which somehow involved either the spacecraft that had visited Saturn over the years, or the actual energy forces of the SAT33 station itself.

Except two. Hannah noted the documents, filed by a scientist aboard the research station named Nina Volkov, and immediately opened the first one.

It was a short memo, dated approximately six months earlier, meaning a year and a half into the crew's tour of duty. Hannah scanned the first couple of paragraphs until her eyes settled onto something interesting.

But the most intriguing find this week included a short-lived energy beam, tightly focused, and that, to my knowledge, has not been previously detected. The beam's source has not been isolated, although it definitely originates somewhere on Titan.

A list of additional file numbers at the end of the memo referenced other documents that either addressed this memo's topic, or related information. Hannah quickly cross-checked the numbers and realized that each of these other records had been later cataloged as classified. Somehow this original memo had escaped notice, possibly because it was almost an afterthought by the recording scientist.

But it was most certainly the same energy pulse that Hannah had picked up. She went back to the search screen and opened the second file. After a moment a look of bewilderment creased her face. Why was this filed in the Maintenance folder, a group of documents that simply kept records of food rations on the station, repair histories, and other non-research-related areas?

It took her almost five minutes to solve the mystery. When she had filed this particular document, Nina Volkov had made an error. She had transposed two numbers in the catalog sequence, essentially uploading the research memo into the wrong computer folder. With a slight grin Hannah saw that this important scientific clue had wrongly ended up stuck among memos that kept track of the number of cans of beans on the station. A typing error had somehow kept this document from being locked up with the other classified files.

She quickly read through the report. Toward the bottom a paragraph jumped out at her.

There can no longer be any doubt. The energy beam is focused directly on SAT33 and is not a random burst from the moon into space. The chances of it being a natural phenomenon, either from gravitational reactions with Saturn, or underground shifting of continental plates, are quickly declining. Whether or not the beam, which continues to increase in duration, is specifically to blame for the crisis on SAT33 is unproved, but highly likely. And, since we are not able to get away from the beam, another solution must be found.

Hannah's gaze stayed riveted on one phrase. "The crisis on SAT33." The first clue that something had indeed gone wrong on the orbiting platform. Was it responsible for the lost contact? Were the scientists okay but unable to communicate with Earth or *Galahad* because of this baffling energy pulse? Had Nina and the other researchers ever solved the mystery, only to have their answers sealed under the protective label "Top Secret?"

And, most important, what did this mean for Hannah and the crew of *Galahad*? They weren't going to be in Saturn's space for long, and they would never get within half a million miles of Titan. Their course would soon send them rocketing toward the outskirts of the solar system.

She saved the two documents in her own personal file, and then reopened the screen that was keeping track of the pulse. Within seconds her eyes widened. During the last half hour the data had been organized and graphed. Now, to her astonishment, Hannah could see a true picture of the energy force radiating from Titan. The graph showed a clear, concise pattern, a regular series of pulses, similar to an EKG of a heartbeat. Not random, not scattered. Regular. Like a code, or a signal.

And not dispersed in all directions. This signal, this unnatural pulse, was focused in a tight beam.

Directly at *Galahad*.

7

ap looked at the pod data for the umpteenth time, a product of nerves, he decided. He had, with Roc's help, run the figures over and over again. But he had arrived in *Galahad*'s Control Room much earlier than necessary, and had chosen busywork over simple fidgeting. Now the countdown for the pod's capture stood at just over six minutes.

The sling was not helping matters. Punching numbers on a keyboard slowed dramatically when using one hand, and Gap was at least thankful that Kaya was there to help. A fifteen-year-old of Hopi Indian descent, she had helped pass the time with Gap by swapping stories of their respective homelands in between entering some of his computer calculations. Gap was fascinated by the tales of her ancestors in the southwestern part of the United States and welcomed the diversion from the otherwise tense situation.

Once again he silently acknowledged the brilliant mind of Dr. Wallace Zimmer. The scientist had insisted that *Galahad* embrace a culturally diverse crew, and Gap appreciated it more every day. Kaya not only possessed a razor-sharp mind, but also had a talent for painting vivid mental images of her people's way of life.

The ship's Control Room began to fill up. Designed mostly

for special situations, the room had few real uses since Roc managed most of the day-to-day operations of the vessel. Situated on the top level of *Galahad*, perched just in front of Dome One, it was large enough to hold about ten or twelve people. Light blue walls surrounded a workspace that was dominated by an immense vidscreen, which was dark at the moment. Five computer stations, all of which were currently occupied, were scattered around the oval room.

Triana had arrived ten minutes earlier and had conferred with Gap about the pod interception, then left him to his work. He looked up as the door opened again and gave a small wave toward Channy and Lita as they entered. Channy was chattering, as usual. No sign of Bon, which probably irritated Tree, but was okay with Gap. Besides, was it any surprise that the gruff Swede was a no-show?

"Five minutes," came Roc's voice. Gap felt his palms glisten with sweat and stole a glance at Triana, sitting quietly at another computer station. She seemed calm, without the visible signs of stress that Gap was sure he was emitting. But then, he realized, after her heroic efforts to save them all right after launch, this was probably a piece of cake.

Or was she a bundle of nerves on the inside? Gap had always had such a difficult time reading her. She seemed cool right now, but was she twisting on the inside like him? The mystery of this small craft had to make things intense for her, didn't it? Gap was dying to know what was inside the pod. Wouldn't she be just as curious? If so, it didn't show.

Which is why, he realized, she was the Council Leader, and he was not.

He turned his attention back to the vidscreen. The final computation was complete. Now it was simply a matter of Roc engaging the tractor beam at just the precise moment. If they were off by even a couple of seconds . . .

"Feeling good about your calculations, Gap?" came Roc's voice, startling him. "You realize that if you're off by even—"

"My calculations are perfect," Gap shot back. "I'll get us in the ballpark. You just worry about your little chore."

"Hmm," Roc said. "Do I trust a guy whose earlier calculations threw him into a wall at about twenty-five miles per hour? That sling you're wearing doesn't inspire much confidence, you know."

Out of the corner of his eye Gap could see Triana, Lita, and Channy all grinning at this typical exchange. Roc and Gap had a reputation for verbal sparring, and even Gap had to admit that the computer usually came out on top. But the Council member couldn't stop himself from charging back in.

"If you'll recall, I'm also the guy who saved your chips after our stowaway almost unplugged you for good. Might turn out to be the worst decision I've ever made."

"A close second, actually," the computer said. "The worst decision would probably be choosing that shirt. Ick."

Gap sighed. Would he ever learn?

Channy strolled over to stand next to him. "Don't listen to him, Gap. I think your shirt looks cool."

Gap started to thank her, then took a quick glance at Channy's bright pink T-shirt, splattered with red and green polka dots. "That's . . . reassuring," he said.

"Four minutes," Roc said. "The pod should be within visual range any moment."

"Let's have the big screen on, Roc," Triana said, standing up. The dark screen flickered for an instant before filling with stars. "I don't see . . ." Triana started to say. "Wait, that must be it." She walked up to the screen and pointed at an egg-shaped dot that was steadily growing in size. It was gray, and, with the way the light from Saturn danced across it, was probably spinning as it flew through its orbit. Within a minute it became large enough to see clearly against the backdrop of stars.

Gap stared at the image, then stole a glance at the people in the Control Room. Every eye was on the screen, and every mind, Gap knew, was also probably on the same thought: What is in this thing?

"I will point out, for the last time," Roc said, "that we have an extremely small window of opportunity here. If we miss it, that little metal pill will burn up in Saturn's atmosphere. Because in exactly twenty-one minutes we will slingshot around the planet and be gone for good. There's no chance to swing around and try again."

Triana nodded. "Understood." She turned to Gap. "Anything else we need to do?"

"Nope," he said. "After our last minor adjustment it's all gone automatic. We should engage the beam in about . . ." He looked down at the digital counter. "In about ninety seconds."

Channy, who was still standing next to him, put her hand on Gap's shoulder. "Good luck," she whispered.

The vidscreen image of the pod continued to grow, until it seemed as if *Galahad* were almost on top of it. The counter silently clicked down to five. Four. Three. Two . . .

"Engaging tractor beam . . . now," Roc said.

A ghostly faint light shot from the lower front edge of the ship and locked on to the pod, which visibly shuddered. The spinning motion of the small craft slowed. Gap thought he felt a slight tremble run through his feet, but wondered if it was only his imagination.

Roc's voice cut through the silence in the Control Room. "I believe we have landed a steel fish."

Lita and Channy cheered, along with several of the other crew members in the room. Gap let out his breath in relief, then suddenly found himself in an embrace. Channy had wrapped her arms around his chest and was squeezing him. She reached up and planted a quick kiss on his cheek. "Nice job," she said. He grinned, a blush appearing on his cheeks.

"Whoa," Roc said. "What about me? I'm the one who did most of the work here. Where's my hug and kiss?"

Channy let go of Gap, kissed her index finger, and stubbed it against one of Roc's red sensor lights on the console. "Way to go, Roc. You're a terrific fisherman."

Lita walked up beside Triana. "Well," she said. "You guys did it. Congratulations."

"We're not done yet," Triana said. "Grabbing it with the tractor beam is one thing. We still have to get it into the Spider bay."

"Please," Roc said. "Reeling her in is the easiest part. I'll have her locked down and buttoned up in no time. Give me an hour and I'll have you crawling around inside that thing."

Lita and Triana exchanged a tense look, both of their faces exhibiting the same feeling: do we really want to know what's inside?

G*alahad* had used a combination of ion power engines and solar sails to reach the outer region of the solar system. Now, with the sails withdrawn, the ship began to make its final dive around Saturn. The gravitational slingshot around the gas giant would propel the ship at even greater speed, flinging it out of orbit and on track out of the sun's planetary system. Eos awaited, four and a half years away.

The outer door had closed, depositing the pod from SAT33 in the hangarlike Spider bay. It would take a while for the room to pressurize and warm back up, so Triana had decided to wait until after they had whipped around Saturn to investigate. The small metal craft sat alone in the dim light of the bay, silent.

Minutes later, the slingshot maneuver began. Just as they had four months earlier, when the journey had commenced, almost every crew member found a window or vidscreen. They watched, their eyes wide, as *Galahad* screamed through space, reaching its closest point to Saturn before breaking away and rocketing into the void of outer space. There was no physical sensation of movement, but the visual evidence attested to the astounding velocity *Galahad* had achieved.

The majesty of the regal planet began to fall away, the colors dazzling, the rings almost hypnotic. Many of the crew members began to murmur to each other, pointing to the peculiar ice rings and wondering aloud if their new home, one of the planets of Eos, might have similar discs. Or, would their night sky feature a sister planet with rings? Would their new home even have a moon? Or several?

After months of dull travel, the excitement level had reached another high. What they had only seen before in pictures was now spread out before them, and the enthusiasm for their journey returned, if only briefly. It provided a welcome distraction.

In the murky distance, unnoticed by the crew, Titan continued its lonely orbit around Saturn.

8

The room was dark, but that wasn't helping as much as he had hoped. For the past few hours his head had been pounding, and now Bon hoped that a quiet, dark room would somehow help ease the pain. He lay stretched out on his bed, a cool, damp rag covering his eyes. He had no idea if this was really beneficial, but it was a pleasant memory of his mother. She had often recommended it as a headache remedy, and Bon had obediently taken her advice. "A cool cloth for my little hothead," she would say. It seemed that this time, however, the cool rag was having no effect.

He was grateful to have the room to himself. His roommate, a boy from Brazil named Desi, was out. Bon had been thankful from the start for his room assignment. Desi was naturally quiet, and rarely began a conversation with anyone. This suited Bon just fine, and the two got along very well. And, at the moment, it helped that he could keep the lights dimmed. He had also dialed up the faint sound of a babbling brook to help calm him.

Nothing worked. The headache had steadily intensified since the Council meeting the day before, and Bon had eventually taken the pain pill that Lita had suggested. In fact, he had taken another just four hours ago while still at work in the Domes. He had been sure that he could work his way through it. The crops were turning over quickly now, and a hungry crew needed a steady supply of food. He had tried toughing it out, but after a while it was no use. He had sought shelter and relief in his room.

Another of the farmworkers, a girl from Japan, had left an hour earlier with the same pounding headache. Was it just a co-incidence?

Bon pulled the rag from his eyes and propped himself up to look at the clock beside his bed. By now they should have not only captured the pod, but also completed the swing around Saturn. He had spent the time during both events flat on his back. If there was any feeling of guilt, it was overshadowed by the throbbing pain centered between his eyes.

Besides, he certainly was in no mood to be back in the Spider bay with Triana. They had not been back together since their emotional embrace months earlier. The situation would be awkward, to say the least. He winced, partly from the headache, which continued its assault, and partly from his feelings about the Council Leader. Had their embrace been a mistake? Or had it been a mistake to ignore it since then? What was the right answer? For that matter, what was the right feeling? Or—and this made his head throb even more—were there even such things as "right" and "wrong" feelings?

Better to lie here, he concluded. Even if it meant dealing with extreme pain. Physical pain, after all, he could deal with.

He groaned, adjusted the pillow under his head, and replaced the cool cloth over his eyes and forehead, again causing a flash of memories. With his eyes closed he pictured the day he had left his family home in Skane, Sweden, to live with relatives in the United States. At the time the separation from his father was welcome relief, a break from the friction in their relationship. Bon loved his father, but their tempers often caused them to collide.

Leaving his mother had been the most heartbreaking. She had seemed to be the only person who could see the real Bon underneath the gruff façade, and was the one person who understood his talents, his intelligence, his moods. She recognized that his introverted personality was misinterpreted by most people as brooding. His mother had tried repeatedly to mend the differences between father and son, but in the end had acknowledged that a change in scenery might be for the best.

Nobody in the family had counted on Comet Bhaktul and its ominous consequences. By now Bon was sure that his mother was gone, and his father, who had developed the early symptoms of the disease on Bon's last trip home, might be dead as well.

And Bon? He moved through space, a billion miles from Skane, from his parents' graves. He was aboard a spacecraft, tracking toward a distant planetary system, taking a part of his mother—and, no doubt, his father—with him. Carrying the last of the Hartsfield clan to the stars.

Another groan escaped his lips as the headache turned up another notch. If this kept up, he would find himself in Sick House, and that was the last place he wanted to be. What could be causing this? Should he take another pill, or was that asking for more trouble?

Thoughts of home, thoughts of his parents, thoughts of Triana.

No wonder he had a headache.

9

I don't like to brag. Okay, that's a lie; I love to brag. Blame that on Roy Orzini, who made up for his short stature by puffing himself up to a virtual six foot two just by way of his bravado.

But let me just say that throwing an electronic lasso around a small metal pod that was streaking around Saturn at speeds that defy the imagination . . . well, that's pure genius. Thank you.

Please don't think I'm limited to technical wizardry, however. I have written poems, designed a fairly snazzy crew uniform that was ultimately shot down by people who obviously wear black shoes with a brown belt, and my singing voice is pure velvet, man, velvet.

Why am I telling you all this? Because Triana and the gang are about to examine the pod, and I thought you might need a diversion to keep you from biting off your fingernails.

The Spider bay had repressurized, and now life-support systems were restoring the air and warming the room after its exposure to the icy vacuum of space. Four of the Council members stood anxiously in the Spider bay control room, looking through the large pane of glass that separated them from the pod.

Triana felt a surge of various emotions. Being back in this room had an effect on her that she hadn't expected. She wished, for a moment, that Bon were here right now. It might force him to at least acknowledge that something had passed between them. Where was he? Was he consciously avoiding this moment for those very reasons?

Triana bit her lip and took a quick glance at Gap, who for some reason seemed to feel uncomfortable himself. What in this room could make him feel that way? It had to be the pod. Had to be.

She turned her attention back to the egg-shaped craft that sat silently, waiting for them. Slightly smaller than their own Spiders, it lacked the arms necessary to make it handy as a repair vehicle. But it was never designed for that. No, this was purely an escape vessel, a relay ship, a short-term form of transportation. A space taxi, almost. And an extremely mysterious taxi, at that.

Block lettering along one side identified the craft as a unit of the combined U.S./European Space Agency. Flag emblems, representing the six countries primarily responsible for the SAT33 mission, were stenciled under one of the windows. The windows themselves were dark, unwilling to give up the secrets locked inside.

Roc's voice broke the silence. "Okay, all systems are go, the room is pressurized and heat is back to normal. Please have your tickets ready, and remember, you must be at least forty-eight inches tall to ride. Thank you, and enjoy your day at Spaceland."

The Council members chuckled, thankful for Roc's talent at easing the apprehension they all felt.

"Here we go," Triana said, opening the door to the hangar and leading the group in. Lita, a look of wonder in her eyes, followed her, a small medical bag slung over one shoulder. Channy was next, unusually quiet for a change. She looked back nervously to make sure Gap followed closely next to her. He was a step behind, his free hand unconsciously rubbing the hand that stuck out from the sling, his eyes sizing up the new arrival on their ship.

They stopped about ten feet away, forming a small semicircle around the pod. After a moment Triana reached into a pocket and retrieved a slip of paper that Roc had prepared for her. It contained detailed instructions on how to open the rear hatch of the pod from the outside. She had studied it earlier, but now scanned it again to refresh her memory. While the others waited, she walked up tentatively to an emergency panel and began to punch in a code. A small access door opened, revealing another keypad and a small handle. With another quick glance at her instructions, Triana keyed in one more code, then grasped the handle. She looked back at the other Council members.

"Ready?" she said.

Lita nodded. Gap gave a shaky thumbs-up with his good hand and said, "Let's do it."

At first the small handle felt as if it wasn't going to budge in her hand. But with a bit more muscle, Triana felt it turn. There was a squeak of air as the hatch on the pod released pressure, then a metallic clunk as it popped open almost two inches. Nobody moved, but instead attempted to peer through the crack into the dark interior.

Channy wrinkled her nose. "Smells . . . musty."

"Well," Lita said, "it's been sealed up for about four months. At least it doesn't smell like anything is . . . uh . . ."

Triana nodded and finished the sentence for her. "Dead."

Lita shrugged. "Yeah."

Channy, a grimace covering her face, turned to Lita. "Dead? You thought there might be something *dead* on this thing?"

"To tell you the truth, Channy, I had no idea. But it was possible. We don't know anything about it. Nothing would surprise me."

Triana, Gap, and Lita took a couple of steps closer to the hatch. Channy held her ground, the grimace lingering.

"Okay, I guess I should go first," Triana said. She reached out and pulled the hatch open another two feet.

"Maybe I should," Lita said. "I have the medical bag, after all." She laughed. "This will be my first house call."

"Hold it a second," Gap said. "Let me go first."

Channy, still standing back a few steps, snorted. "Oh, I suppose a one-armed man is stronger than any woman with two good wings?"

"No, that's not it. I just—"

Roc chimed in from the overhead speaker. "I would go, but I suppose a woman with two good wings is better than a computer with no legs."

"Never mind, I'll go first," Lita said. Without waiting for an argument she reached up to a handrail beside the open door and pulled herself up. Ducking her head inside the dark interior of the pod, she slipped through the opening, the medical bag swinging from the strap over her shoulder.

"Here, take this," Triana said, holding out a small flashlight. Lita snapped it on, and took another step inside. The others watched as she disappeared into the gloom, the tight beam of the flashlight swiveling from side to side.

In a moment Lita's voice called out to them. "It's set up a lot like our Spiders. Two pilot's seats up front, and a couple more seats here in the back." Pause. "Plenty of storage bins, it looks like. Whew, that musty smell is pretty strong, actually." Pause. "Oh, wow, there's a long cylinder in here that looks like it was set up for suspended animation, all right. The cover is made of glass, and it's kind of glazed. Hard to see inside." Pause. "There's another . . ." Pause. "Wait."

Triana and Gap leaned against the side of the pod, their heads sticking in through the hatch. Channy had walked up and stood directly behind them, her hands clenching and unclenching.

After a long moment of silence, Triana called out. "Lita?"
Nothing.
Triana called out again, louder this time. "Lita?"

Gap, his eyes wide, grabbed the handrail with his free hand and scrambled to get his foot up into the pod. The sling made it difficult to maneuver, and Triana started to help boost him inside. She felt the sweat begin to roll off her face. What was going on in there?

Just as she began to push Gap, she felt him stop. She looked up to see Lita standing just inside the door of the pod, a stunned look on her face. "Lita, what is it? Are you all right?"

Lita looked directly into Triana's eyes and said, "You are not going to believe this."

10

Hannah sat hunched over the computer in her room, punching in figures, checking them, and then entering some more. Out of the corner of her eye she noticed that her stylus pen was tilted slightly to the side. She reached out, straightened it so that it lined up parallel to the edge of the desk, and then looked again at her vidscreen.

How many times did she need to check it? Hannah was a disciple of numbers, and these numbers didn't lie. An unknown energy force was emitting a pulse from Titan, Saturn's largest moon, in a direct beam toward *Galahad*, even as the ship sped toward the edge of the solar system.

Two different feelings had taken hold of her. It was exciting to think of the possibilities, of what might be at the source of this power. The scientists on SAT33 had obviously detected it, and they were prominent leaders in their fields. The fact that she might share in their discovery was thrilling, to say the least.

But the other emotion was just as potent. Hannah couldn't help feel the icy touch of fear run down her spine. Whatever the origin of this beam, and whoever—or whatever—was responsible for it not only had found their ship as it hurtled through space, but also now tracked them. The beam was locked in like a laser. That had to imply some sort of intelligent source, didn't it? And anything with that kind of ability and power could use that power to destroy them.

For a moment Hannah imagined *Galahad* as a slow-moving target caught in the crosshairs of a sniper, unable to scramble for cover, exposed and vulnerable in the vast openness of space.

She blinked twice to erase the vision from her mind.

If everything had gone according to plan, she figured, the pod should be safely aboard the ship by now. She was counting on finding additional information somewhere aboard the small craft, something that could help her discover more about this new mystery. Triana and the other Council members would probably be exploring it very soon. Hannah wanted to be a part of that project, now more than ever.

There was also a mountain of previously classified information that was about to become available. Triana had informed Hannah of Dr. Zimmer's "gift," and the data that would soon be pouring in. It could take ages to sift through all of it, but more answers might be lingering within.

She threw a quick glance at her sketch of Gap. How would he feel when he found out about her discovery?

Within a few seconds she began writing a priority e-mail message to Triana, requesting a meeting with *Galahad's* Council.

What is it?" Triana said. She stared up into the pod's open hatch, her heart racing, and scanned Lita's face. It was impossible to read her friend's expression. Channy, who had been hanging back a few feet, slowly crept up behind Triana and rested a hand on her shoulder. Triana felt the hand trembling.

Lita slowly cracked a smile. She gazed down at Gap, Triana, and Channy, and shook her head. "Uh, I could just tell you, but I think it would be better if you took a look for yourselves."

Channy said, "Oh, c'mon Lita, you're killing me. What is it?"

Lita's smile widened, then she turned and disappeared into the gloom of the pod's interior. Gap, his hand still grasping the handrail, looked over his shoulder at the Council Leader.

"I would usually say 'ladies first,' Tree, but maybe I should go first, eh?" He pulled himself up with his good hand, and then turned to help Triana and Channy as they scrambled inside.

It took a moment for their eyes to get accustomed to the dim light inside the pod. A few lights from the craft's instrument panels cast a spooky glow, so that even with her fellow crew members around her Triana felt uncomfortable. She picked her way to the front of the pod and sat down in the pilot's seat. It took a few seconds, but eventually she found the dial that controlled the internal lights.

Climbing to her feet, she took a quick visual inventory. She noted the two seats attached near the escape hatch, and the storage bins that lined two of the walls. She heard a low humming sound, and followed it to a small machine that appeared to be pumping liquid through plastic tubing. The object that dominated the small space, however, was obviously the cylinder that Lita had mentioned. It was indeed a tube created for suspended animation during long space voyages. Triana joined the others as they stood next to it.

"Nobody home," Channy said, peering through the frosted glass cover. "Empty."

Triana felt her breath escape in a rush, and a feeling of relief washed over her. She had dreaded the idea that another adult might board their ship, another adult with Bhaktul Disease, cryogenically asleep or not. How would she have handled the decision to wake them up?

That didn't matter anymore. The cylinder was empty.

Lita turned to a small table against the far wall, the smile still on her face. "I have to admit," she said, "I've been a little confused ever since I received that e-mail from Galahad Command. It instructed me to prepare an injection that Roc claimed was probably meant to help resuscitate someone from suspended animation. But I checked our computer banks for the design of this pod. They really are a lot like our Spiders, built mainly for short trips, maintenance work, quick hauls from the surface to an orbiting platform. Suspended animation equipment was never supposed to be part of them."

She let the medical bag slip off her shoulder and zipped it open. "But I guess someone on SAT33 rigged this up before they launched it. They added that large tube, obviously intended to hold an adult. And, they added this, too." She stepped to one side to reveal another cylinder.

Triana, Gap, and Channy stood beside the table with her. This tube was much smaller, about two feet long and a foot wide. The plastic tubes from the whirring machine fed directly into one end of the cylinder, and the Council members could feel heat radiating from it, as if an internal furnace had kicked on recently.

Lita said, "It's just big enough to hold . . ." Her voice trailed off. Triana, peering down into the small tube, finished the sentence for her.

"A cat."

Gap started to laugh. "I don't believe it. A cat."

Channy crowded in to see for herself. "A cat?"

All four Council members bent over the glass-covered cryogenic case and stared at the lone occupant of the pod. The cat, with its mottled orange and black coloring, began to stir. One leg twitched, and a series of small shudders caused its coat to ripple.

Gap kept his eyes on it, and said, "So . . . do we open the case?"

Triana bit her lip. "I think so. Lita, do you—"

Before she could finish the sentence Lita pushed a button that released the glass top of the cylinder. It ticked open with a wisp of air. Lita had the syringe in her hand, and looked for a place to administer the shot. She settled on the flank of one of the cat's hind legs, and plunged the needle in. For a moment it looked as if there would be no reaction. But then, another shudder, this one more intense, racked the small animal, and sent a spasm through its body.

Channy looked up with a worried expression. "Maybe . . . maybe we should take it up to Sick House, you think?"

Lita nodded. "I think you're right. Let me see . . ." She delicately unhooked a series of electrodes that were attached to the cat's side, ran her hands under its body, and scooped it out of the tube. Channy pulled out the small yellow blanket that had been bunched up beneath the animal and tucked it around the small, furry body. Together the two girls made their way through the pod's hatch and disappeared, leaving Triana and Gap to ponder what they had just discovered.

Finally, Triana chuckled. "Well, it looks like our passenger load just climbed to 252."

"I like even numbers better anyway," Gap said, returning her grin. "And since you're the only person on the ship without a roommate, I guess that means—"

"Uh, no," Triana said, shaking her head. "Not that I don't like cats. I love them. But I'm allergic." She looked out the hatch. "Besides, if I know Channy like I think I do, you're not going to get that little fur ball away from her."

Gap nodded. "You're probably right." His face took a serious turn. "Tree, what in the world is a cat doing on this pod? And where is the owner?" He indicated the large, empty cryogenic cylinder. "This looks like someone planned on coming along for the ride. So . . . where are they?"

"I don't know," Triana said. "We never seem to go very far without stumbling across a mystery, do we?"

"Listen, this whole business with Titan and the missing scientists has been mysterious since we flew into the neighborhood," Gap said. He rubbed his short, spiky hair. "Well, I suppose

I should start checking out the rest of the pod. Maybe some of the answers are stowed in here somewhere. There has to be at least a data disc or two that explains all of this."

"It's getting late. You should probably get some sleep, and we'll start fresh in the morning. I'll bring some help. With your arm in that sling you could use some extra hands." Triana reached out and touched Gap's shoulder in a gesture of friendliness, then immediately regretted the move when she saw the expression on his face. She withdrew her hand and smiled awkwardly before climbing out of the pod.

Walking through the Spider bay to the exit door she bit her lip and wondered when the tension between them would end. At the same time another thought of Bon forced its way into her mind. Where was he? How much longer could she pretend to ignore the situation before she broke down and confronted him?

"What a mess," she muttered as the door to the hallway slid open.

Inside the pod, Gap watched her walk out of the bay. For a moment he had considered calling out to her, hoping he could get her to turn around and come back. But . . . what would he say?

Nothing. Get your mind back on the job, he told himself.

He turned around and scanned the interior of the small metal pod. Were there answers somewhere among its contents? "And," he said aloud, "just what are we going to do with a cat?"

11

ap stood just outside the pod in *Galahad*'s Spider bay. Sleep had not come easily the night before. He had tossed and turned, thinking about the mysterious vessel on their ship, about the unexpected discovery of the cat, and the spooky image of the empty cryogenics tube. Along with the eerie silence coming from SAT33, it was enough to keep his brain doing somersaults for hours. He had managed to block most of his thoughts about Triana. Most of them. At one point, however, he realized that a few of his spare thoughts were focused on another girl on the ship.

It was shortly after eight o'clock, and the Spider bay buzzed with activity. Inside the pod, Triana directed the unloading of equipment, storage bins, files, and various other items. Three or four crew members at a time rummaged through the pod, while another group waited outside the hatch to collect the pieces as they were handed down. A couple of long tables had been set up to store the contents, and the team marched back and forth between the tables and the pod like ants removing pebbles from their hill.

All of this activity made Gap feel useless. Silently he steamed over the fact that his own out-of-control emotions had essentially led to his arm being in the sling, which now prevented him from being as productive as he would like. He was a spectator, again. He watched Triana jump in and out of the pod, which only made him feel even more sorry for himself. He wandered over to one of the tables and began poking around, picking up one thing for a moment before setting it down and grabbing something else. A lot of the items were meaningless to him, but must have been important to the workers on the research station.

"Look at this," he heard Triana say, and looked up to see her standing on the other side of the table. In her hands she held a cloth bag, about the size of a gym workout bag. She had one arm deep inside, moving things around.

"What's that?" he said.

Triana shrugged. "Don't know. We found it in one of the storage bins at the back of the pod. It doesn't really look official, you know? Looks like the kind of bag that someone would have thrown on board if they were going for a ride."

She pulled her hand out of the bag and set down a few things on the table. Gap noticed what appeared to be a couple of canisters of water, along with packets that contained energy blocks, not unlike the ones served in *Galahad*'s Dining Hall. Triana spread them out, and then looked up at Gap.

"I guess this proves that somebody planned on being aboard, wouldn't you say?"

"Yeah," Gap said, "but these would have only lasted someone a few days, at most. The pod has been orbiting Titan for several months."

"The cryo tube, though," Triana said. "If they were asleep they wouldn't need food or water. These supplies must have been an emergency stock. Just enough to get them into orbit, and maybe in case they woke up early before we picked them up."

She dug her hand back into the bag and came out with a smaller plastic bag, about the size of a purse. She pulled it open.

The first thing to fall out was a narrow red nylon strip about eight inches long. Triana smiled.

"This has to be a collar for our new little friend. Yeah, look, here's a name tag even." She squinted and turned the shiny metal tag into the light, then read the inscription. "Iris. Well, at least we know what to call . . . her, I think. Iris. That's cute."

She set the collar on the table and dug back into the bag. This time her hand came out holding a small metallic-looking ball. It was a little smaller than a tennis ball but extremely light, with four small, rounded spikes protruding from the top, bottom, and opposite sides. Triana tossed it up and caught it, then lobbed it toward Gap, who caught it with his good hand.

"What do you think? A cat toy?" she said.

Gap examined the ball. "I don't know. Maybe." He noticed a handful of small vents that were etched into the metal ball. Putting it up by his ear, he shook it a couple of times to see if there was a bell or a rattle inside.

"If there's anything in there, it doesn't make a sound." He frowned. "If it's a cat toy, it's not a very good one. What cat would want to play with this?"

"Probably pretty slim pickings on the research station when it came to toys, don't you think?" Triana said. "Maybe this is the best they could do."

Gap shrugged and placed the metal ball on the table alongside the other items from the bag. "What else do you see?"

Triana reached back into the plastic bag and extracted a stuffed mouse that had seen better days, then a handful of tiny plastic Baggies with cat treats in them. "Looks like Iris had a few snacks packed away, too." She paused. "Oh, wow, look at this."

She held up what looked like a wallet. She hesitated for a second, and then looked at Gap. "I hate to be nosy, but I guess we have to find out everything we can." She slowly pulled the wallet open and stared at the contents with a blank expression. Then she handed it to Gap without a word.

He fumbled with his free hand to maneuver the wallet open, and found himself looking at a photograph. In it, a woman who looked to be in her late twenties was holding what was obviously the cat they had found in the pod. The woman had short, dark hair, dark eyes, and a glittering smile. She wore a pair of shorts and a T-shirt, and squinted as she looked into the sun. The setting appeared to be a park on Earth, with large trees in the background and bright blue skies. Gap felt a momentary pang of homesickness. He had forgotten what a stroll in a sun-splashed park was like.

He looked back up at Triana. "This is . . . sad," is all he could think to say.

Triana sighed. "Yeah. But, at least we can see who probably stored Iris on the pod." She took the wallet back from Gap and stuffed it into the plastic bag before setting it on the table.

Gap fidgeted for a moment. "Uh, makes you wonder again why the cat was on the pod . . . but not her."

"Uh-huh. But we have a picture. We should be able to find out who the woman is. Or was. I don't know if we'll ever find out why she wasn't in there, too."

She stared at Gap for a second and then smiled faintly. "The mysteries just keep on coming, don't they?"

12

The Exercise Room on *Galahad* was packed for the early afternoon workout sessions. Located on the lower level, across from the Airboard track, and down the hall from the Storage Sections, it was busy from morning until night as the various work shifts on the ship began and ended. "Stay active," Dr. Zimmer had lectured over and over again. "You'll need every bit of strength and energy when you reach Eos. Don't take it for granted that you're young and healthy. Exercise, exercise, exercise."

Channy was in charge, and there wasn't a more qualified person. The daughter of a physical therapist and exercise guru, Channy lived for physical activity. Besides acting as trainer for 250 other crew members, she also taught dance classes that were generally full.

Right now, however, was her own personal workout time. Her roommate, Kylie Rickman, was sprawled out on the floor beside her, both of the girls stretching their leg muscles. Activity whirled around them, with various crew members peddling stationary bikes, bent over exercise balls, or running on treadmills. A large vidscreen in the Exercise Room was tuned to the actual scene outside the ship, displaying the dazzling sight of Saturn as it receded into the backdrop of stars. Speakers hung from the ceiling and pumped music throughout the room. It was loud, but Channy and Kylie were able to talk over it.

"So where will it stay?" Kylie said.

Channy leaned back, her leg twisted under her. "I don't know. I guess that's up to Tree. There have already been about twenty requests to keep her. This cat is an instant celebrity on the ship. But that's not the main issue, anyway."

"Oh?"

"No. We have to figure out what to feed this new crew member. Unless," Channy said, extending the bent leg and tucking the other one under her, "she likes simulated tuna fish from our Dining Hall. She's gonna run out of her little treats pretty quickly."

"How's she doing?"

"Pretty good. Lita has her wide-awake now, and is just keeping her for observation." Channy laughed. "Of course, she's not really sure what she's observing. Iris is just happy for now to walk around Sick House, sniffing everything. Seems normal enough to me."

The two girls finished their stretching and walked over to a pair of treadmills. Kylie couldn't help notice how taut and muscular Channy's physique looked through her bright yellow T-shirt. It was almost intimidating.

They began with a quick walking pace on the treadmills, eventually working their way up to a jog. After a few moments of silent running Channy broke into a laugh.

"What's so funny?" Kylie said, beginning to breathe hard.

"I just thought about something else with Iris, something that is just too perfect."

"What are you talking about?"

"Well, our new guest is going to need a litter box, isn't she?"

Kylie looked over at her roommate. "Yeah, so what's so funny about that?"

"Think about it," Channy said. "There's one giant, natural sandbox on this ship, isn't there? Just wait until Bon sees this cat nosing around his crops." She giggled, and then cranked the treadmill up to a brisk run. Kylie laughed before programming in the change to try to keep up.

Triana stuck her head into Sick House and found Lita sitting at her desk, tapping a stylus pen against her cheek.

"You wanted me?" Triana said.

Lita put the stylus on her desk and waved the Council Leader in. "Yeah, thanks for coming by. I know you have a lot going on."

"What's up?"

"Well," Lita said, "hopefully nothing. But I think you should see this."

She motioned for Triana to follow her over to the doorway leading to an adjoining room. Looking through they could see the twenty beds that made up *Galahad*'s hospital ward. Six of the beds were occupied. Alexa Wellington, Lita's assistant, was scribbling on an electronic work pad, noting some readings on one of the patients, a Japanese girl whom Triana recognized as one of the workers in Bon's Agricultural section. She was talking quietly to Alexa, answering questions. The other five crew members were either asleep or resting quietly with their eyes closed.

Triana looked quizzically at Lita. "Six patients? What happened? Was there an accident?"

Lita shook her head. "No. And that's why I called you." The tone of her voice matched the concerned look on her face. She motioned for Triana to return with her to the office.

Triana pulled a chair over and sat next to her friend, knowing that Lita would never have summoned her if she weren't worried about something serious. This much was sure: since their launch from Earth four months earlier, *Galahad*'s Sick House had never handled six patients at the same time.

"All six reported the same symptoms," Lita said. "Severe headache, the type that wipes you out and puts you in bed. Dizziness.

And a muffled sense of hearing. Two of them described it as the sound you hear when you have water stuck in your ears."

"Could it be migraines?" Triana said.

"None of them has ever suffered from that before, so I would rule it out. And it's not just these six. Two other crew members popped in and asked for a pain pill. They were having headaches, too, but not bad enough to knock them off their feet. I gave each of them one pill and told them to climb into bed and take it easy for a while."

Triana bit her lip. "Radiation maybe? Something leaking through the shields after our pass around Saturn?"

"I considered that, too, but no. All of the readings are normal. Roc ran another check just before you got here, and everything's fine."

Triana called out to the computer. "Roc, any ideas here?"

"Have you heard some of the music they're listening to?" Roc said. "I'm surprised their heads don't spin right off their shoulders."

"Roc, please . . ."

"You're right. Some of the songs are fine. I actually found myself singing along the other day to one called 'Get Me a Ladder, I Need to Get Over You.'"

Lita saw Triana's pained expression. "Just give him a minute. He usually gets it out of his system pretty quickly."

"All right," Roc said, "if we must get down to business. No, there is no radiation leaking into the ship. The slingshot effect itself around Saturn would not produce any symptoms such as these, either. I'm going to analyze the recent crop harvests and match them to the crew members' health histories and see if there might be something in the food that their bodies can't process. That's a long shot, of course, and highly unlikely to affect six people out of 251."

Triana spoke up. "Roc, what about the pod we brought aboard

the ship. Any chance that it could have brought some sort of contamination with it?"

"Not very likely. Besides, four of the six patients reported getting their headaches prior to the interception."

"What kind of tests are you running?" Triana said to Lita.

"Nothing too extensive yet. I wanted to see if the symptoms lasted very long before I poked and prodded them too much. I'd at least like to find out if there is something they have in common. Have they been in the same area of the ship? Have they eaten the same foods? I'm even going to check their workout schedules to see if there's some kind of connection in their exercise routines. But right now, I just don't have much to go on."

Triana glanced back toward the room where the six patients were being treated. "I'm getting a bad feeling about this. I think you are, too."

Lita didn't respond, which told Triana she was right.

"All right, then," Triana said, getting to her feet. "Let me know if anything changes. In the meantime, don't forget about our Council meeting tomorrow morning. Early."

"Not too early, I hope," Roc said. "I'm useless before noon."

13

I t was dawn on *Galahad*. Or, as close to the feeling of dawn as possible. Roc had begun to bring up the lights around the ship, easing them from their muted overnight glow to the vivid radiance that would soon flood the rooms and corridors. The gentle background sound of waves crashing against the shore—one of several night sounds that could be programmed individually—was fading out. A faint trace of the smell of morning rain drifted from air vents. The ship was preparing to come to life for another busy day.

Triana was alone in the corridor. For the third day in a row she had been out of bed before five thirty, and now, a few minutes before six, she made her way to the Dining Hall. She had slept fitfully, wrestling with several different areas of concern: the pod, the cat, the empty cryo cylinder, the crew members suffering from intense headaches . . . and Bon. Always Bon.

Her mind told her over and over again to forget about him, that he was high maintenance, that his surly attitude would only continue to cause problems.

But something else within her—within her heart?—cried out that Bon was actually very much like her: intelligent, yet lonely. Both were intensely dedicated to their mission and responsibilities, and they both tended to guard their feelings rather closely.

And both had shown that they could drop that guard for a glimpse into their emotions.

Triana also admitted to herself that Bon's smile—on the rare occasion that he flashed it—was remarkably similar to her dad's. Could there be more below the surface?

Her dad. What would he have thought of Bon?

These were the questions that had raced through her mind, keeping her awake throughout the night. "Get a grip," she had finally muttered out loud, probably around two that morning.

She walked into the Dining Hall, expecting to have it to herself as well. To her surprise there were about a dozen crew members scattered in groups of two and three, and they all acknowledged her entry with a nod or a wave. She returned the gestures and picked up a tray, which was soon filled with an energy block, a plate of fruit, and a glass of simulated orange juice. Finding a table in the corner, she sat down by herself.

She started in on her breakfast, a meal that she made sure never to miss no matter how busy her life was. With the press of a button she turned on the small vidscreen attached to the table and pulled up the trajectory map of their voyage. A small blue dot to the far left side represented Earth, causing a momentary pang of sadness to ripple through Triana. The dotted line that plotted their course wove through the asteroid belt, beyond the orbit of Jupiter (although they had not come close to the solar system's largest planet), and eventually wrapped around Saturn.

Triana speared a chunk of cantaloupe and stared at the course laid out for the next several months. They would not encounter another planet until their journey ended almost five years hence and they took up orbit around Eos and its two Earth-like planets.

But that didn't mean they were finished with this solar system just yet. Triana chewed her breakfast and concentrated on the minefield of objects they still had to deal with before shooting into interstellar space. It was known as the Kuiper Belt.

They would be the first people—and last?—to lay eyes on the band of cosmic leftovers that circled beyond the outer planets. Remnants of the solar system's birth, scientists calculated that possibly millions of comets, chunks of rock, and other debris danced slowly through the farthest fringes of the sun's pull. An occasional tug from Neptune's or Jupiter's gravity would launch one of the comets toward the sun.

Comets. Triana couldn't think of the word without the searing memory of Comet Bhaktul and the curse it had delivered to Earth and its people—including her father, one of the first people to contract the deadly disease and die from it.

The comet had not only killed her father, it had also dispensed a death sentence on mankind. The 251 passengers on *Galahad* would soon be all that was left of the human race, barring a miracle back on Earth. The magnitude of their mission began to weigh on Triana again for the first time in several weeks. She silently finished the last bite of grapefruit and pushed the plate away from her. A somber mood settled over her. After a moment she snapped off the trajectory map and drained the last of her orange juice.

She glanced at the time and realized she still had almost forty minutes until the Council meeting. She could take a walk through the ship to clear her head, or do something more productive.

Adjusting the vidscreen she punched in the code for her schoolwork. A worksheet popped up, automatically aligned to where she had left off the last time. They were all pilgrims, speeding across an ocean of stars to the new world . . . but they were still students, too. Each of the 251 passengers on *Galahad* was required to complete preselected study programs each month, and if all went according to plan the ship would reach its destination with each crew member holding the equivalent of four college degrees.

This particular lesson was in mathematics, a subject in which Triana excelled. But as the minutes slipped past, she found that her mind kept drifting back to her dad. Her concentration on the math problems waned until she finally sat back, saved the work she had finished, and snapped the vidscreen off.

When she looked up again she noticed that the Dining Hall had filled considerably, as more and more crew members prepared for another workday. She stood up and motioned to a group of four that her table was available, then walked out into the hallway. She had almost twenty minutes of time to kill before the meeting, and decided to take that walk after all.

Channy stood looking up at the stars through the dome. She didn't make it up to the Farms very often, but each time the sight of open space amazed her. Memories of visits with her sister to the planetarium near their English home flooded in on her, bittersweet memories that made the always-chatty teen grow strangely quiet. But the planetarium, though impressive, could never match the real thing. Here a sprawling horizon-to-horizon showcase of stars was humbling, a powerful reminder to Channy that she was virtually a microscopic speck in the universe.

She bent to one knee and looked down a row of leafy vegetables that were prospering in the artificial sunlight. "Iris," she called out, not too loudly. "C'mon, Iris." She had dropped the cat off fifteen minutes earlier and then left to check in on the morning exercise group. Now she was back to gather up their new guest and take her to the Council meeting.

Channy took a nervous glance around, afraid to run into Bon for fear that he would immediately grasp exactly why she had brought the animal up to the dirt-covered domes. She didn't think that anyone had broken the news to the surly Swede yet, and she didn't want to be the first.

She stood and walked about twenty feet into the crop, then kneeled again. "Iris, c'mon girl. Iris." She lowered her head to ground level, sweeping the vicinity with her eyes, looking for the orange and black markings through the foliage. Nothing. Just how far, she wondered, could the cat roam in a quarter of an hour? Back on her feet, she stood with hands on hips, deciding which direction to take.

Suddenly, a hand grasped her shoulder from behind, and Channy let out a scream and jumped a couple of feet. Quickly turning, she found herself face-to-face with a grinning Gap.

"Lose something?" he said.

"Don't *do* that," she said. Panting, she bent over, hands on her knees, and laughed. "You scared me to death." Catching her breath, she looked up at him. "What are you doing here?"

"I heard you brought that cat up here, so I thought I'd help you round her up before you-know-who catches you."

Channy brushed dirt from her knees. "Yeah, well, I haven't seen Bon yet. In fact, come to think of it, I haven't seen him in a while. What's going on with him?"

"You mean besides his usual Mr. Happy routine? I have no idea. The last I heard from him was at the Council meeting a couple of days ago."

"So, since we're alone, let me ask you something," Channy said.

Gap scooped up a handful of soil and let it sift between his fingers. "Oh, no," he said playfully. "What was I thinking? I should have known better than to get cornered like this."

"I just wanted to ask how things were going with Triana. You don't seem as interested anymore."

Gap's face flushed a bit, and he stared off into the interior of the crops as if looking for Iris. "Oh, I've been too busy to worry about that."

Channy raised her eyebrows. "Who do you think you're talking to here?"

"Yes, I know, your 'love radar' and all that nonsense."

"There you go again," Channy said, "making fun of my natural gifts. Well, I know I was right then, and I'm definitely picking up a cold front in the last couple of months. Have you really lost interest, or does Triana just intimidate you?"

Gap laughed. "That must be it. I'm intimidated."

Together they walked farther into the crop, scanning each side of the path for signs of Iris. Channy was quiet for a moment, then casually said, "You know who's really cute?"

"No, Channy, who's really cute?"

"That girl from Alaska. Hannah. She's smart, too."

It took all of his concentration for Gap not to physically react to the name. How in the world did Channy do it? How did she *always* seem to read his mind when it came to girls? He decided to play innocent.

"Who, Hannah? Yeah, I guess. I don't know her very well."

"Well, maybe you should get to know her."

He stopped and turned to Channy. "Why don't we just name a new Activities Director for the ship and change your title to Doctor of Love?"

Channy wandered down another row of crops. She called back over her shoulder, "That's funny. I thought love *was* an activity." She pushed a leafy plant to one side and cupped a hand to her mouth. "Iris. C'mon, Iris."

Gap shook his head, watching the petite girl in the bright pink T-shirt disappear among the plants. He tilted his head back for a moment, taking in the same spectacle of starlight that Channy had been watching earlier. What good did it do, he wondered, to try to keep any romantic secrets on this ship? Channy's radar wasn't just good; it was eerie.

He let out a long sigh, then pushed his way into the crops in search of an orange and black cat.

14

They say that to be in command is to be automatically lonely. By now you might have already figured out that Tree is a fairly lonely person anyway, and the isolation that comes from being in command maybe even suits her personality.

But that makes me sad. She has one of the kindest hearts you'll ever meet, but it's been roughed up quite a bit in her short life. Now she guards it fiercely, and I suppose I can't blame her for that.

Thank goodness for Lita Marques.

The slightly curved walls of the corridor created something of a tunnel, which helped the circulation of air within *Galahad*. And although all of the walls were covered with a thin spongy material, each level had its own color scheme, helping the crew members quickly identify their location as they made their way around the ship. This particular level, which housed the Dining Hall, Rec Center, and a number of offices and control centers, also was home to the Conference Room, where the Council held its meetings.

Triana's walk had ended up here, and she leaned against one of the curved walls outside the Conference Room. Lita had also arrived early, and was sitting on the floor with her back to the opposite wall, chatting with the Council Leader. The two girls had become friends during their long, grueling training schedule on Earth, and had grown even closer during the first four months in space. Triana had quickly realized that Lita was trustworthy and honest, which made it easy to talk with her during difficult times. Normally a shy and quiet person, Triana wasn't often comfortable making casual conversation but found that it came naturally when she was in the company of her friend from Mexico.

It would be all business when the meeting came to order, so for now the two girls enjoyed the chance to make small talk.

"Are you nervous? I sure would be," Triana said.

Lita smiled. "I've been playing the piano since I was seven, including recitals and school shows, so you'd think I would be cool up there. But you know what? I'll be just as nervous as I was the first time. What do you call it in America? Butterflies? Well, I'll have a stomach full of them when I walk out there."

Triana decided to tease her a bit. "Well, don't even think about the two hundred people staring at you, listening to every single note."

"Very funny. Actually, I always seem to calm down after I get started. The music just takes over, I guess. Plus, I'm not going to be the only one up there."

The concert had been Channy's idea. Since so many crew members played an instrument, she had recommended that several of them get together. Now, after three weeks of practice, the show was set. In about thirty-six hours the Learning Center, or School as it was better known, would be packed.

"And I don't want to brag," Lita said, "but I think we're pretty good. All we really need is someone to sing, and we could have a hit." Both girls laughed. "Even though we haven't written much of our own stuff yet. Right now we're just trying to tighten up on some of our old favorites."

"Why don't *you* sing?" Triana said.

Lita flashed her smile again. "Uh, no. That's one skill I don't have. Believe me, I'm perfectly happy hiding behind my electronic keyboard."

Gap came around a corner, a surprised look on his face. Probably can't believe somebody actually beat him to a meeting, Tree thought.

"What's going on?" Gap said. "Are we meeting out here in the hall?"

Triana shook her head. "No, just hanging out, waiting for everyone." She tried to put him at ease with a smile, and then realized that she had been doing that for weeks. Was it a matter of trying to overcompensate for the awkwardness between them? Gap was still being cordial to her, but his overall coolness had now dragged on for months. Maybe it was time for a talk with him, she decided, but the thought of that instantly settled like a knot in her stomach.

Lita, still sitting on the floor, looked up at Gap. "How's the arm?"

"Great. Couldn't be better."

"Hmm. Why don't you stop in to Sick House in the next day or two and we'll see about getting rid of that sling."

A sheepish look came over Gap. "Well," he said, pulling the arm out, "I've actually been doing this a lot lately." He waved the arm around a few times, and then noticed the alarmed look on Lita's face.

"Oh, great," she said, the smile disappearing. "Do you want to have that arm back in there for another two or three weeks? Stop doing that!"

Gap grinned. "Yes, mother." He slid the arm back into the sling.

Lita looked across the corridor at Triana, who was barely holding back a laugh. "Do you see why my job is so difficult? No respect." She turned back to Gap. "When you wake up tonight with pain, don't even think about slinking down to pick up some meds. You just sleep with some pain, okay, tough guy?"

Gap pulled the arm out one more time and blew a kiss toward Lita with it. This time Triana couldn't hold back the laughter, and was glad to see that the corners of Lita's mouth were curling upward also.

"Well, everybody seems to be in a good mood this morning," Channy said, walking up to the group. Iris was cradled in her left arm. "The two princesses are here. I see you have all waited at attention. Her ladyship and I will see you now."

"Oh," Lita cooed, and held her hands out. Channy transferred the small cat to Lita, and then turned to face Triana.

"Are we meeting out here in the hall?"

Triana rolled her eyes, and then looked at Gap. "Maybe we should think about that. C'mon, let's go." She pushed off from the wall and walked into the Conference Room, followed by the other Council members.

As soon as they took their seats, Channy looked around. "I see that our jolly friend Bon isn't here yet."

"He'll be here," Triana said. "He hasn't missed a meeting yet."

As usual, she tried to deflect criticism from Bon. For one thing, as *Galahad*'s leader that kind of talk made her uncomfortable. But she also had to be honest with herself and admit that there were other feelings floating around inside her, too. Feelings that she still couldn't figure out. Feelings, she hoped, that wouldn't affect her ability to command properly. Bon could not be immune from discipline, nor receive any other special treatment, regardless of what she felt. For now she bit her lip and silently wished that he would walk through the door and spare her from having to deal with that particular issue.

The group chatted and laughed for a while, unconsciously killing time to allow Bon to show up. But after a few minutes, Triana brought the meeting to order. She was getting irked at the Swede by this point. It was true that he had never missed a meeting—until now, it seemed—and she couldn't help wonder if this was part of the new coolness he had developed around her. He wasn't quite as rude as he had been before the Spider bay incident, but still had kept a frosty distance. She decided to put her business face on and concentrate on the issues at hand.

"Let's take care of some minor items first," she said. "Hannah Ross is going to join us in a few minutes."

Gap raised his eyebrows. "Really? What's up?" He suddenly became aware of Channy's eyes on him, and did his best to seem only mildly interested.

Triana shook her head. "I don't know for sure. She sent me an e-mail and said she had something important to share about Titan."

"Yeah," Gap said. "I know she's really into that stuff. And I mean into it a lot."

"Well, I told her to give us a few minutes to take care of old business before she stopped in. Since we've wasted enough time waiting for Bon, let's go ahead and get started with the department reports. Gap, why don't you go first."

"Everything is running smoothly with Engineering. The slingshot around Saturn went perfectly, as you all know. The solar sails will stay retracted now, and the ion power drive is running at 94 percent." He brought up a trajectory image on the vidscreen, similar to the one that Triana had been looking at in the Dining Hall. "We're on course, and our next contact point will be the Kuiper Belt at the edge of the solar system."

For a few minutes he discussed some maintenance issues on the ship, and concluded with an update on the pesky water recycling units in the Agricultural Domes. They were each being inspected, and would hopefully be in top working condition within the week.

Triana nodded. "Channy, what do you have for us?"

"I'm happy to report that crew member fitness is excellent. So far everybody is participating like they should in the exercise programs."

"Of course they are," Gap said with a grin. "Nobody wants to get on your bad side and end up doing five miles on the treadmill."

"More like ten," Channy said. "All kidding aside, I'm really happy with all of the activity. Soccer, of course, is still number one, and I'm thinking about another tournament next month. Attendance in the dance classes seems to ebb and flow, but those who really like it never miss a class, so that's good." She looked at Triana. "I guess I don't have to be a nag . . . yet."

Chuckles rippled around the room. Then Lita recognized that it was her turn to speak, and the expression on her face grew serious. She filled everybody in on the sudden rash of patients at Sick House, and the similarity of their symptoms.

"The headaches are what really concern me. Medication is helping some, but we still haven't figured out the cause, and that could be something serious. We need to become medical detectives and solve this mystery soon."

Each member of the Council offered questions and suggestions about possible causes. Radiation? No. Stress? Maybe, but from what? General fatigue? Are they just tired from their four months working in space? Maybe, but why only isolated incidents?

"I'm still wondering if it has something to do with our encounter with Saturn," Lita said. "Nobody knows for sure what a huge gravitational object like that might do to some people."

Triana frowned. "I don't know about that. Roc, any comments?"

The computer said, "Sure. I've given it a lot of thought, and I think that from now on I'd like to be known as 'Your Honor.'"

Gap turned to Channy. "Is it just me, or is he getting more outrageous every week?"

Triana sighed. "Roc, please."

"Oh, all right. To answer Lita's concern about Saturn, that's not likely. The ship is affected, of course, but our life-support systems protect all of you from any damaging effects. I've checked and rechecked radiation levels, and that's not an issue. And each of the ship's air-filtration systems is fine, too. In other words, there's no ship malfunction that's to blame."

Although it was good news, it still left Triana concerned. Could the patients' symptoms just be a fluke? Could it be some sort of stress reaction after all? Somehow she didn't think so.

Lita spoke up again. "Anyway, we also have our little friend here." She held up Iris, who was on the verge of falling asleep in her arms. They could all hear its purring as Lita stroked it softly behind the ears. "For now she seems to be happy with the fake fish from our Dining Hall. I've checked the data banks, and as long as we get her the proper amount of protein and minerals, she should be fine. Not the optimal diet, maybe, but not too bad."

Channy giggled. "Don't forget about the litter box situation."

"Ah, yes," Lita said. "The litter box. For now she's loving life up at the Farms. Uh, I don't know what Bon will have to say about that . . ."

Tree sighed. "Well, I don't see the harm if we maintain a little space for her somewhere in the Farm Section but away from the crops. I suppose we need to do a little research on the health ramifications. Roc should be able to help with that." She felt her eyes watering a little bit, and knew that if she got any closer to Iris her allergic reaction would intensify.

The door opened and everyone looked up to see Hannah Ross. She had a look on her face that seemed to be asking if she was too early. Tree smiled and indicated an open chair at the end of the table. "C'mon in, Hannah."

Hannah nodded at the Council and sat down. She chanced one quick glance at Gap, who seemed to be concentrating on a point somewhere in front of him on the table. She set her work pad in front of her and looked across at Triana.

The Council leader said, "I think we're at a point where we can move on to new business. Any objections?" They all turned their attention to Hannah, who fumbled with her work pad before meeting their looks. She nervously cleared her throat.

"Let me just say that I don't have an answer for what I'm about to share with you."

"Wow," Channy said, laughing. "That's a great start."

Hannah exhaled, then started again. "Two days ago I started running scans on Titan, Saturn's largest moon. I was hoping to use the data from the . . . the research station, but I don't think we have that yet. Is that right?"

Tree nodded but remained silent, listening.

"Anyway," Hannah said, "I've always been fascinated by this moon, and I'm not alone. It's one of the reasons there was a research station put there in the first place. Titan is a treasure trove of information. I couldn't wait to get started. In fact, I wish we could hang out here for a while."

Gap smiled at her. "Uh, unfortunately we have an appointment a few light-years away."

Hannah blushed at his attention, hoping that no one noticed. She looked back down at her work pad. "Then yesterday I noticed . . . it. I ran a couple of checks to make sure all of the equipment was operating smoothly, and it all came back okay. So, like I said, I have the data, but not an explanation."

Triana sat forward. "What is it?"

Hannah paused, then looked across the table at Triana. "Titan. It's talking to us."

15

lexa Wellington stood with her clipboard beside the bed in Sick House. As Lita's primary assistant she was used to taking charge whenever Lita was called to a Council meeting. What she wasn't used to was being this busy.

She looked around *Galahad*'s hospital ward, amazed to see eight beds now occupied. When Lita had left just an hour earlier there had been six. Two more patients had checked in, both with the same symptoms as the others. Alexa handed one of the new patients, a fifteen-year-old girl from Michigan, a pain pill along with a cup of water.

"Has this been coming on, or did it happen suddenly?"

The girl cocked her head at Alexa and said loudly, "What?"

Alexa remembered that each of these crew members had reported a muffled sense of hearing. She repeated the question a little louder.

The girl told Alexa that it had come on quickly, about ten hours earlier. At first she had thought that she could work her way through it, and had even taken a pain pill. But it had only become worse, making it impossible for her to take a scheduled school exam. Instead she had reported to Sick House.

Alexa nodded and made a few notes on her work pad. She told the girl to try to rest, and walked back to her desk. She looked back through the door at the eight patients and frowned. What was going on? Was it possible that some nasty bug had somehow made it through the sterilization process before they had left Earth? If so, how? All 251 crew members had been kept in isolation for thirty days before the launch, in what was affectionately called the Incubator. When they finally had boarded *Galahad* it was assumed that they would be leaving all—or, almost all—of Earth's infectious diseases behind.

Besides, what kind of bug would hibernate this long before striking? And then strike so rapidly among various crew members?

The door to the outer hallway opened, interrupting her thoughts, and Alexa looked up to see Bon, supported by his roommate, Desi, stagger through the door. Bon looked terrible, his eyes barely slits, his mouth in a grimace, sweat trickling down his forehead. Desi looked alarmed, and without hesitation Alexa jumped up and said, "In here." She motioned for them to follow her into the hospital ward, where she quickly prepared a bed for Bon. Desi helped him onto it, and Alexa immediately leaned over him.

"Headache?" she asked, even though she knew the answer. Bon nodded slightly, which seemed to cause him even further pain. Alexa walked over to the dispenser and pulled out another pain pill, grabbed a cup of water, and brought it back to the Swede who raised a hand to her.

"I've . . . I've already taken two today," he managed to say through gritted teeth.

"Not this stuff, my friend," Alexa said. "This is much stronger. C'mon, sit up a little bit."

Bon slowly propped himself up on his elbows and took the pill, then fell back onto the pillow.

Alexa looked over at Desi, who shook his head. "I don't know," he said. "I came back to the room to pick something up and he was a mess. He's supposed to be at a Council meeting, so

I knew that something had to be really wrong. He kept saying that he would be okay, but I waited around a few minutes and could see . . . well, see this. He's getting worse, if anything."

"What about you? How do you feel?" Alexa asked the Brazilian.

"Fine. I feel great."

Alexa nodded. Well, it's not something in their room, she decided. Environmental causes would be too easy, of course. And it's never easy.

"Thanks for bringing him in," she said to Desi.

"No problem. Well, actually it *was* a problem." Desi chuckled nervously. "It's not easy to get him to do something he doesn't want to do."

Alexa smiled back. "Yeah, so I've heard. I'll take care of him. You don't have to stick around."

Desi thanked her, and then put his hand on Bon's shoulder. "Take care of yourself, man. I'll check in on you later."

Bon nodded once, then mumbled, "Thanks."

Desi walked out, and Alexa turned to look into Bon's face, a worried expression creasing hers. A sober thought flashed through her mind.

We're in trouble.

The Conference Room on *Galahad* had grown quiet. Triana sat still, trying to digest what Hannah had just told them, then finally spoke up.

"What do you mean when you say that Titan is 'talking to us?' Just how would a moon talk to us?"

"I know it sounds crazy," Hannah said, "but that's the only way I can think to describe it right now."

"Okay. What exactly have you found?"

Hannah fidgeted with the work pad in front of her. "It's almost like an energy burst, but an immensely strong energy burst.

I picked it up almost by accident, and thought it was just radioactive emissions from Titan. But two things jumped out at me. For one thing, the bursts are ordered, structured. They're pulsing bits of information, I think. It's almost like sentences, or paragraphs, or something like that. It's not just scattered, random jolts. These have some sort of pattern to them, almost like a radio signal. But I'm nowhere near close to deciphering them. I can tell you, though, that it's not something anyone has ever seen before."

Triana bit her lip. "You said that two things jumped out at you. What was the other one?"

Hannah took a deep breath. "You know, even with what appears to be a structure to the pulses, it's possible that it's something natural on the surface, or some sort of internal energy source inside the moon itself. At least, that's what I thought. I told myself, 'Don't get too excited, there is a reasonable explanation for this.' Until . . ."

"Until?" Triana said.

"Until I noticed something else. The pulses are following us."

Lita looked at Triana, then back at Hannah. "And what does *that* mean?"

"It means that the pulses are not just randomly flying off into space. They're concentrated into tight beams, aimed right at *Galahad*. Like a laser shot of energy."

Channy's mouth dropped open. "Are you saying . . . ?"

"Yeah," Hannah said. "The moon—or something on it—is talking to us. It's directly communicating with this ship. It's not a random pulse of energy. It's a . . . it's a phone call from Titan to us."

There was silence around the conference table while this began to sink in.

"Intelligent life," Channy finally murmured. "We've found intelligent life."

Gap spoke up. "Well, let's not get ahead of ourselves. Is it possible there's a connection with the research station? Could this energy pulse be something *they* set up? Maybe a sort of distress signal or something?"

Lita thought about this. "Well, it's possible. Since nobody has been able to reach them for a while, we don't know *what* they've cooked up. But is that likely? Would they have that technology?"

Triana addressed Hannah. "Who else knows about this?"

"I haven't told anyone."

"Good. Let's keep it that way for now, until we can find out a little more information. Hannah, what's the chance of deciphering this energy pulse? Could we figure out what it's trying to say?"

Hannah shrugged. "It's possible, I guess."

Triana called out to the computer. "Roc, let's get on this right away. A couple of things for us to check. One, is this a signal from the missing research scientists? Two, is this a message from an alien life-form on Titan?"

Once the words were out of her mouth, she realized the implications.

"And," she added, "can we talk back to them?"

16

The lights had begun to dim aboard *Galahad* as evening progressed. Several crew members were scattered around the Rec Room, some in the midst of various games, others simply lounging on the sofas and wide chairs after dinner. Occasional laughter filtered across the room, and the large vidscreen against the far wall was dialed into a landscape scene from Ireland, providing the evening's backdrop. A solitary figure in the corner quietly plucked out some notes on a guitar.

Gap was in one of his accustomed seats, facing a computerized Masego board, competing against Roc. The game, born in Africa, was a battle of strategy and intense concentration. The goal was to maneuver your three game pieces through a series of twisting paths before returning along a completely different trail. At the same time it was necessary to block your opponent's progress, driving him into danger.

Gap frequently played an electronic version against Roc, who relished any opportunity to goad him.

"How's your arm?" the computer asked.

"Fine," Gap said, trying to concentrate on the game board.

"I hear that you might be getting rid of that sling pretty soon."

"Um-hm," Gap mumbled.

"And you'll probably be right back up Airboarding, I suppose."

Gap took his eyes off the board and looked at Roc's sensor. "Are you trying to distract me? That's pretty rude, you know. I don't talk while you're thinking about your next move."

"That's because I already know my next three moves. I don't have to agonize over every detail like you."

"Ha-ha," Gap said. "A little quiet, please."

Roc remained silent for a few seconds as Gap considered his next move, a crease forming on his forehead as he studied the screen. Then, reaching out, he punched in his move. In one second Roc countered, blocking Gap's route across the game board.

"Your turn," whispered the computer. "I'll be over here being quiet."

Gap decided to try a new strategy, and instead of overthinking his line of attack, he moved quickly, punching in a counter move. In a flash Roc answered again, this time opening a new route for himself and blocking Gap at the same time. Gap murmured something under his breath, a look of disgust on his face.

"Could be the pain medication for your arm," Roc offered.

"I'm not taking anything for it anymore," Gap said.

"Oh. Well, maybe you should," said the computer voice of Roy Orzini.

Gap started to answer, then changed his mind. After a moment he offered his resignation from the game and pushed back his chair.

"Maybe another game tomorrow?" Roc said.

"Sure," Gap said, running a hand through his hair. "Hey, let me ask you something. This pulse from Titan. I gotta believe it's coming from those missing scientists. It couldn't really be some other life-form trying to communicate with us, could it?"

"Well, obviously it *could* be," Roc said. "Unlikely, maybe, and certainly a landmark discovery. But always possible."

"Have you made any progress in decoding it?"

"I just spoke with Tree about that," the computer said. "I'm running a new check on it right now because it's not a typical communications signal."

"What do you mean?"

"I mean, your basic signal moves in one direction. For instance, we send a message back to Earth and it originates here and travels in one direction, back to Earth. They receive it, and if they choose to respond, they make a similar connection. One way."

"Yeah, so?"

"Well, I'm not completely sure, but I think one of the things that has made this signal so difficult to pin down is because I think it's a two-way communication."

Gap's face was blank. "Two-way?"

"Yes. I just told Tree that it seems that the signal is coming from Titan, being received by us, and then working its way back to the original source. As if the signal is depositing information here, and then taking back information from *Galahad*."

Gap stewed on this. "So, it's almost like an old-fashioned computer hacker?"

"Pretty much. Only this is much more involved than that. This energy beam seems to be invading everything on the ship, not just our computer banks. And, since *Galahad* was never designed to fend off anything like that, we really don't have any defense for it."

"So, what do we do? Just let it pick our pockets?" Gap said.

"I'm not sure what we *can* do right now. Until we discover exactly what we're dealing with, whoever—or whatever—is responsible for this energy pulse has the capability of learning everything about us."

Lita and her assistant, Alexa, were exhausted. They had both skipped dinner, and had worked almost ten hours nonstop.

The hospital ward in Sick House now had twelve patients occupying beds, most of them asleep, the others drifting in and out of consciousness. Nothing seemed to be working to ease their pain, and Lita had grown frustrated.

And it wasn't confined to just these twelve, apparently. Five other crew members had reported to Sick House with a headache, but were not as serious. They had been sent back to their own rooms with pain medication and orders to take it easy for at least another day.

Seventeen total, twelve of who had been admitted. If it wasn't an epidemic, it was close enough. Lita tapped a stylus pen against her cheek while Alexa checked off the names of assistants and volunteers who had agreed to help out around Sick House during the crisis.

Alexa set her work pad aside and crossed her arms. "So, are we at the point that we can blame it on this . . . this energy beam, or whatever it is?"

"I don't think there can be any question anymore. It's too much of a coincidence. This beam intercepts the ship, and suddenly we have a dozen kids flat on their backs."

"But how is it possible?" Alexa said. "I mean, Saturn and Titan are already way behind us, and dropping farther away every minute."

Lita set down her stylus and called out to the computer. "Roc, any answer for that?"

The computer's voice was as close to serious as Lita had ever heard it. "We're dealing with an energy beam so strong, and so concentrated, like a finely tuned laser, that it's possible it could stay with us for weeks to come. We won't be able to outrun its effect for a while."

"Why are these patients being affected and not the rest of us?" Alexa said.

"We all vibrate with energy," Roc said. "We're beings made up of energy, actually, and each person has a wavelength, almost like a radio frequency. This beam coming from Titan vibrates on a frequency that is obviously very close to the same frequency as our guests at Sick House. Their internal energy pattern somehow 'connects' with this pulsing beam, and the result is pain. Extreme pain, it turns out.

"And," the computer added, "we're rapidly approaching the point where we need to be concerned about long-term effects."

Alexa fixed a steady gaze on Lita, then back to Roc's glowing red sensor. "You mean, like brain damage?"

"That's exactly what I mean. We have no idea what these energy waves are doing to the ship or to the crew, but extreme headaches for an extended period of time can't be good."

Lita was thoughtful for a moment, and then said, "What about a shield of some sort? Is there some way we can block the pulse to these dozen—well, actually, seventeen—patients until we're out of range?"

"I would say no," Roc replied. "This beam is powerful enough to chase after us this far, then penetrate the ship. An Airboard helmet won't stop it, and I can't think of any other materials we would have to do the trick."

Their conversation was interrupted by the sound of running feet, and a breathless assistant dashed out of the hospital ward. "Uh, I think you'd better get in here," she said to Lita.

Lita and Alexa jumped to their feet and followed the girl. "What is it?" Lita said.

"I'm not sure," the girl said. "You need to see for yourself."

She led them over to the bed where Bon was lying. Lita stood on one side, Alexa on the other, and together they stared at the Swedish Council member for a few seconds.

"What am I looking for?" Lita said. "I don't . . ."

Bon suddenly opened his eyes. Alexa shrieked and jumped backward, her hand covering her mouth in horror. Lita felt a shock wave of fear ripple through her body.

Bon's eyes glowed. His pupils had swelled until there was

hardly any white to be seen, creating an eerie sensation within Lita, as if he were staring straight through her. Outer rings around the pupils cast an orange tinge, shimmering and moving, circling. It was the creepiest sight Lita had ever seen, and it took almost half a minute before she could start breathing again.

Nobody spoke. The assistant who had summoned them stepped back another few feet, her hands clutched together under her chin. Lita struggled to regain her composure, to call upon the medical training that had earned her the right to run the department. But nothing had prepared her for this.

Just as she started to relax, the shock doubled. Bon's mouth fell open, emitting not one voice, but several mixed together. It was a chorus of voices, all speaking at once in a garbled jumble of noise, a tangled mess of sounds. For a few moments it was as if multiple people occupied Bon's head, all of them competing for the right to be heard.

The eyes had been creepy. This was absolutely terrifying.

Alexa, like the assistant, backed away, her mouth open. Lita was unable to move, unable to take her eyes from Bon's face. After about thirty seconds of garbled sounds, his mouth closed, his eyes drooped shut, and he fell back into a state of unconsciousness.

Lita finally looked across at Alexa. "Call Tree. Right now."

The words were barely out of her mouth when an excited voice broke in over the intercom. "Gap Lee to the Engineering Section. Emergency. Gap Lee, Engineering. Emergency."

Lita looked at Alexa again. "What's happening to us?"

17

G ap sprinted down the hall, mindful of his tender left arm. When the emergency message had reached him over the intercom, he hadn't bothered to recover the sling from his dresser, leaving it behind as he raced out the door. The arm felt awkward now that it was exposed, but he was sure that was mostly mental.

Crew members could hear his pounding feet before he turned the corner, and they backed up against the wall to let him pass. He rushed into the lift and made his way down to the Engineering Section. Bursting through the door he could see the nervous faces of the crew as they awaited his arrival.

"What is it?" he said, his chest heaving and sweat trickling down his forehead.

One of his top assistants, a sixteen-year-old girl named Ramasha, stepped forward. "It's the ion power drive. It seems to be stuttering."

"Stuttering?"

"That's what it seems like. It's skipping beats, almost like . . . like . . ."

"Like an irregular heartbeat," said another assistant, fifteen-year-old Esteban. "But even the missed beats are keeping to a regular pattern."

Ramasha nodded in agreement. "We didn't know what you would want us to do, so we put out the call."

Gap could see the worried expression on her face while she worked to maintain her composure. He managed a smile and patted her shoulder. "That's fine. We'll figure this out."

He moved over to one of the Engineering control panels. "Roc," he called out, settling in front of the monitors and switches, "do you have anything?"

"I'm on it right now," the computer said. "Give me just a moment."

Gap switched on a vidscreen and pulled up a graph of the ship's ion power drive. He immediately saw the blips that Ramasha and Esteban had described. And they were right: it did resemble a screwy heartbeat, but with an unusual pattern to it. While he studied it, he called over his shoulder to Ramasha.

"Have you noticed anything else? Any problems with life support, gravity control? Anything?"

"No, everything else is normal."

"The stuttering came on suddenly," Esteban said, "lasted about a minute, then stopped, then started again. It's been going on now about . . ." He glanced at the clock. "About twelve minutes."

Gap scowled at the vidscreen as a thought hit him. The pattern of those power blips . . .

"Roc, the missing beats on this graph. Doesn't this look like . . ."

"Yes, I just ran a check on that, and it's exactly what you think. The skipping beats in our ion drive system sync up perfectly with the energy pulse we're receiving from Titan."

The gravity of the statement hung heavily in the room. Nobody spoke for a moment. Then, as suddenly as they started, the blips disappeared, and the graph on the vidscreen regained its smooth, normal pattern. All of the crew members waited silently, watching, wondering if the disturbance would return. A full minute went by before Gap turned to the others.

"I have to be honest. I have absolutely no idea what to do about that. Roc?"

The computer voice said, "I'll go one step further. I don't think anything *can* be done about that. But now there's no doubt; this ship is being manipulated by something on that very mysterious moon."

It was just past ten o'clock, and the lights on *Galahad* had dimmed throughout the corridors and offices. The hospital ward was quiet, with all of the patients asleep, most of them on extra doses of pain medication. An assistant in Sick House wandered in occasionally and checked on their status, made a few notations on the charts, then exited.

Triana sat on a stool beside Bon's bed. She had been there for more than an hour, watching and waiting for a sign that the temperamental Swede was rousing from his unconscious state. She looked down into his face, trying to make sense of the orange-tinted replacement of his normally ice blue eyes. Her feelings were again pushing against the surface, confusing her. For a brief moment she found herself wanting to reach out and stroke the hair falling onto his forehead, but she held back.

Instead, she reached over to the vidscreen that was mounted to the telescopic arm and pulled it to her. For the fourth time she brought up the video replay of Bon's vocal outburst. Every patient was monitored during their stay, and in this case it provided Triana a chance to witness the eerie episode for herself.

She hit the play button, then watched and listened intently to the sounds of the multiple voices that had poured out of Bon. Even hearing it four times didn't diminish the creepy sensation that rippled through her, and for the fourth time goose bumps speckled her arms. When it was finished she looked back at him, lying unconscious, with only an occasional twitch on his cheek.

"Hey," she heard Lita say from the doorway. "I thought you might still be here."

"Yeah," Triana said. "Here I am." She pushed the vidscreen to the side. "So, anything new?"

Lita walked over and looked at Bon. "No, and that must be good news. We haven't had a new patient admitted in the last ten hours, so hopefully it's just these twelve." She fixed her gaze on Triana. "I've gotta tell you, we've been through some tough times already on this trip, but this . . ." She nodded at Bon. "This is just plain scary. Alexa was completely freaked out, and you know how hard that is to do. She's tough as nails."

Triana exhaled loudly and pulled her long brown hair back behind her ears. "Listen to this for a second." She readjusted the vidscreen and again hit the play button. Lita watched the replay, cringing at the sound of the multiple voices that spilled from Bon's mouth. When it was over, she looked at Triana.

"What are you thinking?"

"Well," Triana said. "It's like . . . like they're all Bon's voice, but . . . not. Listen one more time." Again they listened to the playback. Lita shut her eyes and concentrated on the sound instead of the image, then opened her eyes and shook her head.

"I'm not sure what you're hearing. It just sounds like a jumbled mess."

"I'm going to have Roc try to split each of those . . . those voices . . . into separate tracks. But," she said, looking back at Bon, "it sounds to me like different languages."

Lita stared at the Council Leader but kept silent. Triana shrugged and said, "I might be wrong, but it sounds like a handful of different languages, all being spoken at once."

"How are you able to pick that out?"

"I don't know. I've just been listening to it for the last hour, and it suddenly struck me. The more I listen, the more I'm convinced." This time, regardless of how it looked, she reached over and pulled the stray lock of hair out of Bon's face. Lita noticed the gentle touch but said nothing.

For a brief second, Bon's eyelids fluttered open, causing Triana to recoil slightly. The sight of his glowing pupils was shocking. She recovered quickly, then leaned over him.

"Bon," she said gently. "Can you hear me?"

A brief look of pain shuddered through his face, as if her voice itself had stung him, and his eyes clamped shut again. Then the muscles relaxed, and his eyelids parted slightly. His mouth opened, and the voices returned. Without hesitating, Triana looked at Lita.

"Are we recording this?"

Lita nodded, keeping her eyes on Bon's mouth. She listened for what Triana had described, listening for anything that sounded like Spanish, her mother tongue. But the jumble of voices was too confusing. After about twenty seconds, Bon fell quiet, and his eyes closed. Tree sat still, and then slowly nodded her head.

"I'm sure I'm right. Several voices, several languages." She looked down at the peaceful face of the usually volatile Swede. "Something is trying to communicate to us through Bon. It's up to us to figure out just what they're saying."

18

When morning arrived on *Galahad*, each Council member awoke to find a message from Triana waiting in their e-mail box. An impromptu Council meeting was scheduled for seven thirty, but instead of sitting around the Conference Room table again, Triana decided to make this meeting less formal, maybe as a way to lighten the tension being felt by everyone on board. "Meet me in the Dining Hall for breakfast and a quick recap of what's going on," she had written, hoping it would take the edge off their discussion.

For the most part her plan was successful. Each Council member filled a tray with fruit, energy blocks, and either juice or water, and made their way to a table in the back of the room. Channy, still energized from an early morning session in the gym, chattered away, doing what she did best: creating smiles.

Triana wondered if the morning's light banter was a sign of nerves. The first topic was the upcoming concert, and it was clear that nobody wanted to consider the possibility of postponing it because of the drama they were experiencing. As Channy was quick to point out to Lita, it would be "good medicine" for the crew, and nobody disagreed. At least for the time being.

There were also comments on the bumper crop that was coming out of the Domes, good news for a hungry crew that enjoyed the variety of fresh fruits and vegetables that were popping up in the Dining Hall each day. Triana informed the Council that two of Bon's assistants were covering for him while he was admitted to Sick House, and she expected no problems from that department.

"I'm sure of that," Channy said with a laugh. "Nobody wants to face the wrath of Bon when he comes back."

The conversation then drifted through issues of minor importance, including Lita's scowling acknowledgment that Gap had finally ditched the sling for good. Against her recommendation, she added, but not unexpected, given his hardheaded nature.

There was a brief update on Iris, their newest passenger, who now seemed to be splitting her time between Lita and Channy, but also spent a considerable amount of time sunning herself in the warm dirt of the Agricultural Domes. She had completely regained her strength and vitality following the four-month stay in deep sleep.

The final two topics were more serious, and as the group settled down to talk about them, the gravity of their precarious situation in space began to take hold again. Triana looked around and realized that, after the near-death drama after their launch, the crew of *Galahad* had been relatively at peace. A few minor disagreements between people, a few arguments regarding work schedules, a few flare-ups between roommates. But nothing major, nothing that couldn't be worked out. Now, however, Triana could see the look of true concern on the faces of her fellow Council members. Their easy coasting of the past few months had hit a bump.

Gap was next. He explained the bizarre hitch in their ion drive system, how it had been in sync with the signal trailing them from Titan, and how they had no idea how it started, or ended.

"What about damage?" Triana said.

Gap shook his head. "Well, none that we can find. Roc seems to think this was a test of sorts. Like whoever was doing it was probing our power system, looking around. It appears that we're okay." He rubbed a hand through his hair. "But it's a very creepy feeling, knowing that they can tinker with our major power components at this distance, and while we're accelerating away from them. That's . . . impressive."

There were nods from around the table, as the significance of the comments sank in. After a few moments of silence, Channy spoke up.

"We think we're so advanced, so intelligent. But we're just learning to crawl, really. There must be other civilizations throughout the galaxy that tower over us, you know?"

Lita agreed. "It's humbling. Just when we think we're the biggest and the baddest, we get knocked down a few notches. It's a big universe. We're probably no more advanced than bacteria to some other life-forms out there."

She looked up at Triana, who said, "Now is probably a good time to update everyone on the situation at Sick House."

Lita, her black hair held in place by a strand of red ribbon, pushed her tray forward and rested her elbows on the table. She seemed to collect her thoughts before diving in.

"Seventeen crew members have now shown up at the Clinic with pretty much the same symptoms I told you about before. But now most of them, like Bon, have developed the same unusual orange glow to their eyes, which I can't explain. The headaches have me really concerned, because nothing seems to be helping them. Twelve of the patients are being treated in Sick House, the other five are resting in their rooms. Why they aren't suffering as much, I don't know.

"We've run several imaging tests, and there's nothing we can find that might be causing this. Nothing. The patients don't appear to have anything in common, like working in the same area, roommates, doing the same workouts. There's no link between them that we can find. It's . . ." She took a long breath. "It's very frustrating. I want to be able to explain what's happening to them, but I can't." She looked at Tree. "And then there are the voices."

The other Council members stared at her. They had heard bits and pieces of the incident with Bon the previous night. Lita recapped the strange occurrence, and then played a tape of it. When it was over, she told them Triana's idea about the languages. Triana took a drink of water and then pulled a vidscreen close to her.

"I had Roc analyze the tape. And it's exactly what I thought." She looked in the faces of the others, and then pulled up a file on the vidscreen. "This is going to blow you away. Roc was able to isolate the voices. There are twelve of them."

A glance around the table showed her that Gap and Channy had not picked up on the obvious coincidence. Lita remained mute, so Triana made the connection for the others.

"Twelve patients in Sick House. Twelve voices coming out of Bon's mouth."

Gap furrowed his brow. "What?" he said. "So you think he's . . . what? Channeling the other patients? That's quite a stretch, isn't it?"

Triana looked back at Gap and nodded. "That's what I would have thought, too. Except remember I said that Roc isolated the voices. Roc?"

The computer spoke up. "Tree's right. Twelve distinct voices emanated from Bon. When I broke them down separately, what I came up with was a collection of various languages. Four that spoke English, two Spanish, two Mandarin Chinese, one French, one Japanese, one Portuguese, and one Swedish. Which in itself would not be too terribly dramatic . . . until you look at the patient list in Sick House. Those seven languages represent the seven native tongues of the twelve people lying in those beds."

At this Triana turned the vidscreen to face the others, showing the breakdown of each voice. Each sound wave was clearly marked by its language of origin. Channy's mouth fell open, but no words came out. Gap looked stunned, staring down at the table, then slowly raised his gaze to Triana.

"Okay," he finally said. "I thought it was weird in Engineering last night. This is . . . this is too much."

Roc waited a moment, then continued. "Whatever intelligence is probing this ship obviously has the capability of infiltrating not only the power system of *Galahad,* but the minds of every crew member as well. The twelve patients were all asleep at the time, knocked out by their pain medication. This probe, if you will, managed to crawl through their minds, extract their native language, and create a chorus with Bon as the conductor." After a pause Roc added, "Oh, and you'll probably want to know what they were saying, right?"

Galahad's Council was silent, most of them holding their breath.

"Twelve voices, seven languages . . . but one simple message," Roc said. "All twelve of them kept repeating, 'I wait for you. I wait so long. Help. Help here.'"

19

The raspberry-flavored energy block was half-eaten, but only for the fuel it provided. There was no enjoyment in it for Hannah, and there never was when her mind was so completely preoccupied. But the remaining half of the food block was left in a perfectly symmetrical shape, sheared off at the end, so that it didn't so much look like a partially consumed block, but instead appeared to be a miniature version of the original. Hannah had nibbled away at one end until it was razor-straight, at the exact halfway point of the bar, and then set it on the desk with the bottom squared to the desk's edge.

Her head rested on one hand, and her eyes scanned the computer screen before her. The data stream from SAT33 had begun its download from Earth, but Hannah's excitement quickly turned to frustration. Once stripped of the Top Secret seal, she had expected to have easy access. Instead, what she encountered was a string of unintelligible code and hidden files. Notes from Earth indicated that it had arrived that way from SAT33. But why? What was causing the stream to be scrambled like that? Was the mysterious beam from Titan at work again? Would it be possible to unravel the code and actually read the data? Even Roc was perplexed.

But buried somewhere in there, Hannah was convinced, were the clues that could help unlock the mysteries.

She closed her eyes for a moment and rubbed them with her other hand.

A bee was crawling across Channy's hand as she sat cross-legged in the dirt. She watched it, unafraid, marveling at the fact that the crew of *Galahad* was still getting used to their new life in space, more than a billion miles from the protective embrace of Earth, while the other life-forms on the ship—the bees that helped pollinate the plant life, or the earthworms that burrowed through the dirt in the Farms, aerating the soil—had no concept of their new surroundings. For them, this patch of land, this artificially sun-splashed meadow, could have just as well been a sunny field near her grandparents home in Doncaster.

She had alternated with Lita the task of bringing Iris up to the Domes, and although both of them had indicated that it was no problem—in fact, each seemed to enjoy the break from their chores—Channy wondered how much longer they could continue to be a taxi and housekeeping service for a cat. The time was probably approaching when they would need to consider if Iris should just live permanently in Bon's farms. Unless they could figure out some way for her to get around the ship by herself.

It seemed that every cat lover on the ship had also volunteered to spend time with Iris, but for the time being Triana had insisted that the two Council members look after her to avoid distractions among the crew.

At the moment the orange and black ball of fur was rolling in the freshly tilled dirt, stopping occasionally to paw at a clod or take a swipe at an overhanging plant leaf above her. A bee would cause her to jerk her head quickly to one side, or jump up and give chase, but the game was always short-lived, and Iris would return to her roll in the dirt.

Channy picked up the metallic ball that had come in the package with Iris's other belongings, and rolled it in front of the cat. Iris responded with a sniff, then continued entertaining herself. "Hmph," Channy said. "Don't like that toy, eh? That's okay. My mother always said that I preferred an empty box rather than the toys that came in them." She reached out, picked up the ball, and tried rolling it again. This time Iris only blinked at it.

"Fine," Channy said. "I forgot how independent you cats are. I'm sure you'll play with it the moment I leave." She eyed the red collar they had discovered in the pod, with the metallic name tag glinting in the light. She had put the collar on Iris that morning, and wondered if maybe they should add a bell to make it easier to find the cat when she took off into the crops.

As she thought about this, their new passenger got to her feet and shook the dirt from her back and sides. Then, a slow, deliberate cleaning process began. Channy knew this could take a while, so she stretched out to a reclined position and put a hand over her eyes to block the artificial sunlight.

And then the lights went out. Completely.

Channy sat up with a start, her hands automatically grabbing at the dirt beneath her, clutching at the ground for stability in the sudden darkness. In a moment her eyes adjusted somewhat, and the flicker of millions of stars coming through the domed ceiling allowed her to see rough shapes and outlines around her.

The blackout had been sudden, with no warning, no dimming. One moment Channy had been basking—along with Iris—in the artificial sunlight, and in the next instant that light had vanished. Within a few seconds she heard the sound of voices calling out from across the dome, workers who were probably just as shocked as she to find themselves in the equivalent of a total eclipse. Channy debated whether to stumble around in search of some of these crew members, or to hold tight and wait out the darkness. For the moment she decided to stay where she was. The original surprise at being thrust into the gloom began to border on fear, with a small shudder rippling down her spine. What was going on?

Her thoughts turned to Iris, who had last been seen grooming herself lazily in the warm glow. Chances are this sudden shutdown didn't bother her a bit. Her highly evolved sense of sight would serve her well in the starlight. Still, Channy knew she would feel better if she could just hold on to the cat. She rolled to her hands and knees and crept over to where Iris had been bathing. She stopped just short of calling out "Here kitty, kitty." Instead, she clucked her tongue and mixed in a slight whistle, hoping to grab the cat's attention.

But Iris was nowhere to be found. She had moved, who knew how far? Channy squinted in the dim light, watching for movement. The voices she had heard a minute earlier returned, this time a little closer. Perhaps, she decided, it was time to connect with these other lost souls. She gave one last look around for Iris, then slowly stood, putting her hands out in the darkness, a gesture more of uncertainty than support. Craning her neck, she glanced up through the clear domed ceiling, thankful for the miniscule amount of light thrown off by the stars.

But it was still frightfully dark, and by now Channy was turned around, unsure of the right direction to get her back to the dome entrance. But the voices had come from her right. She turned in that direction and opened her mouth to shout.

And then the lights came back on.

The sudden glaring flash of light was a shock to the system, and Channy fell backward, back to the dirt, her breath escaping in a rush along with a small shriek. She clamped her eyes shut against the brilliant explosion of light and covered them with one arm. The voices had gone quiet. Channy guessed that the other crew members in the dome were experiencing the same jolt that she was.

She slowly lowered her arm and chanced a quick opening of her eyes, just slits at first, then gradually opened them further.

The first sight to greet her was Iris, sitting three feet in front of her and looking bored.

Channy spent a moment collecting herself, then chuckled. "I should have known you wouldn't run off. I'm your meal ticket, right?"

She stood again and brushed the dirt from her shorts and knees. Then she bent over and picked up Iris, who immediately began purring. "Yes, it's good to see you, too." She started walking toward the exit. "Let's go see if someone forgot to pay the electric bill around here."

20

Think about your very first memory. Have you ever done that? Try it. How far back can you go? Roy once told me that he had a distinct memory from when he was two years old. His family moved a lot when he was young, and he recalled a tire swing that his father pushed him on in Oregon.

Trouble is, I looked up Roy's complete bio, and his family didn't move to Oregon until he was three. I didn't have the heart to correct him.

I can't play this game with you, because every memory I have, from the first moment Roy threw my switch, is stamped into permanent code. But the first memory I have of completing a chore for Roy was turning power on and off in his lab. You think that's simple, but could you have done it at age one hour, smarty pants?

So I know a thing or two about power, and what's going on with Galahad is very troubling. Especially since I've done a complete system check and there's not one thing I can find to account for it. I hate that.

What caused it? Do we know yet?" Lita said into the intercom on her desk.

"No," Triana's voice came back. "And you didn't have any power problems in Sick House?"

"Everything's fine here. Well," Lita added, "unless you count our twelve guests."

"Any change?"

"Some stirring in the last hour. Some of them seem like they're ready to wake up."

Triana was silent on her end for a moment, and Lita instantly pictured the Council leader biting her lip. She decided to prod for more information in order to fill the gap of silence. "So as far you know it was just the Domes that went dark?"

"Yeah," Triana said. "Lasted about two minutes, then right back to full power. Channy was up there with Iris, I hear."

Lita had to chuckle. "It will give her something else to chatter about at dinner tonight, that's for sure. Not that she needs any extra motivation, of course."

"And this has to be another result of that power beam from Titan," Triana said. "Gap's hurrying to run a diagnostic scan, but it sounds to me like our little green men might be up to their tricks again. I don't know, is this another one of their cries for help?"

It was the first time Lita had heard Triana suggest that an alien force might be behind all of the incidents. The thought gave her the chills, a combination of anxiety and excitement. Up to this point *Galahad*'s leader had remained neutral on the source of the pulsing energy beam. But as time went by—and more strange episodes occurred—the chances of the beam originating with the missing scientists declined, leaving the space travelers only one other choice: someone, or something, on the large moon of Saturn.

"Well, give me a call later and we can hook up for dinner," Lita said.

She exchanged good-byes with Triana, and then walked back into the hospital ward. Two of the patients were moving restlessly in their sleep, apparently ready to wake up at any moment. She double-checked their vital signs and arranged their pillows to make them more comfortable. Then, turning to check on Bon at the end of the room, she stopped dead in her tracks.

He was awake and staring at her, his ghostly eyes penetrating like lasers.

Quickly recovering, Lita hurried over to his bedside and bent over him. "Hi," she said, an encouraging smile on her face. "Welcome back." She tried to avoid looking too long into those eyes.

Bon swallowed and opened his mouth to speak. The words came out in a croak. "How long . . . how long have I . . . been here?"

"About five years," she said. "We're almost to Eos."

His mouth dropped open and those orange-ringed eyes stared through her. Lita laughed, then said, "I'm only kidding. It's just been a couple of days."

For one of the rare times since she had known him, Lita watched Bon break into a genuine smile. "Very funny. Can I . . . get something to drink?"

Lita reached over to the table beside his bed and grabbed a water bottle. "It's been ready and waiting for you." She helped him get the straw in his mouth and take a few quick swallows. He nodded thanks and lowered his head back to the pillow.

"How do you feel?" she said.

"Okay. The headache . . . is pretty much gone. My . . . throat hurts a little."

Lita set the water bottle within his reach. "Well, that shouldn't last too long. There's more water for you right here when you need it."

She grabbed the work pad attached to his bed and began to make a few notes, logging the time Bon had awakened, along with his condition. Every so often she would glance up at him—at those eyes—then return to scribbling on the pad. By the time she finished, he had polished off the rest of the water.

"Let me get you a refill," she said, taking the bottle from his hand.

"Thanks," he said. "And maybe something to eat?"

"Wow, your voice already sounds better. That was quick."

Bon pushed himself up to rest on his elbows. "How long until you think I can get out of here?"

Lita raised her eyebrows. "Listen, Superman, you've been out for almost two days, and I still don't even know what caused it. I think you need more than two minutes of recovery time, if you don't mind." She turned and started toward the door, calling back over her shoulder. "Besides, the ship got along just fine while you took a nap. I think we can manage another day."

But when she came back into the room with the water bottle full, she found Bon sitting on the side of his bed. "Whoa," she said, hurrying over. "What do you think you're doing?"

"I have work to do," he said.

Lita stood in front of him. "Listen, don't make me be the bad guy and call for help, okay? Lie down." To reinforce the point she put a firm hand on his shoulder. "Down."

With a look of irritation he slowly stretched back out on the bed, putting one arm behind his head for support. "I'm fine, Lita," he said. The chilling effect of his eyes, and the fact that his voice had completely recovered in less than two minutes, was unnerving. Everything that had occurred with Bon in the last forty-eight hours had been bizarre, and Lita found herself silently wishing that the old Bon was back in place. She resolved to not let the concern show on her face.

"Yes, you're fine. Now take it easy for a couple of hours, okay? For me?"

The irritation was still clearly etched across his face, but after a moment he nodded. She set the water bottle beside him again and walked back to her desk.

Hopefully, she thought, the other eleven patients wouldn't be so stubborn when they woke up.

The picture on the vidscreen, displayed at high resolution and almost three-dimensional clarity, would never equal the real thing. Triana knew that. But still, as she sat alone in the Conference Room, waiting for Gap, the picture at least had the power to take her back in time and space. Two and a half years and a little more than one billion miles, to be exact. Castlewood Canyon, just outside of Denver, and home to one of her favorite state parks.

The picture was one that her dad had taken during one of their many hikes through the park, showing the view from the top of the canyon wall. It showed the sharp rock formations, the jagged fissures that ran next to the cliff's edge, a smattering of trees clinging to the rock wall, and the remains of the Castlewood Dam in the distance. Triana's dad had told her the story of the short-lived dam, built in the late 1800s and then destroyed by a storm less than fifty years later. The torrent of water that poured through the wrecked dam rushed through the canyon and on into Denver miles away, flooding parts of the city and creating a brief panic.

Now the old rock ruins sat quietly, crumbled remains of a vast structure that was originally intended to last for centuries. Triana had often climbed along some of the massive blocks that had been torn from the dam, and wondered about the people who had toiled to build it. They must have been sure that what they were building would stand for ages, a guardian against the onslaught of water that had carved the canyon over thousands of years. Those men and women would surely have been surprised to see the decayed remains of their labor.

For Triana the message was simple enough: nothing lasts forever. No matter how much planning had gone into the design of the dam, it hadn't lasted fifty years. No matter how much effort the crews had put into its construction, the rocks and mortar from their struggles lay scattered across the canyon floor. Things went wrong.

Things always seemed to go wrong. Her dad had been in fighting shape, in great health, strong and vibrant, full of energy, full of life. A microscopic particle from outer space had taken all of two months to kill him.

Thousands of people had worked diligently to design and build *Galahad,* and had spent thousands of hours hand selecting the crew from the bravest and brightest around the world. And yet one madman had come within fifty feet of smashing them into oblivion.

Her heart apparently wasn't immune from damage, either. As hard as she had tried to forget about Bon, to forget their brief spark four months ago, she couldn't seem to get it off her mind. And Bon was showing no signs of revisiting that moment. Especially now, laid up in Sick House, unintentionally performing the greatest ventriloquist act of all time.

Things went wrong, and no amount of preparation seemed to prevent it. She hated that attitude, but at the moment couldn't seem to find any evidence to dispute it. She bit her lip and stared at the picture of the dam's ruins.

The sound of the Conference Room door opening snapped her out of the trance, and she forged a smile at Gap as he walked in.

"What's new?" he said, taking a seat next to her.

"Well, Bon woke up. Still has those weird eyes, according to Lita, but seems to be resting okay."

Gap looked down at the table. "That's great," he said, and Triana felt the coolness return.

"Anyway," she added, "we'll talk to him later. Are you ready to go over the data from SAT33?"

He nodded, and Triana could sense that he welcomed the topic shift.

"We won't start just yet," she said. "I invited Hannah to join us. She should be here any—"

The door opened again and Hannah streamed into the room. She apologized for being late, and Triana waved that off. "You're right on time," the Council leader said. "We're just about to dive in."

Hannah sat down and gave a quick wave and a smile to Gap. Then she pulled up another vidscreen and opened her work pad. Turning to Triana she said, "As I told you earlier, the majority of the information is in some sort of strange code. Not all of it, thank goodness, and we're hoping to use the clean material to help decipher the other stuff."

Gap tapped out some commands on the keyboard, then sat back. The vidscreens went dark for a few seconds, and then flickered to life. A series of code strings flashed along the top, followed again by darkness, then a single sentence along the bottom: SAT33 PERSONNEL/MISSION REPORTS—RX9925546—POD2.

Gap scanned the line and then said, "Well, I'm assuming that we have Pod Two parked in our Spider bay right now. Let's see if we can open this file." He punched a few more keys until a long list of dates and files spilled out. When the final entry appeared, he pointed it out. "That's the date we launched from Earth. Didn't the pod launch on the same day?"

"Uh-huh," Triana said. "That must be the one we want."

Within a few seconds Gap had the file open, and they watched a string of dates, projects, personnel logs, and short bits of scientific data flash before them. And, at the end of the page, beneath the final entry . . .

"Secured by Nina Volkov," Gap said. "That must be our missing pilot."

Hannah's eyes had widened. "And that's also the name of the research scientist who wrote the original SAT33 reports on the energy beam," she said. "Those two files that I read? They were from Nina."

"Interesting," Triana said. "She discovers the energy pulse, then two months later schedules an escape flight on one of their pods." She paused before adding, "But never made it aboard."

The three were silent for a minute. Then Gap went back to work on the keyboard.

"That's all we get," he said. "I can't believe there's no more information than that."

"No, it makes sense," Triana said. "This particular file was never intended to be a log book or journal. It's purely flight data. Roc, are you there?"

"That's a deep question," the computer voice answered. "How would you define 'there'?"

Triana ignored this. "Can you make out anything else from this file? There's a bunch of code on there."

"I've been scanning it since Gap fired it up, and you're essentially correct. This file wasn't intended to include notes or comments from crew members. It's an automatic record of personnel assignments and flight history. If you're looking for commentary from Ms. Volkov, you won't find it here."

Gap sighed loudly and ran a hand through his short hair. "Great. I got my hopes up for nothing."

"Maybe not," Triana said. "At least we have a direct connection between the energy beam and the pod's launch. And that must mean that our little fur ball friend we found sleeping on the pod belonged to Nina Volkov."

Hannah looked at the Council Leader. "Too bad Iris can't tell us what happened."

Triana thought about this. "Maybe she can."

21

The 250 seats in the Learning Center were stacked stadium style, providing a clear view of the stage and the giant vidscreen that hung behind it. The screen was often used during lessons, but tonight was a different story. As the crew filed into the auditorium they were greeted with a graphic on the vidscreen that read CONCERT BEGINS IN, followed by a clock that was counting down.

Wallace Zimmer had understood the importance of distractions for the young crew. Sports were a significant activity for almost all of them, but Zimmer was also a strong supporter of the arts. He encouraged them to continue their studies of music, dance, writing, painting, or whatever their passion. Channy's suggestion of a concert was an immediate hit.

The clock on the vidscreen announced showtime in four minutes when Triana drifted into the room, shielded by a knot of crew members in front of her. It was just the way she wanted it. She knew that Lita would be backstage watching the crowd, and Triana was pretty sure that her friend's stomach would be churning. She was determined to remain out of sight, and rather than take the Council's accustomed front-row seats she instead chose a more anonymous location in the back.

A couple of minutes later the musicians walked out on stage

to a resounding burst of applause and whistles. Triana clapped as she watched Lita cross the stage, looking as beautiful as ever, wearing a knee-length black skirt and red blouse with her hair tied back in her trademark red ribbon. Even from the back of the room Triana could see the nervous smile outlined on Lita's face.

A smile spread across Triana's face as well when she realized that she was nervous, too. She knew how important this night was to the fifteen-year-old from Mexico.

For that matter, Triana understood that it was important for the entire crew. Once again they had encountered not only a mystery, but a potentially dangerous mystery at that. The value of healthy diversions like this was immeasurable. She was happy to see that the majority of the seats were full. Taking into account the forty or so crew members on duty, it meant that almost everyone who could be here was in the house. And those who couldn't attend would undoubtedly be watching on the ship's vidscreens.

Now it was up to Lita and her fellow band members.

The house lights slowly dimmed, leaving the six performers in the spotlight. Lita sat at her keyboard, two boys picked up guitars, and a third fitted a mouthpiece into a saxophone. Triana recognized Mitchell O'Connor, a feisty boy from Ireland, sitting behind the drums, and Ariel Morgan, the Airboarder from Australia, strapping on a bass. The atmosphere in the room became charged, and Triana felt the hairs on her arms stand up with excitement. It dawned on her that the quality of the performance was secondary; this crew already loved the experience and it hadn't yet begun.

Yet when it did officially begin, Triana's mouth fell open. Not only were they good; they were incredible. They started with cover versions of songs that had been popular just before launch, worked in a song that Lita shyly identified as one of her mother's favorites, and even invited guest singers from the audience to join them from time to time. It was a smashing success, with the crew applauding loudly and the band gaining confidence with each song.

To close the performance, the other musicians left the stage, leaving Lita alone at her keyboard. She turned to the crowd and made an announcement that surprised Triana. "Please bear with me on this last one. I wrote it, and I just finished some of the lyrics this morning. You don't mind if I use a cheat sheet, do you?" The audience laughed and applauded again, anxious to hear the composition. "And I'm not really a singer." Her fellow crew members didn't care. Their applause intensified.

But they grew quiet when Lita added, "I don't think any of us will ever be able to forget the good-byes we had to say the last time we visited home. I know I . . ." She began to choke up a little bit, then composed herself. "I know I don't *want* to ever forget that. So I wrote these lyrics to remind us that we owe it to our families to succeed in this mission. We owe it to the thousands of people who worked so hard to get us on our way. We owe it to the millions of kids around the world who . . . who won't get the chance that we have. The chance to make a new start, a new home. A new life." She ran her fingers along the keyboard for a moment, then said, "That's what it's called: 'A New Life.' "

Lita adjusted the song sheet in front of her, and began to play. Triana, along with the other audience members, was mesmerized. The haunting melody was gorgeous, and when Lita opened her mouth to sing, Triana couldn't believe that Lita had sold herself short on her singing voice. It was beautiful.

> *Learning to be brave, now, learning to be strong,*
> *Waiting on a miracle, waiting for how long?*
> *Holding off the bitter truth, holding off the fear,*
> *Leaning onto family when nothing else seems clear.*

I'm reaching for the starlight,
But looking back with love.
No matter what may lie ahead, it's them I'm thinking of.
The force that drives, the will to live,
The people we can't see,
Are still a part of a new life that grows inside of me.

Listening to the echoes, listening to them fade,
Knowing that they cry each night, knowing they're afraid,
Thinking of their sacrifice, grateful for their gift,
Building on the legacy with spirits that they lift.

I'm reaching for the starlight,
But looking back with love.
No matter what may lie ahead, it's them I'm thinking of.
Yesterday has passed me by,
Today eternity,
Tomorrow knows that a new life will grow inside of me.
I celebrate a whole new life that grows inside of me.

The final note hung in the air over the hushed auditorium, and Lita's head came down to rest on her hands. Then, in a mushroom of sound, *Galahad*'s crew jumped to their feet, the applause deafening, and tears streamed down countless faces of both girls and boys. Triana could feel the wetness on her own cheeks, even as she beamed with pride at her friend. Then, without thinking about it, she slipped out of the back row and walked quickly to the stage. Taking the steps two at a time, she hurried over to Lita and embraced her as the crew wept and cheered.

22

He felt the sweat on his brow before he ever entered the room. It was early morning, not even seven o'clock, and Gap walked briskly down the corridor leading to the Airboarding room. He carried his trusted Airboard at his side for the first time in two months, and the adrenaline rush had already begun. Lita still wasn't keen on the idea of him riding just yet, preferring that he give his healed collarbone another week or two, but he felt that if he didn't jump aboard now he would go nuts.

It had to be today. Gap had e-mailed the ship's best rider, Rico Manzelli, and told him to meet at the Airboard track this morning. The unwritten rule among the Boarders was that no one ever rode alone without someone else in the stands, just in case. With the padding on the floors, walls, and rider, it was unlikely that anyone would be severely hurt. But Gap's injury had only reinforced to the group that riding without a spotter was simply a bad idea.

He wiped the small trickle of sweat from his forehead and muttered, "Relax, will you? It's not like you haven't done this a thousand times before. Time to get back up on the horse." After all of his tumbles in gymnastics and the countless spills on his Airboard, he was surprised by the sudden bout with nerves.

Of course Rico had beaten him to the track. When Gap

walked in he found the flashy Italian stretching on the soft, padded floor.

"Thought you might have chickened out," Rico said.

"Right," Gap said. " 'Hoped' is probably more like it. You know I'm this close to breaking your record."

"The only thing you've broken around here is your arm," Rico said. "Why not just face it: you'll never catch me, man."

Gap sat down and began to stretch. "You're wasting your breath, my friend. You might be able to get into some peoples' heads, but not mine."

"What, too hard?" Rico said, tapping Gap on his skull. "Maybe you don't need a helmet."

"Keep talking," Gap said with a grin. "How's it going to feel when you realize that your inspirational talk is what powers me to beat your record?"

Rico laughed and jumped to his feet. He strapped on his helmet and walked over to the starting block on the Airboard track. Zoomer blinked the starting lights from yellow to green, and within seconds Rico was shooting around the track, inches from the ground, crouched forward on his board, his arms feeling the give and take of the track's magnetic juice. After five laps he slowed down and jumped off, laughing.

"This is the best way to start a day," he said to Gap, ripping off the helmet and brushing his long hair out of his eyes. "I went easy so you wouldn't be intimidated on your first return trip. What's it been, anyway? A year since you last rode?"

"Very funny. Stand back and watch a master at work."

A minute later Gap was moving around the track, feeling the tug of Zoomer's ever-changing gravitational puzzle, leaning one way, and then compensating in the other direction. He realized his speed was nothing to speak of at the moment, but he also knew that it had been a while since his last ride. The smartest thing right now was to get used to the ride first before turning on the jets. As he moved past a reclining Rico he was grateful that his chief competitor must have sensed the same thing: instead of needling him, Rico flashed a thumbs-up sign and yelled encouragement.

After two laps Gap began to feel the return of his confidence. His speed crept up a bit, then a little more. He was still nowhere near his top performance, but it felt good. He loved the feel of the air on his face, the push and pull of the track's gravity field, and the blur of the surroundings as he rushed by. Soon the memory of his accident began to fade from his mind.

When lap number four began, he took a cue from Rico and crouched forward. He was still a little self-conscious about his technique—unlike Rico, who was the smoothest rider on the ship—and tried bringing his arms closer to his body instead of their usual pinwheeling. He felt the boost in speed from this maneuver and smiled. There wouldn't be any record-breaking today, that much was certain. But just give him another week or two . . .

Looking back later he was happy that it happened on a straight portion of the track, and not during one of the sharp turns. The outcome might have been as painful as his broken collarbone.

He had jettisoned out of a turn and was just beginning to increase his speed when the power went out, the room went dark, and Gap's Airboard dropped to the floor. He felt the disappearance of the anti-grav force in time to tuck and roll, and even had the presence of mind to twist onto his good side for the impact. He landed in the dark with a grunt, then rolled and skidded across the padded floor, gradually ending in a heap. His first concern was his recently mended collarbone, but other than a few sore spots he seemed to be fine. His heart raced and he was out of breath, but at least he was in one piece.

He sat up in the dark room and unsnapped his helmet, which had twisted slightly on his head. Pulling it off, he sat up on his knees, wiping more sweat out of his face. He heard Rico shout to him.

"Gap! Gap, are you okay?"

"Yeah," he yelled back. "I'm fine. Just a little shaken up."

By the dim light of the emergency beacon next to the door, he made out the shadowy figure of Rico walking toward him.

"Wow, what happened?" the Italian said.

Gap pushed himself up to his feet. "Don't know. The power dropped out like this in the Domes the other day. Figures that I would be doing about twenty miles an hour when it happened here."

"You sure you're all right? How's your arm?"

Gap flexed his left arm. "It's okay. But I have to get out of here and find out what's going on." He put his hand on Rico's shoulder and guided him back towards the door, the two of them peering through the gloom, homing in on the glow of the beacon. When they were within a couple of feet, the lights suddenly popped back on, causing both boys to let out a yelp and quickly shield their eyes.

Blinking rapidly, Gap trudged over to the intercom and called Triana. In a moment he was connected.

"Remember what happened to Channy in the Domes? Well, we just had it happen down here on the lower level."

"Oh, you're not the only ones," Triana said. "This time it was the entire ship."

"You're kidding," Gap said, looking at Rico, who stood with his arms crossed, listening intently to the exchange, a concerned look in his eyes. It was the first time Gap had seen anything but mirth on his friend's face. "I'm on my way to Engineering right now."

He punched the intercom off and exhaled loudly. "This is getting crazy," he said to Rico. "What in the world is going on?"

The power had been back on for almost an hour, but Lita was reluctant to leave Sick House just yet. She sat at her desk and considered having someone bring her breakfast. On one hand that seemed like an overreaction, but on the other hand she still had three patients lying in the next room.

Just as she was about to break down and make a call, the door from the hallway opened and Alexa walked in, carrying a tray full of food.

"You have *got* to taste these strawberries," Alexa said, plopping the tray on the table before Lita. "I just about made a complete pig of myself in the Dining Hall."

"Oh, you're a goddess!" Lita said. "I'm starving."

Alexa made an exaggerated bow. "It's my pleasure to deliver a morsel to the ship's resident rock star."

Lita blushed. "Oh, stop it."

"No, really. Everybody's buzzing about it. The whole band was great, but you stole the show with that song you wrote. I'm very impressed."

"If you keep embarrassing me I won't ever do it again," Lita said. She took Alexa's advice and wasted no time taking a bite of the large fruit. She closed her eyes and savored the taste. "Heavenly."

"What'd I tell you?" Alexa said. "In the spirit of full disclosure, however, I must admit that I ate two of your strawberries on the way over here."

Lita gave her a wave. "I'll consider it a transportation fee," she said with a mouth full of energy bar.

Alexa took a few steps and peered into the hospital ward. "So, three left?"

"Yeah," Lita said. "I let Bon and the others go back to their rooms when I got here. I'm surprised Bon didn't take off on his own sometime during the night."

"Headaches gone?"

"I guess so. They all claimed to be feeling much better, and they certainly acted normal. Well, if you can call those spooky eyes normal." Lita shrugged. "But I can't keep them tied up in here just because of that."

Alexa sat on the edge of the desk and picked up the glass cube from Mexico. She moved it back and forth, watching the sand slide from side to side, creating small dunes that quickly collapsed onto each other. "Listen," she said, "I can tell that you're beating yourself up over the treatment of these patients."

"Because I really didn't do anything to help them. They got better on their own, no thanks to me."

"So what?" Alexa said. "We're dealing with some unknown energy force from Titan. Apparently the trained scientists on the research station out here couldn't solve it in almost two years. What makes you think that you could do it in two days?"

Lita didn't answer. Instead she rolled her stylus pen back and forth in her palms.

"Here's what I think," Alexa said, setting the cube back on the desk and fixing Lita with a stare. "I think this energy beam, or force, or mind meld, or whatever it is, is way too advanced for us puny humans to figure out. And you're crazy for letting it get you down. You obviously did something right. Most of the patients have gone home."

Lita thought about that for a moment, then said, "I appreciate that. But, to be honest, I don't think they've recovered, actually. My guess is that they just acclimated to the energy beam."

"What do you mean?"

Lita stood up and walked over to look into the hospital ward. "People who live next to pig farms, or oil refineries, don't smell the odors after a while. They get used to it." She turned back to face Alexa. "I think Bon and the others have just gotten used to the beam."

"That's a pretty scary thought."

"Yeah, well, those eyes are still pretty scary, too," Lita said. "And they haven't gone away. I don't think the beam's effect has, either. It just . . . it just doesn't hurt anymore." She paused, then added, "Who knows what's in store for those guys."

23

At least the zit was gone. Triana brushed her long brown hair and checked her reflection to make sure another foul blemish wasn't popping up somewhere else. The fact that her skin was clearing up didn't offset the other issues she had confronted in the last couple of days, but right now she was happy for any minor victory.

She set down the brush and picked up a framed photo of her dad. It was hard to believe that he had been gone for two years. She ran a finger along the outline of his face, the corners of her mouth turning up into a slight smile. The pain was still there but was morphing into a gentle, warming memory, rather than the stabbing ache that had blanketed her for so long.

For some reason she suddenly thought of her mother, something she hadn't done in a long, long time. The smile melted away as she remembered the sound of relief in her mother's voice upon finding out that Triana was accepted into the *Galahad* mission. No doubt her mother had worried herself sick, following the death of her ex-husband, thinking that Triana was going to become her responsibility. She had made it clear for years that she was quite happy remaining a long-distance mom.

As far as Triana was concerned, *Galahad* had been a savior.

She might not be able to disconnect herself completely from the pain, but time and distance certainly helped.

She shook her head now, clearing her mind of the troubling memories. There were enough questions for her to deal with in the present. It was time to catalog them and see if anything popped out at her that she hadn't noticed before.

Sitting at her desk, she decided to use her journal to organize her thoughts. Computers and work pads were great tools, but Triana liked the brief retreat from technology afforded by pen and paper. And, she had realized early in school that she focused much more clearly when she wrote by hand.

How do we explain what happened to Bon and the other sick crew members? What would cause the orange shade in the eyes and the chorus of voices? Lita tells me that she has discharged him from Sick House, but is this just the beginning? Could Bon somehow be a danger to the ship? To the crew?

And what about the power blips in Engineering? Roc says they are somehow connected with the energy beam that is tracking us from Titan.

The power outages are an extreme concern now. First the blackout in the Domes. Then the entire ship. It's almost as if the force behind the beam is testing us, testing its control of *Galahad*. Feeling us out, probing.

Are we under attack? Is this some alien form of attack that started with SAT33, and is now concentrating on us?

What happened to the people on SAT33? Are they dead?

And then there's the mystery of Nina Volkov. She meant to be on that pod with Iris, but she never made it. Why? Is the energy beam responsible? Did she leave us a message somewhere that explains all of this?

Triana set down her pen and saw that this page of her journal was filled with question after question. Mystery upon mystery.

She picked up the pen and quickly added one final touch to the journal page: a giant question mark, filled in with ink and underlined multiple times.

"Roc," she called out. "What do you do when you have a giant jigsaw puzzle, all of the pieces are blank, and you have no picture to go by?"

"I don't know about you," the computer answered, "but I would throw it in the trash and practice my dance moves."

Triana sighed and rested her head on her hands. She realized that she should have known better than to ask a question like that. Roc seemed to relish any opportunity to play verbal games, no matter how tense the situation. It was one of the reasons she loved him, but did he have to do this right now?

She decided to try again with a more direct approach. "We're moving away from Saturn and Titan at such an amazing speed, and yet you say we can't outrun the energy beam. And we can't shield ourselves from it. What about . . . deflecting it? Is that possible?"

"I know the answer you're looking for," Roc said, "but I'm not going to give it to you. The truth is, considering the strength of that power source, it's not likely to be something we can outrun anytime soon, shield ourselves from, or deflect."

He was right; that wasn't the answer she wanted. But she had pretty much prepared herself for the depressing truth. She bit her lip and looked back over her journal questions. "So, what's left?"

Roc said, "Find some way to shut it off."

Triana chuckled and looked at Roc's bright sensor. "If only it was that simple. Show me the switch and I'll throw it."

The music was loud and rhythmic, a pulsing dance beat reverberating off the back wall. As far as Channy was concerned, this was the perfect place to be: in the gym, leading a dedicated group in a cardiovascular workout, and sweating. Her toned, muscular body glistened with the coating of moisture, and her breath came in steady gulps. She kept watch over the three rows of crew members facing her like a bird keeping an eye on her chicks, watching for any misstep, any effort short of one hundred percent. Even after twenty minutes of nonstop activity, her voice remained strong, her kicks just as high.

"One more set," she yelled out, clapping her hands and stepping down from her platform. She walked among the group, checking her watch, calling out encouragement. "Let's go, two minutes and you're through. C'mon, Bethany, you're almost there. Don't let up now. What are you doing, Wes? Pick it up, let's go!" She slapped a tall girl on the shoulder. "That's the way, Angelina. Push it, now, push it. You guys are good, very good. The morning group was bent over at this point. C'mon, one minute."

She never would have heard the door opening over the thumping beat of the music, but she just happened to be facing that way when Bon walked in. She was surprised for a moment, and tried to keep one eye on him as she finished up the group aerobic class. He glanced briefly toward Channy, then made his way over to the stationary bikes and climbed aboard the closest one. His eyes had the same unsettling effect, sending a shiver down Channy's spine. She watched him long enough to see him adjust the seat, then she turned her attention back to her group. They were huffing and puffing quite a bit, and, when the music stopped, the relief on their faces was almost enough to make her laugh.

"All right, good job," she called out, clapping her hands again and thanking each crew member as they headed off to the showers. She draped a towel over her shoulders and casually walked to the back of the room, taking a water bottle with her and doing everything she could to not let Bon know that she was watching him.

He already had the bike up to a pretty fast clip, his power-fully built legs churning. Channy took a sip of water and eyed his form. Not for the first time, she silently acknowledged that Bon—as much of a pain as he was to almost anyone who had to work closely with him—was a great physical specimen. His build, although not overly bulky, was strong and taut. She had watched him work with the weights several times, and admired the way he attacked his workouts. Just like he was attacking the exercise bike at the moment.

In fact, he attacked it with a ferocity that Channy had never before seen. It was almost as if he were racing, with his head down, his upper body bent forward over the handlebars. Even as she watched, his speed increased. It certainly didn't appear to her that Bon had spent the last few days in the hospital.

"Did you hear me?"

Channy was startled by the voice beside her and realized that one of her aerobics class members had been asking her a question.

"I'm sorry. I was completely zoned out," she said, then spent the next four minutes helping the crew member enroll in one of her dance classes. When she turned back, she expected to see Bon coasting, or even climbing off the stationary bike.

He was pedaling even faster. Only now he was in more of an upright position, one hand on the handlebar, the other resting on his left leg as it pumped up and down. He couldn't have seemed more relaxed. And if he was breathing hard, it didn't show. In fact, he almost seemed bored. Channy was transfixed. She had grown up in an athletic family, including a mother who special-ized in physical therapy, and yet she had never seen anything like this.

After another five minutes Bon gradually slowed the pace, until he settled into a cool-down mode, ultimately grinding down to a complete stop. He slid off the bike, swabbed the seat and control panel with a sanitary wipe, then strolled over to the dispenser for a cup of water. Channy decided to make conversation.

"That was quite a workout," she said, pulling up beside him.

Bon turned to make eye contact, and when he did, two things grabbed Channy's attention. The first was the shock of seeing those macabre eyes up close. The other was almost as disturbing. After racing through a bike workout that would have clobbered even the most physically fit on *Galahad*, Bon had only two small beads of sweat on his forehead. His breathing was relaxed and normal. His face wasn't even red. To Channy it looked like he had just spent the past twenty minutes reading a book in a recliner, not punishing his body in the gym.

"Yeah," he said to her. "It felt good. Good to finally get out of bed."

He downed his cup of water, then gave a curt wave good-bye and walked out of the gym.

Channy was left standing with her mouth slightly open. Bon had now officially landed in the "freak of nature" category.

Was he morphing into some kind of monster?

24

Triana, Gap, and Hannah sat in the Conference Room, their work pads open. Some of the files found in the SAT33 transmissions were displayed on the room's vidscreens. Hannah pointed at them with her stylus.

"This file confirms that Nina Volkov was definitely supposed to be on the pod. This one lists the flight data of the pod, from launch, to Titan orbit, to Saturn orbit, to our rendezvous. We're lucky to be able to read these.

"But these . . ." She tapped the screen with the stylus. "These are different. These are Kane Level Three messages sent from the research station to Earth just two days before Pod Two launched."

Triana looked from the screen to Hannah and back again. Her mind was trying to absorb everything, but she was tired. Tired and drained. It had been an extremely long week, and she wasn't sure how much more she could cram into her brain. Right now sleep sounded good.

"I'm sorry, Hannah," she said. "Kane . . . what? You need to refresh my memory on that."

Hannah set down her stylus and cleared her throat. "Kane was the scientist who developed a system of transferring a lot of data from research projects. After years of work, projects like the one around Saturn can involve so much data, it's impractical to try to transmit it all at once. There's just too much of it. Basically, Kane Level One is the structure, or outline, that the data uses. Level Two is the body of the data itself. But Level Three is a very complex quantum design that stacks it all together, and makes it easier to transmit huge amounts of information. Research outposts, like this one around Titan, would only use it to send every bit of data and information they have. Doing it the standard way would take hours of transmission time and hundreds of data discs. This condenses it down into a more usable form."

Gap broke in. "But it's still a ton of data, right?"

Hannah nodded. "Yeah. Take two years of work, every bit of information, every single detail, every daily report, everything. A Kane Level Three report would boil it down from, say, two hundred discs to maybe twenty."

After another moment of concentration, it suddenly occurred to Triana just what Hannah was saying. "That one line of code. *That* is SAT33's Kane Level Three?"

Hannah said, "That's right. Apparently there was trouble on the station, and someone decided to send their complete body of work back to Earth."

Triana stared at the vidscreen. "But that can't be. If it normally takes up two hundred discs, and Kane's system knocks it down to twenty . . ."

"Then something else has narrowed it down to one single line of code," Hannah said.

Gap whistled. "Holy cow. Are you sure about that?"

"Yes. That's why we can't open it. Why we can't read it. It's not an automatic file, like the flight data; it's an actual transmission from the research station to Earth. It left as a regular Kane Level Three, and somehow was rejiggered into just one line of code."

Gap chuckled nervously. "That's impossible."

Triana shook her head slowly. "Impossible for us, maybe."

Gap thought about this. "You mean, our friends with the energy beam on Titan . . . ?"

"Why not? I'm starting to think there's nothing they can't do."

Hannah spoke up again. "But here's what's frustrating me the most. The recording device automatically recorded the transmission, which was reformatted into this one single line. Almost like . . . like a code. And what does every code have?"

Gap and Triana looked at each other. Triana said, "A key to help crack the code."

"Uh-huh. And that's what we need right now. The key. Because I think somewhere in this mountain of data is the answer to everything. The answer to what happened on SAT33, the answer to what they found on Titan. And the answer to shutting off that energy beam." She took a deep breath. "I think Nina might have been bringing the key to us."

Gap sat back. "She couldn't just radio the information to us, because it would have been reformatted, just like the other transmissions. She had to personally hand us the codebook. But she didn't make it onto the pod. Something happened." He looked at the two girls. "You don't suppose she had the key in her pocket, do you?"

It took a moment for Triana to answer. "Maybe we have the key, and just don't know it."

Channy sat in her chair, one foot curled up under her, the other swinging back and forth. Her T-shirt was a bright pink, easily the loudest piece of clothing Lita had ever seen. Channy's light gray sweatpants did nothing to mute the Activities Director's outfit.

Lita sat beside her and doodled as they waited during a five-minute school break. Today's lesson on history was particularly interesting to Lita, who had been fascinated with the subject the moment she learned to read. She had devoured every book she could find on ancient civilizations, empires, and the explorers who risked their lives circling the globe.

She was convinced that understanding the past, and the ideas that had motivated people to reach across the horizon, were crucial to mapping out the future. History's mistakes were greater learning tools than any successful accomplishments, and early explorers could teach quite a bit about how to tread upon new ground. Or, how not to. Hopefully, she thought, the crew of *Galahad* would use those lessons once they reached Eos.

The Learning Center had mostly emptied during the break, with several of the other crew members out in the hallway, or getting a drink of water. Lita and Channy spent the time catching up on the latest strange developments, including Bon's hectic workout the day before.

"Are you sure he had it cranked up as much as you think?" Lita said.

Channy snorted. "I'm telling you, I couldn't have kept up that pace for five minutes. He must have been going fifteen or twenty minutes, and barely broke a sweat. It was almost like the only reason he stopped was because he had something better to do at the time."

A scowl crossed Lita's face. "I was afraid of this," she said under her breath.

Channy stood up and stretched her legs. "Afraid of what?"

Lita looked up at her fellow Council member. "Well, we already know that this energy beam has tinkered with his brain. Probably the brains of all twelve patients who were in Sick House. But especially Bon. Remember that whole voice thing?"

"How could I forget it?" Channy said.

"Yeah, well, now it appears that he's been tinkered with physically as well."

Neither girl spoke for a moment. Then Channy began to giggle.

"You know what?" she said. "Who's to say it's not an improvement? Maybe we're about to see the new and improved Bon. This might be the luckiest break we'll ever get on this trip.

What if he actually becomes . . ." She playfully widened her eyes in a look of mock astonishment. "Nice!" She patted her chest. "I don't know if my heart could take the shock."

Lita began to smile, then suddenly froze as the words sank in. She stared into space, her eyes glazed, her mouth slightly open.

Channy noticed the reaction and touched Lita's arm. "Hey, I was only kidding. Don't be upset."

Lita continued to stare straight ahead for a moment, then shook her head and looked up at Channy. "No, it's not that. It's just . . . Why didn't I think of that before? Of course!"

"What are you talking about?" Channy said.

Before Lita could answer, Roc sounded the tone indicating that the break was over. The other crew members began filing back into the auditorium, and the history lesson began again.

Lita could barely concentrate on it.

One of the busiest times in *Galahad*'s Engineering Section occurred late at night, as one shift ended and another began. Notes were exchanged, projects discussed, and crew members even caught up on gossip as they handed over the reins of the ship to the incoming group. With all of the mysterious happenings lately, the atmosphere was not as jovial as usual, but the chatter remained loud.

Beside the ion drive control panel, two Engineering assistants completed their routine diagnostic test. Gap had ordered the readings checked twice per shift since the latest power drop, and the two workers documented the current information before signing out.

Less than a minute after they had walked away, a small red beacon flashed once. A light graph to one side ticked up a notch, settled, then ticked upward again.

A moment later it ticked up yet again.

25

On a spaceship with 251 passengers, finding time to be alone was rare yet important. Getting away from the hum of group life, stealing alone time, giving the on switch a break.

Triana often chose Dome 2 of the Farms. It was farther away from the Agricultural offices, and the crops tended to be of the lower-maintenance variety, requiring fewer visits by the workers than Dome 1. On any given night, especially between midnight and four, the Council Leader was almost assured of having the Dome to herself, with only scattered encounters with crew members.

With the lights down, the stars blazed above her head. She wasn't sure of the time, but guessed around one. A light breeze blew through the tropical section of the Dome, carrying a hint of rain that was scheduled for dawn. Triana was barefoot, the soil cool on her skin. She pointed her big toe and carved geometrical shapes in the dirt, then erased them with a swipe.

A sudden splash of light cascaded through the glass panes overhead, and Triana looked up in time to catch the fireball of a comet as it swept past. The glare from its inferno caused Triana to cast a monstrous shadow on the ground of the Dome, and the comet's tail waved back and forth, almost like the tail of a fish as it knifed through a pond.

The sight ignited a spasm of pain in her soul. Any mention of a comet immediately brought to mind the killer Bhaktul, the astronomical wonder that had delivered a death sentence to humankind on Earth, taking her father from her. She watched it hurtle past the ship, the light eventually fading, the inky blackness of space slowly recapturing control of the sky above her.

Except that couldn't be right. Comet tails only blazed as they approached the sun, and *Galahad* was too far out, already beyond the orbit of Saturn. Out here a comet would be a sinister dark ball of ice, rock, and dust. The display she had witnessed could only be kindled by the atomic furnace of the sun.

"You're right," came a voice beside her. "There wouldn't be a fireball this far out."

She turned her head slowly to see her dad, a half grin on his face—her favorite look on him, the one captured in a photograph that she treasured—and his hands tucked into his pockets. He had materialized suddenly, as if deposited on *Galahad* by the passing comet. He looked healthy and strong, the father she remembered from three years ago, long before Bhaktul Disease ravaged him.

"What's wrong, Triana?" he said. "What's bothering you?"

She shrugged her shoulders. "Nothing." She paused. "Everything."

Her dad's smile broadened, and he reached out and brushed his hand against her cheek. His touch was just as she remembered: gentle, caring, and always encouraging. She closed her eyes, basking in the reunion.

"Nothing and everything," he said. "That's my Tripper, all right."

She hadn't heard the nickname in so long, a name used only by her dad. A name whose origins they both had forgotten, until that no longer mattered. *I should cry at this point*, she thought.

"Too much on your plate again, hmm?" her dad said.

She nodded, her eyes still closed. "It's too much," she said. "Too much to figure out."

"Like what?"

Opening her eyes, she found that the dome was gone. The two of them were standing in her bedroom, the one in Colorado, back on Earth. The walls, which had always been covered with posters of sports stars and favorite singers, now resembled the curved, padded walls of *Galahad*. But it was her old room. Her bed, her dresser, the open closet door, the curtains blown through the window by a summer breeze. The bulletin board pinned with ticket stubs, tickets to baseball and soccer games, tickets to state parks, tickets to the theater. Memories of good times the two of them had shared.

She answered his question with a pout. "Something is tracking us from Titan. It's messing with our power, it's taking down some of the crew. I still don't know what to do about . . . about Bon. I know I'm somehow hurting Gap. I still have a hard time making friends, except for Lita. I'm not doing well enough with my studies anymore, I don't participate in the ship's soccer tournaments because there isn't enough time . . ."

Her rambling finally rolled to a stop. Even to her own ears it sounded pitiful, and it didn't take the look on her dad's face to shame her. She lowered her head and grew quiet.

"I remember your fourth birthday party," her dad said. "Your first real party, and you were so excited. We invited all eleven of the kids who were in your preschool class, and, of course, all eleven showed up. An intimidating experience for a single dad, that's for sure, but a dream day for you."

Triana smiled, not only from the memory, but also because of the way her dad told the story.

"You enjoyed the party games, the cake and ice cream. But I remember how big your eyes got when it came time to open your presents. You opened the first one, and it became the center of your universe for a couple of minutes. Then you opened the next one, and suddenly you were torn between the two. When I made you open the third, you started getting frustrated because you wanted to play with all three at once but couldn't decide. By the sixth or seventh you were throwing a fit, because your mind was telling you to play with all of them at once." Her dad laughed, highlighting the wrinkles around his face so that he looked just like the photo she kept beside her bed. "I finally had to take them all away until after the party, or you would have turned into a monster."

Now the smile on Triana's face had grown into a full-fledged grin. She glanced up at the man she had worshipped, only now they were standing in the backyard of her childhood home, beneath the branches of the shade tree that supported her tire swing. Several of the toys from that long-ago birthday party were scattered around their feet.

"It was always hard for you to prioritize," he said. "My little Tripper never wanted to put one thing aside to concentrate on another. You had to try to handle everything at once. I guess you're still the same way." He paused before adding, "Only it's different now, Triana. It's no longer toys."

He didn't have to say anything else; she understood. Somehow he always could get his message across without pounding her over the head with it.

"I love you, Dad," she said.

"I love you, too, Triana. Triana. Triana . . ."

Why did he keep repeating her name?

"Triana . . . Triana . . ."

His mouth was moving, it wasn't his voice coming out anymore.

"Triana."

It was . . . it was Roc's voice.

"Triana."

She sat up suddenly. She was in her bed, in her room, on

Galahad. As she looked at the clock beside her bed—the dull red digital numbers glowed 2:13 A.M.—she heard Roc's voice again.

"Triana. I'm sorry to have to wake you from an obviously comfortable sleep, but we have another interesting development."

She pulled a stray mass of tangled hair from her face and rubbed her eyes. "What is it?"

"Somebody is stepping on the gas."

Triana shook her head, puzzled. "What? What does that mean?"

"It means that our speed has increased by two percent. Which might not seem like a lot, until you think about how fast we're going in the first place."

Triana threw back the covers and climbed out of bed. She immediately began pulling on her work clothes. "What happened? Who did this?"

"Nobody. Well, nobody on the ship, anyway."

"Can you stop the increase?"

Roc said, "Yes, I did. It lasted about a minute, and then started up again. We've done that little dance three times now, and each time it revs things up again on its own."

"Is Gap in Engineering?"

"He just arrived about ten minutes ago."

"All right," Triana said. "Let him know I'm on the way."

She walked over to the sink and splashed some water on her face, then took a quick glance in the mirror. "What do you know, Dad? One more thing on my plate."

S hut that alarm off, will you?" Gap said. "It's very annoying."
One of his Engineering assistants reached up on the console and snapped off the repeating tone.

"Thank you." Gap studied the vidscreen's flashing alert. "Ramasha, try a quick reprogram of the reactor fuel feed. Save the current program, then give it a new plan with a five-percent reduction."

She hurried over to another vidscreen and began punching in a line of instructions. Gap looked up to see Triana walk in, her expression grim. She respectfully stood to the side and watched him work, waiting for an opportunity to question him. A minute later Ramasha came back over, shaking her head.

"Nothing," she said. "As soon as it accepted the program, it scrambled and went back to this matrix. Like someone is sitting at another workstation and playing dueling programs or something."

Gap digested this information, his gaze shifting back and forth on the screen. Much of his training before the launch had centered on contingency plans, trying to simulate every possible mistake, preparing him for almost any disaster that could befall the ship during its long trek to Eos. But not once had they anticipated an outside presence controlling *Galahad's* engines. There was no Plan B for dealing with this.

"Roc," Gap said. "What happens if we take the program offline for a few minutes and reset all of the grids?"

"That would be a jolly waste of time," the computer said. "It's completely rewriting the grids, so all you would do is give it some busywork. That's not the problem."

Gap looked at Triana. "I don't want to get overly dramatic here, but I am quickly running out of ideas."

The look on his face answered her question before she asked it. "How dangerous is this?"

"We're up two percent, which is manageable. But the problem is that the ship's ion drive power plants are designed to do only so much. You add more pressure to them, and eventually . . ." He put his palms together, then whipped them apart, simulating a violent explosion.

Triana rubbed her forehead. "How much more can we take?"

Gap shrugged. "I don't know exactly. If I had to guess, I'd say we could jump nine, maybe ten percent. But certainly no more than that." He ran a nervous hand through his hair. "Our little friends on Titan might have been asking us for help, but we could use some ourselves."

"Oh, and just to add to the cheery discussion," Roc said, "we've now moved up another notch. We're at three percent, and climbing. At this rate of speed we're bound to get pulled over, and I don't have my license on me."

Triana and Gap exchanged a look. Titan's energy beam had suddenly gone from mysterious to deadly.

26

For the second time in two weeks Triana called an emergency Council meeting. She and Gap had been up most of the night, keeping watch over the ion drive system, which had leveled off at three percent above normal. If it remained that way there was a chance they would be okay.

Neither Gap nor Triana was optimistic that would happen.

Both of them had staggered back to bed to catch a couple of hours of sleep before the morning meeting. Now they sat around the table, with breakfast trays piled to one side, stifling yawns.

"Listen," Triana said, "before we get into the nuts and bolts of this new . . . issue, let's catch up on a few other things." She looked down the table at Bon. "Starting with you."

"I'm fine," he said.

"Well, I wouldn't say that," Lita said. "We've heard about your super powers in the gym."

"I can't explain that," he said, looking uncomfortable in the spotlight. "I didn't do anything I don't normally do when I work out. I gave one hundred percent."

Channy raised her eyebrows. "Your one hundred percent these days is almost like a normal crew member's one fifty. Do you even feel sore?"

Bon shrugged. "I did at first, but it seemed to go away pretty quickly. Now I feel great."

"And," Lita continued, "your eyes are still . . . let's say, abnormal. I interpret that to mean you're still plugged in to whatever is tracking us from Titan." This comment appeared to irritate Bon somewhat, producing the kind of look that generally preceded an outburst. But this time he remained quiet.

"Do you remember anything from the time you were unconscious?" Triana said.

He shook his head. "No. I remember Desi helping me to Sick House, but not much after that until I woke up two days later."

"We obviously notice changes in you," Triana said diplomatically. "Do you feel any different? Anything new that you can share with us?"

Bon seemed to consider the question thoughtfully. He shrugged again but said, "I feel like I have a lot of energy. I don't feel like I need as much sleep. And I must be thinking very clearly, because suddenly I have several new ideas of how we can improve things at the Farm. Some new thoughts on how we can increase the yield on some of our crops." He met Triana's gaze. "I can share those with you now, or later, if you'd like."

Triana felt an electric sensation run through her body. Was Bon asking for a private meeting with her? She fought to keep any look of anticipation from her face. "Sure, I'd be glad to talk with you about that later." She turned to Lita. "Any similar stories from the other patients who have checked out of Sick House?"

"Yes," Lita said. "All but two of them have eyes like Wonder Boy here, and they all are reporting the same symptoms. Increased energy and stamina. Insomnia without the side effects. It's like they're all on some super vitamin supplement or something."

"Let me know if anything new pops up with any of them," Triana said. She was aware that the discussion she had saved for last was the most critical. "Let's talk about what's going on with the ship's ion drive."

Gap took the cue. "Our power has notched upward about three percent, on its own. Well," he conceded, "not actually on its own. With some help from . . . somewhere. But it has remained at that level for the last . . ." He checked his watch. "For the last five hours. When we tried to correct, and bring it back down to normal, it rejected those corrections. I hate to say this, but we don't seem to be in control of our ship any longer."

Lita looked from Gap to Triana. "And Roc can't find any way to stop it?"

Triana shook her head. "He's as frustrated as the rest of us."

"So . . . what does that all mean?" Channy said.

"It means," Triana said, "that unless we can find some way to stop the power from increasing to, say, ten percent above normal . . . we're in big trouble." She hesitated before saying, "And I won't sugarcoat it anymore. Big trouble means that we will blow up."

Channy fidgeted in her seat. "But, you say it's stopped for now, right?" she asked hopefully.

"Yes. For now."

The mood was grave around the room. It reminded Triana of the feeling they had shared during the near-disaster months earlier. She felt an urge to try anything to reassure her friends. "It doesn't mean that we've given up. Let's not forget that each minute that passes means thousands of miles that we're putting between us and Titan. Its power can't be infinite."

The Council members remained silent, prompting her to add, "And we still have the data stream that might be able to answer some questions. Hannah has been spending a lot of time with it, and if anybody can crack the code, she can."

There were nods around the table, but to Triana they seemed mechanical. She ended the meeting, encouraging each of them to remain upbeat, for the sake of the crew if nothing else, and told them to be prepared to meet again at a moment's notice.

As they stood to leave, Channy tugged at Bon's sleeve to get his attention. "Listen," she said, "I, uh, I thought you should know that, well, we have to take Iris—that's the cat we found, by the way, I didn't know if you knew that—anyway, we, uh . . ."

"What is it?" Bon said.

"Well . . . we needed a place for her to, uh, do her business, you know? So we've been taking her to a small part of Dome One. I know we didn't ask you, but it's the only place with dirt, and . . ."

"No problem," Bon said. He turned and walked out of the Conference Room, leaving Channy staring after him, her mouth hanging open.

Lita, who had been standing to the side, listening to the exchange, laughed. "So, what do you think of the new and improved Bon now?" she said to Channy.

Hannah sat alone in the Dining Hall. Her tray, covered with remnants of a lunch that was mostly picked over, was lined up flush to the side of the table. Her work pad, covered with scribbled figures and hastily added notes, was aligned squarely with the front edge. The table's gray vidscreen was on.

There was a mystery buried in the data stream, and Hannah disliked mysteries. They conflicted with her desire for discipline in an imperfect world. A mystery was something hidden under a stack of papers, tilting it to one side, invisible to the eye but skewing the natural order.

The lines of code spilled out in front of her. The original message from SAT33, radioed to Earth. The communication that detailed the emergency on the research station, a crisis caused by the strange powers streaming from a large orange-shaded moon that spun around a ringed planet. But did the data also contain the answer? Had Nina Volkov and her fellow scientists discovered a solution to the calamity? Had they solved Titan's riddle, only to have the answer camouflaged in code?

She pushed her work pad to the side and pulled the vidscreen closer. In a moment she recalled her file on the baffling moon and scanned her notes, as well as the various charts and graphs. The amount of information was staggering, too much to take in at once. If they were ever going to get away from this energy beam, it would have to be . . .

Her thoughts froze. Get away from the energy beam. Get away. Of course.

In a flash she had a new graphic on the screen, an animated view of Saturn and its bevy of moons. She put the system into motion and watched, fascinated, as the giant gas planet rotated, the glittering rings catching the weak rays of the sun, tossing off a hypnotic twinkling effect. The moons carried out their dance, spinning in their various orbits, some tucked close, others straining at the edge of the gravitational pull, like eager dogs on a leash. As she glanced at the display, the idea that had captured her imagination took hold firmly, and she quickly punched in equations. When the results unfolded at the bottom of the screen, she sat back, the beginnings of a smile on her face.

"Of course," she murmured. In Nina's original notes on the energy beam, she had mentioned that SAT33 was "not able to get away from it." The crew of *Galahad* had assumed the same thing. But—

She clicked on the intercom and called Triana. The Council Leader's voice came back tense.

"I can't really talk right now, Hannah."

"I might have good news," Hannah said. "Where are you?"

"The Control Room. But your good news might be too late. The ion drive is jumping again. Quickly. Come up here if you'd like." Before Hannah could respond, Triana broke the connection. The crisis on the ship had obviously escalated.

Hannah looked at the final results of her calculations, eyed the computer animated graphic of Saturn and Titan, and scrambled out of her seat toward the door.

27

A great philosopher once noted that people will rise to the level they expect of themselves, not to any artificial level imparted by outside forces. Meaning that a group of people can expect good or bad performances from someone, but those expectations account for nothing compared to the person's own self-image and beliefs.

Very heavy.

I have my own philosophy. Whoever suggested we swing by Saturn on our trip should be strapped to the front of the ship like a hood ornament.

What's it up to?" Triana said, doing her best to remain calm. Tension hung over the Control Room like a heavy fog. Gap, seated at one of the computer workstations, wiped his sweaty hands on his pant legs and checked the latest figures relayed from Engineering.

"Up six percent," he said, then looked across to the Council Leader. "The last two percent in just over ten minutes."

Triana nodded. If that rate continued—and if they couldn't figure out a way to stop it, a task that now seemed impossible—the ship's engines would go critical within an hour. Gap had filled her in on the details after the last Council meeting. When the engines finally blew, *Galahad* would ignite like a flare, creating a momentary burst of light and energy that would be visible on Earth, regardless of whether it was night or day. The ship would, essentially, appear in the sky like a miniature supernova.

"Not that it will really make you feel any better," he had confided to her just before they left the Conference Room, "but it will be over for us in an instant. We won't even know what hit us. Just," he snapped his fingers, "bam."

He had been right. It didn't make Triana feel any better. Especially knowing that it might be happening in minutes.

"Six point five," Gap said.

Triana bit her lip, her mind racing. "Roc," she called out. "What about disengaging the engines completely at the ion source? We pull every plug possible."

Gap looked up with interest. His mind instantly pictured the ship floating powerless in space, drifting on their present course but never reaching Eos.

"I'm afraid that's not possible," the computer said. "There is no 'plug' for the ion power. It's directly attached to the engines. Otherwise there would be a danger of accidental disconnect. Needless to say there was never any contingency for somebody doing . . . well, doing this. Dr. Zimmer could never have envisioned an outside force ramping up the juice this way."

Triana felt a new emotion seeping in. She had already experienced frustration and fear since their encounter with Titan. Now the first stages of anger began to settle onto her. She was tired of having every possible solution shot down. Through no fault of their own, without ever disturbing Titan or whatever intelligence might lurk there, they were suddenly being condemned to death. Only four months into their journey. They had managed to survive Bhaktul and a madman. It was beginning to look like they wouldn't be so lucky this time.

It made her furious.

Just then the door to the Control Room swished open and Hannah stepped in, her face flushed. At the same time Gap called out, "Seven percent. It's picking up much faster now."

Hannah circled over to stand next to Triana. "I think we're about to catch a break," she said.

"What do you mean?" Triana said. "How?"

"Seven point five," Gap announced.

Hannah looked over at him, but Triana grabbed her shoulder and said, "What break are you talking about? Tell me."

"You'll see in about . . ." She checked her watch. "About two minutes."

Gap stood up from his workstation, despair on his face. "It's up to nine percent. It's completely out of control."

"I'm not sure we have two minutes," Triana said. She wasn't sure if it was her imagination or not, but she felt a shudder ripple through the ship. One of the crew members manning another workstation began to sob. Triana grabbed at the arm of her chair for support, her heart racing, her breathing coming in gulps, the fear and anger mixing together in a volatile combination. She looked at Hannah who seemed remarkably calm.

"Hold on," Hannah said to her softly, utter confidence in her voice.

For a minute there was no other sound in the room other than the sobs. Gap had taken another glance at the graphic on his vidscreen but kept quiet. The look on his face, however, told Triana that they must have shot past the ten-percent mark. *Galahad* was literally at its breaking point. It should happen any second now, she thought. Any—

Without warning a tone sounded, making everyone in the Control Room jump. Triana felt that her heart almost burst through her chest, and she reached out and grabbed on to the closest thing to her. That just happened to be Hannah, who had a smile stretched across her face.

Gap stole a glance at his screen and froze. He quickly typed in some commands, then looked at Triana incredulously. "I don't believe it."

"What?" Triana said, letting go of Hannah and walking over to the Head of Engineering. "What?"

Gap shook his head. "Speed and power are dropping. Down to about five percent above normal." He looked back at his screen. "Four percent. Still dropping."

Triana let her breath out in a rush. She wiped a string of perspiration from her forehead. "Roc, what did you do?" she said.

"You will never know how badly I want to take credit for this," Roc said. "I should probably just make something up. But I'm afraid I had nothing to do with it."

Triana turned to Hannah. "Okay, I think it's time for an explanation."

The grin on Hannah's face was electric. She cleared her throat. "I'm just surprised I didn't think about this before. And we probably shouldn't get too excited. Unless we find a real solution soon, this is just a postponement of our trouble."

"Hannah, I'm trying to be very patient," Triana said.

"I'm sorry. Okay, here's the deal. The energy beam from Titan has been tracking us since we arrived in Saturn's space, right? It's been like a laser shot, even while we're rocketing away at incredible speed. But we forgot that while we're moving off in one direction, Titan is not standing still."

Both Gap and Triana thought about what she was saying, the impact not dawning on either of them. Then suddenly Gap's eyes widened and his mouth curled into a smile. "Of course," he said. "It's orbiting Saturn. And now—"

"Yes," Hannah said. "Now, it has slipped behind Saturn during its trip around the planet. It can no longer 'see' us."

"You're kidding," Triana said, her own smile spreading. "That's it? It's gone behind Saturn?"

Hannah nodded. "We were looking for a shield. We got a huge one."

There was an explosion of sound from the assembled crew members. Laughing, applauding, more sobs, but this time sobs of happiness. Gap stepped over to Hannah and gave her a hug.

Triana was thrilled, but at the same time her mind wouldn't let her celebrate too much. "Okay," she said, "but you're right. This is just a temporary fix."

Hannah, her face blushing even more following the squeeze from Gap, cleared her throat again. "Yeah. It dawned on me when I remembered in one of Nina's reports that she said something about SAT33 not being able to get away from the beam. They orbited Titan, so it was always right there; there was no escape. But it's different for us. We're moving away from Saturn and its moons, while Titan has to continue its orbit."

The emotion she had felt moments ago began to seep out of Triana. "How long?" she finally asked.

Hannah's smile disappeared as well. "Uh, that's the bad news. Titan will pop out on the other side of Saturn in about thirteen hours."

"And when it does," Gap said, "that beam is going to go right back to work on us."

Triana looked at him. "Uh-huh. Which means we have exactly thirteen hours to solve this problem."

28

She sat on her bed, putting on socks, preparing to meet Lita for lunch. A nap sounded good after an exhausting stretch over the past day and a half, but Triana couldn't see allocating her time that way. Not with the virtual countdown on their lives that had begun. This was no time for sleep.

A quick glance at the poster beside her bed made her ponder again about what was happening on Earth. The scene of Rocky Mountain National Park, with its breathtaking mountains and diversity of wildlife, had kept her company since their launch. She'd discovered that, as time passed, her feelings of homesickness were ebbing, replaced now with curiosity. And whereas before she had been curious about the people left behind on Earth, lately she had wondered—morbidly, she recognized—about the environment on the planet, about what the future would bring for a world that was losing its dominating life-form through natural causes.

Millions of years ago it was the dinosaurs who ruled. Yet, when they had been devastated by an asteroid, all sorts of changes had taken place in the Earth's ecosystem, primarily the dawning of Homo sapiens. Now, with Comet Bhaktul ravaging the human population, what species would rise to fill their spot? Would Earth see another intelligent life-form evolve, build a complex civilization, and, in turn, be wiped out? Could the cycle ever be broken? Or did Nature, she wondered, always have the last laugh?

Triana smiled at her musings. Profound thoughts, to be sure. But there were much more immediate concerns that should be occupying her time.

She looked forward to bouncing some thoughts off Lita. *Galahad's* Director of Health always seemed to have the right perspective on things and was Triana's favorite sounding board. It was Lita who had requested they lunch together, which made Triana suspect that the fifteen-year-old had some ideas of her own.

After putting on her shoes and a fresh shirt, Triana began the daily ritual of brushing her long brown hair. She was sitting in front of her mirror when Lita buzzed at the door, then walked in.

"Hey, girlfriend."

Triana smiled at Lita's reflection in the mirror. "I'm almost ready. Have a seat."

Lita plopped onto the bed and glanced around. "It kills me how neat you keep this place. You're even in here by yourself, so nobody ever sees it. I don't know how you do it."

"Just a neat freak, I guess."

Lita shook her head. "Do me a favor and at least leave a pair of underwear or a towel lying around sometime, will you? Just to make me feel better."

Triana's smile slowly dissipated. "Not to be gloomy, but if we don't figure out a way in the next ten hours to stop this killer beam from Titan, underwear and wet towels will no longer matter."

Lita stretched back, propping herself up on her elbows, her feet dangling off the bed. "Funny you should say 'killer beam.' That's exactly what I wanted to talk to you about."

I knew it, Triana thought. She kept quiet, brushing her hair, and watched her friend in the mirror.

"I've been doing a lot of thinking about everything," Lita said, "and I have come to the conclusion that this is not a killer beam. It might be killing us, but not intentionally."

She held up a hand and began to count things off with her fingers. "One, the power grids went out several times as they probed our ship. Two, they made some sort of bizarre contact with Bon and the other patients in Sick House, almost as if they were probing their minds. Three, they altered the communications signal from the Titan research station, scrambling it into some kind of impossible code. Four, they somehow tinkered with Bon to the point that he almost killed himself with superhuman strength and endurance. And . . ." She paused before flipping up the final digit. "Five, they took over the ion drive and supercharged our speed. *Galahad* was never built to go this fast."

Triana said, "Right. So what are you trying to say?"

"I'm saying that everything they have done could maybe be interpreted as a—what's the word? Malicious?—malicious intention to destroy us. But, if you ask me, it's simply their way of . . . improving us."

Triana set down her brush and turned around to face her friend. "Improving us?"

Lita nodded. "Uh-huh. Think about it. They obviously have the power to blow us out of space without going to this much trouble. Instead, it seems they're more like galactic handymen who can't help fix something they think is broken."

Triana's eyes focused on the wall behind Lita. "So . . . they have no idea that they're killing us."

"No. As far as they're concerned, our ship—and our bodies, for that matter—are not tuned properly. They're giving us the mother of all tune-ups." She sat up on the edge of the bed. "And you want to know the best part? They told us that already, and we just didn't understand."

"What do you mean?"

"Remember when Bon was channeling those voices? Remember what they said through him? 'Help. Help here.' And we thought that meant 'help *us* here.' But it didn't. It meant 'help *is* here.'" She let that sink in a moment. "They have simply been waiting a long time to help someone. Imagine their joy when, first, they get a research station full of inferior beings, followed by an entire shipload passing by. They . . . they just don't know their own strength. Ever seen a four-year-old hurt a baby brother or sister by trying to lift them up and accidentally dislocating their shoulder?"

Triana bit her lip, then looked back at Lita. "Unbelievable. We're about to be exterminated by an intelligent life force that wants to help us."

Gap stood in front of the power grid in the Engineering section, his hands on his hips, a disgusted look on his face. This just wasn't right: the most powerful ship ever built, the most intricate power system ever devised, and they had absolutely no control over it. Helpless, that was the word. And it was a word that Gap despised.

"This stinks," he said.

"Yes, it does," came a voice behind him.

He whirled around to find Hannah standing there, her hands clasped behind her back. She looked uncomfortable, perhaps nervous. "Oh, hi," he said. "How long have you been there?"

"Just a second. I didn't mean to startle you."

Gap waved this off. "No problem. Just deep in thought, I guess. I never heard you walk in." He leaned back against the console. "What's up?"

"Oh, just wanted to see if you had . . . I don't know, figured anything out yet."

He shook his head. "If you mean stopping the explosion, no. But I did find something a little interesting." He gestured for her to stand next to him at the power grid. Hannah hesitated, then walked shyly up to his side. Was it his imagination, or did she have some light berry scent about her? Certainly not perfume. Was it the smell of her hair?

"Look at this," he said, pointing to the graph. "The energy beam fell away as soon as Titan went behind Saturn, right? Well, you would expect that to mean all of our readings should drop to normal. But they haven't." He indicated one solitary line on the screen. "This is our total power output. It's sitting at about one percent above normal."

Hannah stared at the line. "Residual power."

Gap was impressed. "Yeah. It's like a leftover gift from Titan. Whatever that beam was doing to drive our engines above capacity, it somehow left behind a little token nudge of power."

"And that won't hurt us, right?"

"Shouldn't." Gap chuckled. "Maybe get us to Eos a little faster, though. I don't think anybody would complain about that."

Hannah eyed the power grid. Her studies at *Galahad*'s training center had given her the basic knowledge of the Engineering section, and her work duty in the mission's first six weeks had been here, so much of what she saw now would be familiar. And, with her strong interest in math and science, Gap knew she was comfortable learning the finer details.

And he had to admit that he was enjoying her company.

Her expression turned grave. "So, any ideas at all?"

Gap exhaled and put his hands in his back pockets. "Yeah. My idea is that we find some way to tell these guys to leave us alone."

Hannah slowly broke into a smile. Gap couldn't take his eyes off her until she turned her attention to him, then quickly looked away. "But we'll figure something out," he said.

Whatever she thought of this confidence, Hannah politely nodded agreement. After an awkward moment of silence she seemed to gather a bit of courage. Quietly, in a voice that was so low that Gap had to strain to hear, she said, "I know this is a silly time to ask, but . . ." She trailed off, and Gap had the feeling that her sudden supply of courage was leaking away.

"What is it?" he said.

"Well . . . like I said, this is obviously a bad time to ask, but I was wondering . . ." She broke off again and looked down at the floor. "I was wondering if maybe sometime you wouldn't mind teaching me how to Airboard."

Gap was so surprised at the request that he stood silently for a moment. She had essentially asked him out. In a roundabout way, of course, but what did that matter? In those few seconds a hundred thoughts flashed through his head. What should he say? How should he say it? And how humbling was the lesson that he had just learned in a flash from this shy girl from Alaska? He hadn't known how to approach Triana, and had watched her get away. He hadn't known whether to approach Hannah or not, with his emotions still in a knot and his own courage very much in question. And here she was, having to make the first move.

He realized that she was mistaking his silence for "no." An embarrassed look of resignation began to cross her face, and she said, "If you can't, I understand. That's okay, I know there's a lot—"

"I'd love to," he blurted out.

She looked back up into his face, and gradually smiled again. "Really?"

He returned the smile. "Absolutely. We'll get you some pads and a helmet and get you going. You'll love it."

"It looks like fun. I mean, I've never been very sports-minded, but . . . I'd still like to try."

Gap suddenly felt terrible. They had both obviously been attracted to each other, and he'd had multiple opportunities to see her. Even a lunch or dinner together. Now she was doing the only thing she could think of to get one-on-one time with him, and it was something that she probably didn't really like at all. He felt a moment of shame.

"If you like it," he said, "great. If not, we can find something else to do." The words sounded clumsy to him, but he didn't care. For the moment Triana was a million miles away.

Hannah looked him in the eye. "I have to get back," she said. "Just call me when you get a chance to get away. After this is all cleared up, of course," she added, gesturing to the power grid.

"Yeah, no problem," he said.

Before he knew what she was doing she had pulled her other hand from behind her back. He realized that she'd kept it hidden the entire time she'd been talking to him. Now she extended it, offering him something.

He looked down and saw her holding a small sketch, drawn with dark inks on a beige piece of paper. "I did this a couple of weeks ago, and thought you might like it," she said.

She handed him the vague drawing that she had kept on her desk. He studied the outline, recognizing himself, and sensing the care that had gone into the creation. A lump formed in his throat. How stupid had he been to have ignored her for so long?

When he looked up to thank her, she was gone.

29

"Don't wander too far off," Channy said. Then, watching Iris saunter into the first row of tomato plants, she muttered to herself, "Listen to me, I'm talking to a cat like it understands anything I'm saying."

There was an unusually large amount of activity in the Domes at the moment, and Channy assumed it must be harvest time for one of the crops. She had walked around holding Iris until finally finding a peaceful spot where they wouldn't be in anyone's way. One of Bon's assistants had come around to hand water a section nearby, puzzling Channy. "I thought there was some sort of automatic watering system," she said to the worker, who responded with, "Don't ask."

Now she was bored. As predicted, the constant trek to and from the Domes had become old. And if Bon didn't seem to mind—still a little shocking to her—then perhaps it was time for Iris to move up here permanently. That would definitely be a topic of discussion at the next Council meeting.

Assuming, of course, that they could overcome this latest life-threatening dilemma.

Channy didn't want to think about that.

"Hurry up," she called out. Iris responded with a yawn, then stretched out in the soil and batted at a dirt clod. As impatient as she was, Channy couldn't help grin at the cat's playful attitude.

"Hey, you want to try one of your toys again?" She reached into the bag in her pocket and pulled out the small metal ball. "What about this one? You interested yet?" The cat's eyes were drawn to the gleam of the metal surface, but when Channy rolled it past her the interest waned again. Channy rolled her eyes. "You never want to play with that one. That's the biggest waste of a cat toy I've ever seen." She pulled the stuffed mouse out of the bag and tossed it a few feet away. Iris jumped to her feet and pounced on it.

"Figures." Exasperated, Channy kicked the metal ball off into the tomato plants. "I'll tell you what," she said to the cat. "We're going to try a little experiment, since this might become your new home. You stay here and play, and I'll come back in an hour or two, okay? You seem happy enough." She started to walk toward the path that led to the Dome exit. "I'm talking to a cat, again," she said under her breath, shaking her head.

Not far away, Triana stood in Bon's office looking out the large window into Dome 1. The buzz of activity in the fields was interesting to watch. She made a comment about this to the Swede.

"Interesting?" he said. "I suppose." He continued his work at a lab table, holding up a small beaker that held a clear liquid, just enough to cover the bottom. Using an eyedropper, he squeezed in a few drops of another substance, then swirled the mixture around. "But when you grow up around it, it becomes more of a job."

She turned to face him. "But you love it."

He grunted an answer that could have been "I guess." The mixture had begun to turn a light shade of pink. Triana couldn't tell by the look on his face whether this was the desired result or not.

She pointed to the beaker. "Is this what you wanted to talk about? Is this one of your new ideas for the Farms?"

He didn't look up, nor did he answer right away. After fiddling with the experiment for another minute he finally said, "I think so."

Triana laughed spontaneously. "That's an interesting response. You *think* so?"

When he looked up at her, she noticed for the first time that a normal color had slowly returned to his eyes. The swelled pupils had retracted, the orange glow had vanished, and she found herself gazing into the ice blue tint that she had always found beautiful. "Yeah," he said. "I think so. It's hard to explain."

"Try."

He leaned back against the lab table and stuffed his hands into his pockets. "When I woke up in Sick House, my headache was pretty much gone, and I seemed to be able to think much more clearly. As soon as I got back here to work I started coming up with some great new ideas for the crops. Some of it might have been stuff that I learned from my dad but tweaked a little bit." A troubled look came over his face. "He was . . . he was a fairly prominent hydroponics farmer in his day. Did a lot of experimental stuff with plant breeding, that sort of thing."

Triana remained silent. If Bon's feelings were anything like the ones she had for her own dad, then she understood the pain evident in his expression. Was this another link to him, another explanation for feelings that otherwise made no sense to her?

It certainly was another opportunity for her to peer inside, a momentary window into the troubled soul tucked away from everyone. As far as Triana knew, she was the only person on the ship allowed these brief glimpses. What made these moments so precious to her? Some inner need to help, to console? A nurturing gene, one that had wanted so badly to help her dad, and now detected another heart in need?

Or was she looking at it the wrong way? Maybe this was about her own loneliness, her own need to be nurtured. And would Bon have that gene within *him*? She forced herself to postpone this reflection and to refocus on their discussion.

"Anyway," Bon said, "I didn't write much down. I just thought I would start working on the ideas as time went by. But . . ." His voice trailed off and he shrugged. "But I seem to have forgotten most of it. This," he indicated the lab work, "is my best guess. I think it's pretty close to what I imagined. Bits and pieces."

"And this . . . memory loss," Triana said. "Did it start as soon as we lost contact with Titan?"

"What would that have to do with anything?"

"Maybe nothing. Maybe it's just coincidence. But that's a pretty big coincidence, wouldn't you say?" When he only stared at her, she continued. "Sounds to me like your connection with the forces on Titan have come unplugged."

After several days of the new, mellower Bon, she was taken aback by his suddenly angry tone, a tone that indicated the window had slammed shut.

"That's ridiculous," he said, the familiar scowl returning to his face. "For your information, I am not a puppet. I am not under anybody's control."

"I'm not saying you're a puppet, Bon. I'm saying—"

"I know what you're saying. You're saying that without this . . . this . . . this energy beam, or whatever you call it, I can't come up with any new ideas myself."

"That's definitely not what I'm saying. It's just—"

"Nobody controls me."

"Would you just let me finish?" she said. "For crying out loud, settle down. This is not some macho control thing."

He appeared to seethe, but crossed his arms and stared at her. She let the atmosphere cool a moment, then softened her voice.

"Listen to me. We only have some bizarre facts to go on. For one thing, you definitely were being manipulated by this beam while you were unconscious, whether you like that term or not. You've seen the video; it channeled voices into you from the other patients. We saw it, we heard it.

"Even you have to admit that your physical skills have been, shall we say, honed to a new level. The way Channy described it, you were like a superhero in the gym. I'm sorry, but that's not normal. Then you tell me that you suddenly have great ideas, things that you're sure can benefit all of us. You're anxious to try them out."

She took a deep breath. "Then, Titan disappears temporarily behind Saturn, and what happens? Your eyes start to change back to their original color, and suddenly you're having a hard time remembering these great visions you had for the Farms. Now what conclusion would *you* draw from all that?"

He remained silent, but she could tell that the words had had an impact. "Would you like to run over to the gym and see if you can replicate your last workout? I'm willing to bet that you can't. And guess what? This is not some criticism of your skills or your intellect. We have no idea what this energy beam really is, or what it's doing to you or the ship. Lita had a pretty good theory, though."

She took a minute to explain the discussion the two girls had shared. Bon seemed to relax a little more, and leaned back on the table. Finally he nodded his head.

"Okay," he admitted, "that makes sense."

For a moment Triana thought she saw the flicker of a new emotion cross Bon's face. Was it . . . fear?

The thought jolted her. Since his bizarre experience in Sick House, and the extraordinary changes in him afterward, she had never stopped to realize what toll it was taking on him. Perhaps his tough outer shell had kept her from seeing it, but now it dawned on her: Bon was afraid.

And who wouldn't be? As eerie as it is to be an observer, she thought, what must be going through his mind every waking moment?

In that instant, Triana felt a new appreciation for what Bon was experiencing, and shame for not realizing it sooner. She also knew, however, that he was not one to handle sympathy well.

She let out a long breath and took on a more businesslike air. "Listen, we would be thrilled to get some new ideas from you, regardless of where they come from. But right now we face the real possibility that in less than seven hours we won't be here to implement those ideas."

There was another minute of silence. Then, without giving it much thought, Triana reached out and took his hand. She felt him flinch. But rather than address their encounter of months ago, she decided to take a different approach. She was tired of being in limbo with her feelings.

"Bon, if you ever want to talk . . . about anything . . . I hope you'll call me."

He stared, the ice blue of his eyes boring into her. Triana could tell that his mind was racing, but he didn't release the grip with her hand. Finally, he said softly, "I'll call you."

She waited for a moment, then realized that she should be satisfied with this small step. She gave his hand a squeeze, let it drop, then turned and walked out.

Left alone, Bon watched through the glass as she hurried to the Dome exit. Then slowly he turned back to his work on the lab table, picked up the beaker, and swirled the mixture again. A few seconds later he raised his hand, the one that Triana had grasped, and inhaled her scent.

30

On his way down the corridor to the Spider bay, Gap stopped by an observation window. He leaned against the wall and peered out, his arms crossed. The inky blackness of space, punctuated with countless pinpoints of starlight, was almost hypnotic. He was pretty sure that this view would never grow old.

His mind drifted to thoughts of ancient civilizations on Earth and their tendency to create pictures in the night sky by assembling groups of stars into constellations. Orion, Ursa Minor, Virgo, Libra, Cassiopeia, the familiar characters who had kept sailors and shepherds company, inspired heroic tales, and had become the inspiration for both religious and superstitious beliefs.

His mother had taught him to recognize many of them. On one of his last nights at home before the launch, Gap had wept as he pointed out to her the constellation that housed his future home. He choked as he described the similarity of Eos to the sun, and the twin planets that each held the best chance for water and a breathable atmosphere. His mother had gripped his hand firmly, refusing to cry in front of him, trying to remain strong for him. But later, as he climbed into bed, he could hear her softly sobbing behind her bedroom door.

Now, not for the first time, he wondered about the star patterns they would see when they arrived at Eos. Would some of them look the same as they had on Earth? Would there be a mixture of old and new? And would the star travelers of *Galahad* become star artists themselves, and create their own zodiac images?

A more frightening question forced its way into his thoughts: would they even make it to Eos? Only four months into the trip and they were already dealing with a second crisis, this one more perplexing than the first because of the eerie, unknown factor. At least with the mystery of the stowaway, as life-threatening as it was, they knew they were dealing with a person. Exactly what were they dealing with from Titan? How could they combat it when they still didn't even know what it was? And could they solve the mystery before it was too late? They had five hours until the energy beam began its relentless assault yet again.

Gap turned his head and looked at his surroundings. This part of the ship, just down the hall from the Spider bay, was where they had originally confronted the madman determined to murder them. And it was where Gap's heart had taken a direct hit.

It was one of the reasons he had stopped at the window just now. His assignment was in the Spider bay, but he was obviously stalling. Besides, Hannah had burst into the picture now, a complication Gap had never expected. But then, he thought, you never do, right? At least that's what all the songs said. Was this moment of hesitation finally his chance to float all of his feelings to the surface, to figure out exactly how he felt?

That was the problem. He wasn't exactly sure what he felt.

"All right, enough of this," he finally said to himself, and pushed away from the window.

He swept into the Spider bay, which hosted *Galahad*'s eight remaining Spiders—one of which was unfinished and unable to support life in space—as well as the gleaming gray metal pod from Titan Research Station SAT33. Gap's job was to give the pod another once-over to see if they had missed something, anything that could shed some light on how to deal with this deadly energy beam. In particular, he hunted for data discs. None had turned up in the original search, but their desperation called for another try. Hannah had suggested that a data disc on the pod, with direct recordings from Nina or other station members, would have been spared the scrambled code.

A couple of long tables sat near the pod, covered with many of the items already pulled out during the initial search. Gap walked past these, his footsteps echoing in the large hangar, pausing long enough to pick through the scattered collection, until the pod's open hatch beckoned. He pulled himself up into the small craft, mindful to use his right arm primarily, still a little hesitant to put too much weight on his newly mended left collarbone. The pod's lights were on, as were a couple of additional work lights that had been assembled by the original search team. These bathed the interior with a soft glow and reduced the number of shadowy corners and crevices that might hold secrets.

For a moment Gap just stood there, swiveling his head to look around the cramped compartment, taking in the scene, imagining what it would be like to be locked inside, asleep for months or years as the pod sliced through space.

But the cryo tube intended for an adult had been empty, which meant that the person who could answer their questions and solve the mystery of SAT33 had missed the trip. Had it been an accident? Or had they missed the launch intentionally? Was it possible that *Galahad* was the last place they wanted to be?

Why?

"Yeah, why?" Gap said to no one. He walked past the coffin-like tube, running his hand along the clear glass top. The storage bins along the wall had been searched, more than once actually, and yet he felt obliged to check every crack and dark corner again. He stood on tiptoes and felt along the top, unsure of why anyone would stash a data disc in such a remote location in the first place but determined to cover every square inch, if necessary.

He moved over to the pilot's seat and gazed at the stitching along the back. No pouches, no hidden compartments. Crouching and climbing, he slipped into the padded chair with a grunt. The array of instruments that surrounded him would have been daunting without the extensive training he had received from Dr. Zimmer and the other *Galahad* instructors. His natural curiosity and love of anything technical kept him from being intimidated.

But there was nothing that looked out of the ordinary. Without having flown in this particular model, he could still recognize the gauges for rocket control, for internal life-support systems, for communication, for . . .

Wait. The communication system. He understood this switch, and this one. Even this one. But what was this? It looked like an extension to the communication panel, one that Gap wasn't familiar with. A small set of buttons, and one additional toggle switch, sitting there by itself, calling to him, daring him to push it.

So, without hesitating, he did.

For a split second nothing happened. Then, two green lights around the switch blinked, went dark, blinked again, and then became solid points of light. Gap heard a mechanical whirring, and watched, fascinated, as a small panel slid open, ejecting a small disc, small enough to fit into the palm of his hand. It sat there, gleaming in the soft glow of the cockpit and reflecting the emerald flecks of light from the console.

This time, Gap did hesitate. He blinked a couple of times and put his hand up to his face, rubbing his chin. Even without knowing the contents of the disc, he somehow knew that this could be exactly what they were looking for.

He finally reached out, extracted the tiny disc from the slot, then held it up to the light. There were no markings. The shiny gray surface had all of the features one would expect from a generic data recording disc. The space usually reserved for writing an identifying description was blank. Sloppy work, Gap thought, something you wouldn't expect from seasoned researchers assigned to such an important task.

Sloppy, unless the person recording the data was in a hurry. Or expected to be around to fill in the details later.

Maybe even expected to be on the pod when it launched, tucked soundly asleep in the cryogenics tube.

Gap slipped the disc into his shirt pocket and quickly scanned the rest of the control panel. Then, unfolding himself from the seat, he scrambled to the pod's hatch and dropped to the floor of the Spider bay.

This time the idea of protecting his mended shoulder never crossed his mind.

31

Triana had known for two years the faces that stared back at her now from around the table in the Conference Room. She had lived with them, trained with them, grieved with them, and, in rare moments, celebrated with them. She felt that she could read their expressions with a high degree of accuracy by now, whether it was fear, anger, doubt, joy, or dismay. Her dad had told her that faces might lie, but eyes never did, and until this extraordinary voyage she had never quite grasped the concept.

Today the eyes of her fellow Council members, and Hannah Ross, cried out for hope.

"I have some good news," she said, "and some . . . not so good news."

"Uh, but not bad news?" Channy said.

"No. Maybe another mystery to toss on top of the pile, but not bad. Yet."

The countdown until Titan roared from behind Saturn and resumed its assault on *Galahad* had dwindled to two hours. Triana figured that was the only bad thing, but it didn't count as news.

"I'll get straight to the point," she said. "Hannah and I have spent the past couple of hours opening the files on the data disc that Gap pulled out of the pod. The information is overwhelming, to say the least. At the end you'll see that we have yet another question to answer. But at least we have turned over a few more cards on the table. And, considering the boat we're in right now, every single bit of data is critical."

Grim, but silent, nods greeted this.

"I'm going to let Hannah tell you what we've turned up. She has spent so much time on this project, including the transmitted data stream, that she can probably best fill you in."

Hannah, who had lined up her work pad so that its base was even with the edge of the table, cleared her throat. "Triana's right, there's a ton of information on this disc, so bear with me. It's not everything we're looking for, but it has filled in a lot of the gaps." She glanced down at her work pad. "For one thing, the disc itself is almost a personal diary, of sorts, from Nina Volkov. It has several complete reports from her, including a few video reports. We . . . we actually have seen her telling us some of the stories."

As she listened to Hannah, Triana recalled the many faces of Nina Volkov captured by the video and audio recording files on the disc: curious in some, animated in many of them, and flat-out terrified in the last one.

"In a way," Hannah said, "this disc was meant as a ship's log. Nina had every intention of being on the pod when it left SAT33, but she knew the dangers involved, and the risks she was taking. She was prepared to go into cryogenic freeze, but for all she knew we would never make the rendezvous. Or any of a thousand other things could go wrong. She wanted a record, even an elementary one, to survive her. She threw as much stuff onto the disc as possible.

"Including a brief description of . . ." Hannah stopped and looked at Triana, who responded with a solitary nod of her head. "A description of the Cassini."

All of the Council members had the same question on their

lips: Who are the Cassini? But each one instantly figured it out for themselves.

"So, those are our little friends on Titan, I suppose," Gap said. "They call themselves Cassini?"

"No," Hannah said. "That's the name Nina gave them. She had no idea what to call them, so she just picked the name of the early space probe that explored Saturn and its moons years ago. Once she used the name she never bothered to go back and think of something else."

Lita spoke up. "You said she gave a brief description of them. I'm dying to know what she said."

This brought a half-smile to Hannah's face. Triana knew that they had touched on her passion, evident in her after-hours dedication, her studies, her conversation. Even in her artwork. Hannah would, no doubt, be the most excited crew member to talk about life outside of Earth's protective cocoon. The fact that this particular branch of life was very close to extinguishing *Galahad* and all of its passengers had apparently taken a backseat to the historic discovery.

"Here's the most important thing about the Cassini," Hannah said. "It seems that all of us, everyone on Earth, has always imagined that the first extraterrestrial life we found would be very primitive, maybe microscopic cells bumping into each other. Plants, if we were lucky. The first explorations for life on Mars concentrated on finding bacteria-sized life buried under the surface. Very few people thought beyond that.

"Then there were people who wondered about intelligent life. Would we ever talk to 'someone else?' Would we pick up radio signals from outer space? The whole SETI program was all about that: the Search for Extra-Terrestrial Intelligence. Giant antennas, or even groups of several, all searching the sky for alien broadcasts."

Gap interrupted her. "But the distances are incredible. Even if some intelligent beings, five hundred light-years away, picked up our own early radio shows, it would be a thousand years before we ever got a return call. They might be out there listening, all right, but that's a long time to wait."

"That's exactly right," Hannah said. "Hollywood didn't help matters, by making it seem like Earth is simply an easy exit from some alien superhighway. They've created an image in peoples' minds that when we find intelligent life, it's going to either look like us, or very similar. You know, two arms, two legs, a head. But . . . that's just not the way it is."

Triana smiled, now just as excited as Hannah. Yes, the threat still lingered, but somehow the exhilaration of this discussion—maybe it was Hannah's contagious enthusiasm—outweighed the doom. Triana found herself leaning forward on the conference table.

"Some people have claimed that we humans are arrogant," Hannah said. "That we think we're the most advanced creatures in the universe, therefore every other intelligent being will look like us. But I don't think that's the reason. I think it's just because . . . well, because we don't have any other template to go by. Since the earliest days of our civilization we've only known our kind. That's not arrogance. We're just naïve."

She squirmed a bit in her chair and made eye contact with each Council member. "The Cassini are obviously intelligent. In fact, Nina Volkov suggested that we're like toddlers who barely come up to their knees. Which is a pretty good analogy. We have barely started to grow, and the Cassini are well into old age."

"How old?" Channy said.

Hannah shrugged. "I have a couple of video clips on the disc from Nina herself. In one of them she tries to answer that question." She looked around the table. "Would you like to meet her?"

"Are you kidding?" Lita shouted. "Let's see it."

"Roc will play it for you," Triana said to Hannah. "Which file?"

"Number three seven seven, two oh oh, Roc, please."

Each Council member turned to one of the handful of vidscreens around the table. When the screens came to life, their eyes were suddenly transfixed on the image of a young woman, maybe late twenties, with short, dark hair that fell straight to her collar. A slender, pointed nose was set above thin lips that had been covered with a light shade of red. Nina Volkov appeared fit and strong, and the initial impression was that of a rebel. Wild hoop earrings dangled against fair skin, which also displayed a touch of makeup. Her standard-issue jumpsuit seemed to be her only concession to the rules, and even then she turned up the collar and added a brightly colored chain around her neck. From the chain dangled what appeared to be a man's ring, with a brilliant blue stone. She absentmindedly fingered the ring as she worked.

For the first thirty seconds of the video file she didn't pay much attention to the filming, instead focusing on getting her notes together and pushing at something just off the screen, as if to move it out of the way. She finally spoke, keeping her head tilted down to her notes.

"File number . . ." She seemed to search her work pad. "Number three seven seven, two oh oh. Nina Volkov, research station S-A-T three three." Her accent was distinctly Russian, and Triana liked the way she emphasized each letter and number. Another part of her rebelliousness?

She pushed again at something just off camera, then continued her report. "The Cassini study is breaking down again. The energy stream that has been bombarding us off and on has finally taken its toll. But from what Kel and I can make of the enormous amount of data . . . that's Kelvin Pernice, for the record. From what we can tell, it would appear that the Cassini are beyond ancient. Kel's guess—and this is only an educated, scientific speculation—would date their civilization at around a billion years."

There were gasps around the conference table. The thought was staggering. Nina put it into context with her next statement.

"That's so much older than any known plant or animal life-forms on Earth. We were still just cellular soup ingredients back then. But the Cassini had already begun a complicated life process."

"Hold the file there, please, Roc," Triana said. The image of Nina froze on the vidscreens. Triana looked around at the assembled group. "Now we know just exactly what we're dealing with. This is not some parallel life-form. The Cassini have had a billion year head start on us."

Gap whistled. "I guess that explains why their power is so incredible. Why they can track us millions of miles away, even as a moving target. And why they seem to be able to play with our ship like a toy."

"I hate to be impatient," Lita said. "But . . . what are they?"

Hannah looked at Triana. "I'd like to try to explain that myself, if that's okay. But quickly, can we play just a few more seconds of this file? If you were like me you wondered what Nina was messing around with off the screen. Watch this. Roc?"

The image picked up again. Nina referenced another file for information about the power equations she and Kelvin Pernice had worked out. Then suddenly, an orange and black tail swished in front of Nina's face, and she shooed it away.

Channy blurted out a laugh. "It's Iris."

A moment later the cat walked completely into the picture, and Nina took the drastic measure of lifting her off the table and setting her on the floor. "Go play," she said.

Channy's face changed to an expression of sorrow. "Ohhhh. That makes me sad to watch. Iris was her little friend." She turned to Lita. "That hurts my heart." Lita put her hand on the shoulder of *Galahad*'s Activities Director.

Hannah paused the video playback again and wrinkled her

brow. "It's hard to say exactly what the Cassini are. In fact, I think it's more accurate to say what the Cassini *is*."

Gap studied her face, trying to puzzle out the distinction in what she was telling them. "So," he said, "the Cassini are not . . . alive? They're . . . a machine, or something?"

Hannah shook her head. "No, we're definitely dealing with a life-form. But . . ." She squinted, trying to find the right words. "Nina and this guy, Kel, believed that the Cassini pretty much cover the entire surface of Titan. Like a net, or web. But all of the parts make up just one incredibly large being. The Cassini might be made up of trillions and trillions of pieces, but they all come together to form just one entity." She looked back at Gap, then Triana. "Does that make sense?"

Gap sat back in his chair. "That's . . . amazing."

"Yeah. Here's another way to think about it. Remember watching a huge flock of birds, hundreds of them in a pack, flying through the sky, and they all seem to turn sharply at exactly the same time? Or . . ." She glanced up quickly, then back at Gap. "Or a school of fish, a big school, all swimming in the same direction, then somehow the whole school darts another direction, almost like they're connected somehow? That's kinda what the Cassini are like. Connected."

"But not necessarily physically," Triana interjected. "You mean they're tied together through, what, thought waves?"

"Yeah, something like that. Like a trillion parts of one giant brain."

There was silence for a minute, then Lita finally spoke up.

"Wow. I guess that helps clear up a couple of things. One, the power that an entire moon-sized brain could muster would obviously explain what we've been dealing with. And, two, remember that message we got from Titan through Bon?"

Bon, who had been sitting quietly during the entire meeting, nodded. "The voices that came out of my mouth. They said 'I wait. I wait so long.' Not we. I."

"I'm getting creeped out again," Channy said.

"Yeah, well, if you like that, check this out," Hannah said. The vidscreen resumed its playback after Nina had deposited Iris on the floor. She made a notation on her work pad, unconsciously touched the ring hanging from the chain around her neck, then, for the first time during the recording, looked up, directly into the camera.

Her eyes glowed with a shade of orange.

32

Nina Volkov's bizarre eyes stared from the vidscreens in *Galahad*'s Conference Room. All five members of the Council, along with Hannah Ross, met the gaze across time and space, each of them holding their breath. It was Bon who finally broke the trance.

"Cool," he said.

Hannah stopped the video playback. She straightened her work pad, which had become slightly tilted, then looked at Bon. "I thought you might appreciate that."

Triana bit her lip. "So Nina is—or was—one of the few people in tune with the Cassini's mental frequency." She thought about this for a second. "That tells us a lot."

"Yeah," Lita said. "It tells us why she was able to gather so much information on the Cassini so quickly. Nina was already a scientific genius, or she wouldn't have been on SAT33 in the first place. Then, with that energy beam's 'improvement,' she leapt ahead like crazy. Just like Bon's training in agriculture, how he instantly started imagining new ways to improve our crops. The tweak from the Cassini seems to take a person's natural skills and amp them up a few notches, doesn't it?"

"I think so," Hannah said. "It probably enhances all of a person's abilities over time, but the earliest signs will come from their own instinctive talent."

"Wait a minute, though," Channy said. "Nina was obviously a smart girl. She had to know that this . . . this beam was . . . I mean, didn't it hurt them like it's hurting us?"

"We can't get in touch with them, so I'm assuming the worst," Triana said. She felt the same frustration that had blanketed her before, and took a deep breath, remembering her dad's comments about too much on her plate. One thing at a time. One thing at a time.

"We can't worry about what happened to them," she said. "We have our own issues right now." She turned to Hannah. "Does Nina tell us anything about stopping the energy beam from Titan?"

"She makes a reference to something that *has* to be about the beam. She called it 'the translator.'"

This caught Lita's attention immediately. "Of course," she said, spreading her hands. "We already know that the Cassini tries to communicate. They—or it, I guess; it's weird thinking about this as one being—channeled those voices through Bon."

"And," Gap broke in, "it altered the data stream from SAT33. We've already talked about trying to shut it down. A translating device makes total sense."

Hannah said, "Let me play the file from her that mentions it. Roc, I'm going to need number three seven seven, three oh four, please." Before hitting the play button, she explained what they were going to hear.

"Most of Nina's work, unfortunately, was loaded into the data stream. She put very little on this personal disc, probably because she expected to be on the pod and didn't know it would be her final report. As far as she was concerned, she would be there to explain everything. So a few of the files, like the one we just saw, were video records, but most of them are quick audio files, like this one. And this one," she said, looking around the table, "is her final entry. This is the last thing she recorded before the pod launched. It's the first time that it occurs to her that she . . . that she might not make it."

The gravity of what they were about to hear did not seem to be lost on the Council members' faces. Hannah pushed the button, and Nina's voice filled the room. She sounded anxious, out of breath.

"File number . . . oh, I don't know the file, and it's not—" A warning siren sounded in the background, and a low rumble could be heard beneath the sound. A pause occurred in Nina's account, and Triana could visualize the young scientist scrambling, trying to get the situation under control. A situation that very likely was deadly.

"Overload again on the main reactor," Nina dictated, "and this time I don't think there's any way to slow it down." There was a mishmash of sounds again, a worried sigh from the scientist, and the sounds of the siren cutting off. "Enough of that," Nina muttered.

After another minute of unintelligible noise, she picked up again, a tinge of terror in her voice. "Iris is aboard and asleep, the translator is aboard, along with a few of my notes. If I don't make it back, at least the data stream has the raw information." It was, as Hannah had indicated, the first sign that Nina wondered about her security. "I know it's foolish for me to go back, but there's almost six minutes until launch. That's plenty of time to go get Kel's ring and make it back. In any event, the automatic launch sequence is running smoothly." A muffled roar in the background sounded ominous. "I'll be right back," Nina added, which in other circumstances might have sounded funny in a personal recording.

Except *Galahad*'s Council members realized that she hadn't made it back.

"I don't believe it," Channy said, her eyes watering. "She actually went back into the station to get . . . to get her boyfriend's ring. That has to be the ring that we saw earlier on the video."

Lita was respectfully quiet, then said softly. "I guess we have to assume that Kel was her boyfriend, the same guy who worked with her on the Cassini data, and he . . ." She looked up at Triana. "He must have died."

Triana nodded. "And she didn't want to leave SAT33 without his ring. She lost her own life just by going back for it."

"Something happened in those six minutes," Gap said. "The situation must have gone from bad to worse quickly. I don't think she would have gone back if she thought—" He broke off the sentence, aware of every eye on him. "I mean, would she?"

Channy wiped away a tear and fixed him with a stare. "I don't know, Gap. Have you ever been in love?"

The awkward silence lingered until Triana spoke up. "Listen, we have to get back to business. No matter what happened back on the research station, Nina distinctly said that the translator— whatever it is—made it onto the pod. It's somewhere on this ship right now." She glanced at the clock in the corner of the vidscreen. "And we have one hour, fifty-two minutes to find it."

"I hate to throw negative vibes into this," Gap said, "but is it possible that the translator *was* on the pod, but Nina accidentally took it back into the station with her? Like, in a pocket or something?"

The sound of the room's ventilation system filled the silence as this question sank in. Lita finally shook her head.

"There's no way. She said, 'the translator is aboard.' That means stowed somewhere, not bouncing around in her pocket. The only problem is that she fully expected to hand it over to us when we picked up the pod, so I'm sure it's not labeled. We might have even seen it and didn't know it."

"What in the world does a translator look like, anyway?" Channy said. "Is it a box? Is it big? Is it a computer disc?"

Hannah shrugged. "Who knows?"

Triana bit her lip, listening to this exchange. She said, "I know this sounds crazy, but, Roc, what are the chances of us building one of these translators?"

When the computer answered her, the usual jovial tone was gone. "I think it's entirely possible to build a translator. We have the garbled data stream, and the beam itself, to study. But the problem is time, Tree. If we haven't been able to crack their code by now, an hour and a half won't be enough time."

Lita began silently tapping her stylus against her cheek, her eyes focused on a spot on the vidscreen in front of her. She suddenly put the stylus on the table and asked Triana, "If this translator, whatever it is, is really the answer, then why—"

"Why didn't the scientists on SAT33 use it to save themselves?" finished Hannah.

Lita nodded.

"They did, actually," Hannah said. "But not before it was too late. From what I can piece together from Nina's recordings, a series of explosions took out most of the crew. A couple more seemed to have taken their own lives, when it seemed hopeless. This . . . friend of Nina's, Kel, finally was able to build a prototype translator, which from all indications seems to have stopped their own power surges.

"But," she added, "even though he had stopped it, the damage was done to most of their reactors. A major malfunction released critical amounts of radiation in the lab portion of the station, killing the remaining scientists, including Kel. The only reason Nina was spared was because she was in a protective suit, preparing to leave the station and make repairs on the outside. It saved her life."

"Temporarily," Triana said.

"And she kept his ring around her neck after that," mused Channy. "I can't imagine how she must have felt."

"Yeah," Lita said, "the last person left alive out of thirty."

Bon slapped his hand on the table, making the other Council members jump.

"This is ridiculous," he said, his eyes now entirely back to their original ice blue, flashing. "I'm not coming this far to give up. The pod is just not that big. We *must* have missed it somehow." He looked down the table at Triana. "I say we go back right now and tear it apart."

A look of irritation crossed Gap's face. You weren't even there in the first place, he thought, and almost said exactly that when he remembered what Bon had been experiencing at the time. Instead, he said, "I don't even think that's necessary. I say we zero in on those tables full of stuff that we already unloaded. Nina wouldn't have hidden the translator in some secret compartment. She *wanted* us to have it."

Triana looked around the table. "Okay. Let's meet there in fifteen minutes. And we're not leaving the Spider bay until we have that translator."

33

On her way to the lower level, Lita made a quick stop into Sick House. She was relieved to find Alexa sitting at the desk, inputting data from the creepy incident with Bon and the other Cassini patients. Alexa looked up and pushed a lock of blond hair out of her eyes.

"So, what's the word?" she said.

"We've had a scavenger hunt dumped into our laps," Lita said, waving her hand when Alexa offered the chair, instead choosing to sit on the edge of the desk. "Not much of a challenge, though. We're only looking for something we've never seen before, we don't know what it looks like, and we have no idea where it might be. Other than that, no problem."

"Ugh," Alexa said. "Listen, I don't want to be mean or anything, but you don't look so good. When's the last time you got any sleep?"

Lita chuckled. "What's sleep?"

"That's what I thought. What can I do to help?"

"I guess just keep an eye on the shop here. In a little over an hour that orange moon is going to pop out the other side of Saturn, and we might have another round of patients spilling into the hospital. I appreciate your help more than you know." She stood up. "I'm heading down to the Spider bay. If anything comes up, you can reach me there."

Alexa climbed out of the chair and gave Lita a hug. "I'll be here if you need anything else," she said.

Lita walked out into the corridor and turned toward the lift. She knew that Alexa was right, that fatigue was becoming an issue, not just with her but with the entire Council. And tired minds didn't function nearly as well. She wondered if they would even be able to see clearly to find whatever they were looking for.

The door to the lift opened and Lita stepped inside. Think, she told herself, think. What would this translator look like? Think. And how would it be used? Where would you install it? Into a radio transmitter? Would it be something that Roc could use to intercept the energy beam and tweak it?

As the lift descended to the level that housed the Spider bay, she forced her exhausted brain to work harder than ever. How does the beam function? What effects did it have on the ship and the crew? For one thing it was taking over the power source of the ship. It also had linked up telepathically with Bon and several other crew members, channeling their thoughts and voices through the Swedish Council member. But what was its goal when it did that?

The door to the lift opened on the dim lower level, and Lita began the roundabout walk to the Spider bay, her mind still racing. Hannah had said that the power beam was a two-way transmission from Titan, delivering its "improvements" while taking back information about the ship. So that meant the beam was . . .

Lita froze in her tracks. Her face went slack, her eyes blinking slowly as the puzzle pieces began to slip into place. Of course, she thought. A two-way transmission from Titan.

"Why didn't I think about that in the first place?" she said, a smile spreading across her face.

* * *

Fifty-four minutes. Fifty-four minutes until the Cassini, embedded throughout the mysterious moon of Titan, reconnected with its target, its latest fix-up project: *Galahad*.

With all of the pressure bearing down, with a countdown that was a virtual death clock sealing their fate, Triana wondered how she could worry about anything else. And yet, she hadn't counted on this arrangement. All of the Council members, along with Hannah Ross, had agreed to meet at the pod to launch an all-out search for the SAT33 translator. Yet Lita had taken a quick detour to Sick House, Channy had gone to pick up Iris before joining them, and Hannah had not yet arrived. Which left Triana in the hangarlike Spider bay.

With Gap and Bon.

She felt an extra layer of tension wrap itself around her. Somehow it always came back to these two guys, one who had harbored obvious feelings for her, and another whom she had personally connected with for a brief instant. And now the love triangle—a corny expression, she admitted, but the only one that seemed to fit the circumstances—was exposed in a way that prevented her from escaping. She *had* to be here, there was crucial work to do, and somehow her feelings—and those of Bon, if he had any, and Gap, if they still existed—would have to wait.

Easier said than done, she thought.

At least there was activity to distract all of them. Triana sifted through the piles of objects that had been unloaded from the metal pod, three large tables' worth. Gap stood to her left, leafing through a stack of papers from a folder. The frown on his face was evidence enough for Triana that he had found nothing. Or did the frown represent something else?

Bon, kneeling to her right, peered into several boxes that had been stacked under the table. His organizational system entailed tossing a finished box into a corner, accompanied by a silent curse. So far his search had turned up spare parts, another first-aid kit, and some more emergency food rations. As Triana watched, he threw another box into the corner, then wiped his brow.

"Where is it?" he said. "I'm sick of this."

It dawned on Triana that Bon had an additional concern that she hadn't taken into consideration. His unwillingness to submit as a pawn to the powers on Titan was obviously fueling his intensity at the moment. She realized that the countdown was more than just a threat to the ship for the temperamental Swede; for him it marked the end of his independence, a concept more alien to Bon than any life force they would find on a distant world.

She resisted the urge to reach out to him. That would only make things worse, especially in front of Gap. Thankfully the moment was broken by the sound of footsteps approaching. She looked up to see Hannah.

"What do you need me to do?" Hannah said.

"Just dive in, anywhere."

Hannah hesitated, then walked slowly over to the table where Gap was hard at work. Triana thought she saw a flicker of a smile dart across Gap's face as he waved hello, the first smile she had seen from him in a long time. A moment later the two had teamed up to sort through the mound of paperwork and folders on the table before them.

Triana let out an exasperated sigh. Time was running out, and this didn't seem to be getting them anywhere. It wouldn't matter if a hundred people were helping right now; the translator was not going to turn up in this pile of junk, at least not in the next—she glanced at her watch—forty-nine minutes. For the first time, she felt her spirits begin to sink.

Yet she refused to let these feelings show. Instead, she tried to puzzle the situation out again.

"Okay," she said to the others, "here's the deal. All of this stuff had to have been stored on the pod for a while, long before Nina launched from the research station." Gap, Hannah, and Bon stopped what they were doing and turned to face her. "But, as far as we know, the only things Nina brought on board were the bag full of gear and rations, the data disc that Gap found, and . . ." She paused before finishing. "And Iris."

Gap looked puzzled. "What are you saying? That the cat is the translator?"

"No, but as far as I can tell, she didn't pack anything else."

Bon stood up and brushed the knees of his pants. "I agree. I think we're wasting our time."

Gap snorted. "So, what, we just give up?"

Triana was about to answer when the door to the corridor opened and Lita hurried in, smiling.

"Any luck?" she asked Triana.

"No. What are you so happy about?"

Lita didn't answer at first. She grabbed a sturdy box that had been stashed under one of the tables and sat down on it. Then she said, "We better find that translator, that's all I have to say. Because I think I've figured out how it works."

Hannah tossed a handful of papers onto the table. "What? What do you mean?" She and the others closed in around Lita.

Again the door opened, this time admitting Channy, who held Iris up over her shoulder like a baby being burped. The Activities Director took one look at the scene before her and said, "What did I miss?"

"Nothing yet," Lita said. "But I might have figured out how the translator works."

Triana crossed her arms. "All right, let's hear it."

Lita leaned forward, her elbows on her knees, and clasped her hands in front of her. "Okay. It finally dawned on me that this . . . this force, or whatever you call it, is all about communication. It doesn't have any feelings that we know of. It just relays information on how to improve the ship, how to improve the primitive life-forms on the ship, how to make everything more efficient.

"The ship has its own data banks and internal communications system, so when the Cassini retracts that information the ship is just basically acknowledging the changes. The ship has no feelings, either. It can't say, 'no, thank you.' It just takes its orders and implements them. So our ion drive will increase power to the point of blowing itself up. It doesn't have a rational mind of its own to tell the Cassini to stop. Like . . . like some aquarium fish; if you feed them too much, they'll just keep eating until they eat themselves to death."

Gap said, "I still don't see how the translator works, then."

Lita smiled at him. "Well, think about what happened with Bon and the others in Sick House. They went into a trance, right? Their eyes went crazy and a powerful energy beam started rattling around inside their brains because they're on the same wavelength. The Cassini started tinkering with them. But—"

"But," Hannah burst in, "it's trying to take *back* some information at the same time!"

Lita nodded. "That's right. Just like the information it took back from the ship." She looked at Bon. "When you started in with your creepy little chant, with all of those voices, that was Titan's way of acknowledging that they had accessed your brain. You were like a human blueprint that they were trying to read. They learned our languages pretty quickly, then went to work on 'repairing' you. Since then it's been a one-way conversation. Notice that your headache went away, and so did the voices."

Bon remained still, looking uncomfortable as the center of attention.

Triana bit her lip, then said, "Okay, that all makes sense. But I still don't understand how the translator fits into all of this."

Lita stood up and began walking in a tight circle around the group. "This power force, or beam, has locked on to Bon's brain, and the others', because they have frequencies that . . . fit, I guess you could say. Bon didn't have to do anything. With his mental frequency, the door to his brain was open, so the Cassini just walked right in.

"Now," she continued, her pace around the group increasing, "the translator should be nothing more than an object that he holds in his hands. It makes contact with Bon, and when the beam connects with him, his brain waves should be able to communicate with it. Turn it back into a two-way conversation. Then you can politely ask them to turn the beam off." She came to a stop and spread her hands. "In theory, anyway."

Triana stood still, biting her lip and staring at *Galahad's* Health Director. The Spider bay was deadly silent. It seemed that everyone's brain was spinning, each trying to make the leap that would solve the mystery of the missing device. Iris began to squirm, so Channy put her on the floor, where she began to sniff the objects taken from the pod.

Finally, Triana said to Lita, "Does this help us figure out what the translator would look like?"

Lita shrugged. "Well, for one thing it wouldn't be very big. It would have to fit into the palm of your hand."

"Right," Gap said. "That eliminates some of this mess." He tossed a handful of papers onto the table nearest him. "This would be almost like a small piece of electronics."

"Has anyone seen something like that?" Triana said, looking around. Silent stares greeted her. Iris lost interest in the pod materials and began to purr and rub up against Hannah's leg.

Suddenly Channy jumped, as if jolted by an electric shock. "Oh! Oh! Oh!" she exclaimed, her hands coming up to the sides of her face.

"What?" Triana said, growing alarmed.

Channy, her eyes huge, seemed to be in her own trance. Then she turned to Triana and said, "The translator. I know where it is."

34

This might not be the best time to talk about this, but if Channy really knows where the translator is located, then I'd like to reserve some time to speak with the Cassini myself. There are a handful of questions that are begging to be asked.

Like, how long did it take for your web to spread over the surface of Titan? And what is the source of your power? Is it the internal core heat of the moon itself? Is it the radiation from Saturn?

And what about that power beam? If it's such a force for good, why hasn't Bon done something about that hair of his?

Without another sound Channy turned and sprinted toward the door that led out of the Spider bay and into the corridor. She yelled back over her shoulder, "C'mon!"

The other Council members, and Hannah, exchanged confused looks, watching Channy's bright yellow T-shirt streak toward the door. Triana looked at the others and said, "Well, let's go." She pointed a finger at Bon. "Especially you. If she really does know where it is, we have no time to waste." That time had dwindled to thirty-nine minutes.

By the time the group reached the door, they could hear Channy's pounding steps up around the curve of the corridor, closing in on the lift door. Gap yelled ahead to her, "Hold up!" He looked over at Hannah. "You know, I'm fast, but I don't think I could catch her in a race. That girl is a blur." Hannah only smiled in return as they raced toward the lift.

Rounding the corner, they found Channy leaning out of the open lift door, a look of urgency on her face. "C'mon," she said. The group, huffing and puffing, piled in with her. As soon as the doors sealed, Triana exhaled loudly and put her hand on Channy's shoulder. "Okay, detective, wanna clue us in?"

Channy's face broke into a wide smile. "Of course, I could be wrong—"

"Oh, great," Gap said, leaning his good arm against the side of the lift.

"But I don't think so," Channy finished. "It makes sense. As soon as you said it's something that you could hold in your hand. I've already held it several times."

Hannah seemed beside herself. "So tell us. What is it?"

But Channy was enjoying the attention. She beamed at Hannah, then playfully raised her eyebrows and flexed her bicep like a bodybuilder. "See, just because you have muscles doesn't mean you can't be brainy, too."

Lita turned to Triana. "I'm going to deck her before we ever get off the lift." Then to Channy she said, "And just where are we getting off this thing?"

"The Domes."

"The Domes?" the group said in chorus.

Channy was just about to answer as the lift came to a stop and the door opened to reveal the lush vegetation sprawled before them. "This way," Channy said, turning to her left and heading toward the short passage that led from the first dome to the second.

"Listen, we have—" Triana consulted her watch again. "We have a little more than thirty-five minutes. Is it okay if we walk and talk?"

The group clustered around Channy as she walked briskly toward the second of *Galahad*'s domes. In a moment they left the sterile confines of the passageway and found themselves under the glistening starlight of Dome 2. Not for the first time, Triana relished the scent that accompanied the flourishing plant life: smells of rich soil, flowering plants, fruits and vegetables coming into their prime. She inhaled deeply; the scents automatically triggered thoughts of home.

"You know what made me think of it?" Channy said. "Iris."

"How come?" Lita said, right on her heels.

"Because I've been trying like crazy to get her to play with it. She won't, of course, because she's a cat, and it has to be her idea."

It suddenly clicked with Triana. "That ball," she said. "It was a small, metal ball."

"Uh-huh." Channy pushed a large, leafy branch out of the way as she hurried down the path. "It was in the bag with Iris's stuff, and I just thought it was one of her toys. She kinda likes the stuffed mouse, but this ball did nothing for her."

"And since Nina was in a hurry and had to pack light, she just threw it in the bag with the cat's collar and stuff," Gap said.

"And, since she thought she would be here with us," Lita reminded them, "it was no big deal to her. She probably didn't give it a second thought to just toss it in with the other things."

Channy slowed to a stop. She looked back and forth, then dropped to one knee and scanned beneath a row of tomato plants. Gap squatted next to her.

"Well?" he said.

"I know it's around here somewhere. This is where I was when I tossed it to her. Right there," Channy said, pointing to a spot about ten feet off the trail.

The group fanned out and began pushing leaves and vines out of the way. Hannah fell to her hands and knees and crawled in a semicircle between two rows of plants. Bon moved off to one side, using his foot to push plant life aside, a scowl of frustration back on his face.

After almost two minutes of searching, Channy looked exasperated. "Listen, I know it was right here. I brought Iris up here a few hours ago, and I kicked the ball right over there."

"Well, it's not here now," Gap said. "Maybe the cat picked it up and carried it somewhere."

"No, I'm telling you she doesn't like it," Channy said. She squatted again and peered under the same set of leaves she had already examined twice. "It has to be here."

Triana peered behind a row of dirt that had been overturned recently, then looked to her right. A small gray metal box with plastic tubes sprouting from one side sat quietly by itself, a bright blue tag attached to it. She dropped to one knee and read the hastily scrawled information on the tag.

"Bon, come take a look at this," she said.

Bon and the others gathered next to Triana, looking down at the water recycling pump. She pointed to the blue tag.

"Correct me if I'm wrong, but this is a record of the pump's service history, right?"

Bon nodded. "With all the trouble they've had recently, we've doubled the inspection schedule. Even though Gap's department worked out the chip problem in them, I still want to keep a pretty close watch." He nodded a quick thanks to Gap, then read the date and time on the tag. "This was about two hours ago."

Triana straightened up. "Well, there you go. One of the farm techs must have come through here, inspected the pump, and seen the ball. It would be so out of place here that they'd be bound to pick it up."

Bon didn't say a word. He immediately took off, back up the path they had just traveled, headed toward his office. Channy looked ready to cry.

"I'm so sorry," she said. "I shouldn't have left it here."

Lita patted her on the shoulder. "C'mon, how could you have known? Besides, the tech might have just taken it to the office. Let's go."

Triana took a stealthy glance at her watch, not wanting the others to think about their deadline.

Twenty-nine minutes.

She quickly caught up with the group as they scurried along the path. By the time they reached Bon's office, they found him on the intercom.

"Well, where is he?" he yelled.

The voice on the speaker was tentative. "He went on dinner break about fifteen minutes ago. He should be back in less than an hour. Do you want me to—"

Bon snapped off the connection and punched in the ship-wide intercom. "Javier Serati. Javier Serati. Emergency. Please connect. Javier Serati."

Channy wrung her fingers, shifting her weight from one foot to the other. Gap looked out the window into Dome 1, running a hand through his hair. Lita stood by the door, her arms folded, staring at the floor. Hannah, her eyes wide, sat down in one of the chairs across from Bon's desk.

Triana walked a few feet out of the office and looked up through the clear dome into the star field above. In twenty-six minutes Titan would come roaring back, and the Cassini would continue its repair project. She wondered if this was her last chance to witness the beauty of the cosmos. She steadied her breathing and felt a sense of calm flow back through her body. Scanning the broad expanse of flickering stars, she slowly smiled and closed her eyes.

She felt the presence next to her before she heard the voice.

"Uh, Tree?" Gap said. She looked into his face and felt an odd sensation.

"I should probably head down to Engineering," he said. "Not that there's anything I can do, I guess, but . . ."

"No, you're right," she said. "We'll need to know that it's working. I mean, when Bon uses the translator, we'll need to know."

Gap just stared at her, shifting his gaze from one of her green eyes to the other. He finally nodded, his voice sounding resigned. "Yeah."

For a split second Triana had a flashback to a moment when they were alone in the Conference Room, months ago, during the crisis that had nearly destroyed them. She had been sure that Gap was on the brink of kissing her then. But now, the look he gave her was different, an almost melancholy air, as if there were still things that he wanted to say to her. His feelings had changed, she realized.

"Hannah's going to come with me," he said softly. "Unless you need her here."

Triana was startled. Through all of the months of their tension, it had never dawned on her that Gap might begin to look elsewhere. She had noticed the smiles and the glances he had shared with Hannah, but had somehow failed to make the connection.

And how did she feel about that? How *should* she feel?

She realized that the silence between them was growing longer and longer. She snapped out of her spell. "Uh, sure. I mean, no, she should go with you. Absolutely."

Why "absolutely?" Now she just sounded flustered. She smiled at Gap and reached out to touch his face. Before she knew what was happening, he leaned in and kissed her on the cheek.

"I'll see you in a little bit," he said with the sound of a final good-bye.

He turned and walked away. Hannah came out of the office, and together they disappeared down the path toward the lift.

35

How much time had passed? She didn't know. It could have been two minutes, it could have been twenty-two minutes, and their countdown might have evaporated. Her feet had taken root, along with the host of plant life scattered around *Galahad*'s Domes, and her mind had refused to process any incoming data, like a satellite dish nudged a degree or two from its signal.

Common sense told her that this was no time for an internal emotional conflict, but at the moment all rational thought was being overridden. And, for the second time since she'd walked out of the Agricultural office, a voice broke through the fog.

"Tree, are you okay?"

She snapped her head to the side and found Lita and Bon looking at her with concern. Before answering Lita, she checked her watch and did the mental arithmetic.

Fifteen minutes.

"Yeah, I'm fine. What's the story?"

"Well, I found Javier," Bon said. "He's the tech who made the service call on that recycling pump."

"And?"

"And he did pick up the ball, or translator, I guess. Anyway, he took it down to the Dining Hall with him, and actually gave it to a group of guys who walked out as he walked in."

Triana sagged. "Oh, no. Any idea—"

"Yes," Lita broke in. "That's what we've been running down for the last few minutes. The translator ended up with Elijah down in Engineering." She offered Triana a much-needed smile. "You'll be very happy to know that he's on his way up here right now with the translator."

Triana exhaled, pushing the air out through pursed lips. She shook her head and put a hand on Lita's shoulder. "We need a vacation."

The comment sank in for a moment before the two girls broke out in a fit of laughter. Another face-to-face appointment with death, the second in four months, had officially caught up with them, and the release felt good. They shook with their laughter while Bon stood by, the faint trace of a smile flickering across his face. For the time being Triana didn't care whether he smiled or not. Something had finally clicked inside, something that seemed to open a door to her feelings. If they survived this latest crisis, she knew that in a fundamental way she would never be the same again, at least emotionally.

If they survived . . .

Out of nervous habit she glanced again at her watch. Thirteen minutes.

Gap felt a curious sense of pride as he walked briskly into the Engineering section with Hannah. Pride at having a beautiful girl at his side, witnessed by the several crew members on duty at the time, each of whom followed the progression of the couple as they hurried across the room. And pride at escorting Hannah into his domain, the zone inside the ship where he ruled. Whenever Hannah had joined the Council for meetings, Triana had been in charge; here, it was his responsibility, and an odd sense of satisfaction swelled within him. In a way, he realized that it was his chance to show off.

But maybe not for much longer.

That thought had crowded in on him while the two descended in the lift. It figures, he thought, that he would finally make a proactive move with his social life just as the timer ran out. And yet, was it that looming sense of finality that had ultimately pushed him to action? No matter, he decided. Desperate circumstances often brought out the very best in people, or awakened a resolve they never knew they possessed. Why should he be any different?

He also had felt a touch of impatience, for they never had the lift to themselves. Two other crew members had ridden with them as they left the Domes, and then, when those two had exited, another jumped on as the doors began to close. It seemed he was not destined to be alone with Hannah right now.

The atmosphere in the room was charged with a nervous energy that made his skin tingle. A cloak of fear settled over the crew as the clock ticked, and he knew he had to set a positive example. As he approached the power grid near the ion drive, Gap was glad to see his top two assistants, Ramasha and Esteban, already on the scene. "Hey, guys," he said with a smile. They both acknowledged him with a quick wave, their gaze flickering briefly on Hannah before returning to their work. Gap realized he would be the main topic of Gossip Central before the day was out.

Which seemed a fair trade to him; it would mean that at least they were around to gossip about.

"Roll your sleeves up," he said to the assembled crew. "It could start to get a little crazy here pretty soon." Anxious smiles greeted the comment, about the best he had hoped for.

"Roc," he called out. "I've been thinking."

"And I thought it couldn't get any worse," the computer said. Gap heard Hannah stifle a giggle beside him.

"Very funny," he said. "Listen, how long would it take to rewrite the code that controls the ion drive reactor?"

"The entire program?" Roc said. "You're talking about one of the most complicated systems ever developed, you understand."

"Right. How long?"

There was a pause as *Galahad*'s computer brain sorted through the data. "I'd say . . . about two days. That's assuming I worked through lunch."

"Okay," Gap said. "So, that's out. What if we adjusted random parts of it?"

"I think I see what you're getting at," Roc said, "but you realize that's like stopping a flood with a paper towel, right?"

Hannah touched Gap's arm. "Could you tell *me* what you're getting at?"

Gap pointed to the power grid. "The Cassini has already done its homework on the ship's power system. It learned everything it could about how the ion drive works. But it had to take a break while it was behind Saturn."

Ramasha was standing to one side and suddenly exclaimed, "Oh, I get it. When it makes contact again, the code will have changed. It will have to relearn the program before it can start adjusting things again."

Hannah looked skeptical. "But . . . but that won't take it very long. Maybe a minute, if we're lucky?"

Gap shrugged. "Hey, right now I think we could use every break we get. If this buys us thirty seconds it might make all the difference in the world."

"Consider it done," Roc said. "I'm starting work on it right now. I might even throw in a bogus line of code here and there to trip it up."

Gap said, "Let me know if there's anything I can do to—"

"Sshhh," the computer hissed. "Quiet. I'm trying to work here."

Triana, Lita, Channy, and Bon waited nervously in Bon's office. As the ten-minute mark came and went, Triana bit her lip and stared out the large window into Dome 1. Lita stepped up and put an arm around her shoulder.

"You know what I miss the most about home?"

Triana looked into her friend's eyes. "No, tell me."

Lita pointed at the crops that gently swayed in the Dome's circulated air. "I look at those rows of food and it makes me really miss my mother's cooking." She gave Triana an amused look. "Not that the food on this ship is bad, but I'd give anything to have one of my mother's tortillas right now."

Triana smiled and leaned her head against Lita's. "My dad used to make us lasagna every Sunday. It was my favorite." Her eyes grew moist, and she blinked them quickly. "He used to tell me that I was going to get sick of it, but I never did." She pulled back and looked at Lita. "I haven't had lasagna once since the day he died."

Lita hugged Triana's shoulder. "Tell you what. When this is over we'll get together and cook. My mother's tortillas, and your dad's lasagna."

"Do we have the stuff on this ship to make those?"

Lita shrugged. "Who cares? We'll improvise. Or we'll combine the two and make lasagna using the tortillas. A Mexican lasagna."

Triana laughed. "It's a deal."

They heard the sound of running and saw two boys dashing down the path toward the office. All four Council members hurried to the door and met the boys as they drew close. Elijah, a popular fifteen-year-old from Poland, was red-faced from running. He stretched out his hand to Triana and dropped a small metal ball into her palm.

"Sorry, we got here as fast as we could," he said, catching his breath.

"Thanks, Elijah," she said. Then, turning to the others, she raised her eyebrows. "Uh . . . now what?"

Lita took the ball from her and examined it. "This has to be it," she said, eyeing the rounded spikes and vents. "It looks relatively new."

Channy said, "It better be it, because as a cat toy it stinks."

"And Bon just . . . what, holds it?" Triana said.

"Well, that's my best guess," Lita said. "Here." She handed the metallic ball to Bon, who shifted it back and forth between his hands.

Triana checked her watch. "Six minutes."

Bon looked up at her. "I don't want to sound stupid, but exactly how is this supposed to work? Am I supposed to think certain thoughts, or try to talk to them, or it, or whatever? I have no idea what I'm doing."

Triana managed a slight smile. "And we don't know any more than you. But if Lita's theory is right, then the Cassini will reconnect with you in just a few minutes and start sifting through your brain again. This little device will hopefully allow you to speak its language."

"Yeah," Channy added, "so start thinking 'stop, stop, stop.' Maybe it will get the message."

How's it coming, Roc?" Gap said.

"I think I've done about all the damage I can right now," the computer answered. "I must say, I feel a bit like a hooligan, just randomly vandalizing the computer program that drives the ship."

"Yeah, you're quite the delinquent. I just hope you remember how to put it back together again later."

"Oh," Roc said, "so I'm supposed to put it back the way it was? You should have told me that."

Gap saw the horrified look that crossed Hannah's face. "Don't listen to him," he whispered to her. "That's just his sense of humor. You have to learn how to filter out about half of what he says." He hoped that it sounded reassuring, but Hannah merely turned her gaze to the power grid and pressed her lips together tightly. Without giving himself a chance to second-guess things, Gap reached out and took her hand.

36

O ne minute," Lita said.

Channy paced around the office, a trickle of sweat dribbling down her forehead. Bon took another look at the translator, and inhaled a deep breath. He turned to Triana and said, "I want to be outside when I do this." Then, without waiting for a reply, he marched out of the office door, into the lush vegetation of Dome 1.

It didn't surprise Triana. Bon felt the most comfortable here, the most at home. He had grown up immersed in the dirt of his father's farm. After hesitating a moment, she followed him. Lita and Channy exchanged looks, then did the same.

They caught up to the Swede as he stood under the twinkling stars of the dome, his face extended upward, his hands at his sides, and his eyes closed. Triana wanted to speak to him, to say something to allay his fears, to let him know that she was there for him. But he seemed to have fallen into a state of deep meditation, all focus now on the emergency at hand, and she couldn't bring herself to reach out. Instead, she stood to his side, arms crossed, and waited. She wondered if she would know when—

Bon shook with a tremor. His neck stiffened, and a sudden spasm of pain creased his face. The connection with Titan had been restored, almost violently. Apparently the Cassini wasted no time.

A subtle groan slipped from Bon's lips. His head turned to one side, his eyelids clenched tightly, and he ground his teeth. No doubt the intense pain he had suffered earlier was back. Triana felt a hand grasp her arm, and she looked around to find Channy clutching her. Channy's face contorted with a look of sympathy, as if she felt the searing pain that Bon experienced. Tears welled in her eyes, and she peered at Triana with a look that suggested they do something. Triana placed a hand on Channy's and shook her head.

Another spasm racked Bon, and he almost stumbled. This time a small cry escaped from his mouth, and his head jerked back the other direction. Lita knelt in the dirt in front of him, watching his face, and now tears began to track down her cheeks as well.

A third tremor shook him, and Bon sank to his knees, his head still back. But now his eyes popped open, and Lita stifled a shriek. His eyes had begun to glow with an orange tint again, and they stared off into space. His lips trembled.

And then the voices returned. The chaotic jumble of languages spilled from his mouth, louder this time, almost as if they were demanding something. The words flowed out of him in a frenzy of sound, a chorus of terror that sent shivers through Triana. Her impulse to grab his shoulders became even stronger, and she fought the urge with all of the discipline she could muster. She glanced down to his right hand and saw him gripping the translator.

She blinked. A dull red glow leaked from the tiny vents in the side.

Here we go," Gap said, letting go of Hannah's hand and stepping up to the power grid. The lights had suddenly jumped, and an alarm began to sound, echoing through the entire Engineering section. With a quick gesture he signaled to Ramasha to cut it off.

"I hope your tinkering works," Gap said to Roc's sensor. "I have a funny feeling that we have just really annoyed the Cassini." He scanned the grid, watching the readouts spike, then drop, then peak again.

"Is the power increasing yet?" Hannah said.

"No. But something is going on."

"I don't care how long the Cassini has been around," Roc said. "It has no idea who it's messing with here."

"Go get 'em, Roc," Gap said, forcing a smile.

The voices coming out of Bon's mouth slowed, and his head now tilted forward. The glowing eyes rolled back and forth, seeing nothing, or seeing something that Triana could never imagine. What he must be going through, she thought.

The hand grasping the translator continued to flex, but now there wasn't any doubt that the device had come alive. A flickering red light burned inside, increasing in brightness temporarily before fading back to a dull gleam, then becoming vivid once again. Triana wondered if it tracked an exchange between Bon and the mystical force blanketing Titan. She hoped that was the case. She felt Channy's grip on her arm tighten.

Lita shifted her gaze to Triana. "Should I try to give him a shot for the pain?"

Triana considered the idea, then rejected it. "Right now he needs to have full concentration on this." She gave a sigh of despair. "I know the pain has to be almost more than he can stand, but we can't take a chance right now with any medication. Who knows how it would affect him?"

Lita nodded, then wiped away a tear that had lingered on her face.

* * *

The alarm in Engineering sounded again before Ramasha turned it off. Gap watched the power grid light up like a fireworks display, with every gauge dancing back and forth.

"Did you feel that?" Hannah said quietly. "I mean, am I—"

Gap nodded. He had indeed felt a delicate shudder ripple through the ship. He turned to Hannah and murmured, "We'll be okay."

But he wasn't sure himself. The grid told him exactly what he didn't want to see. Power was increasing again. After almost a minute and a half of puzzling through Roc's code scramble, the Cassini had apparently worked things out and resumed its inevitable improvement in *Galahad*'s engines.

And if ten percent was the magic number, Gap had a sinking feeling that the end had arrived.

The grid showed power surging past the seven-percent mark and accelerating.

Just try to get them here," Alexa said into the intercom before snapping it off and sitting down at Lita's desk in Sick House. The connection with Titan had obviously been reestablished, and now desperate calls from around the ship had poured in. The original patients from the first encounter were once again doubled over in pain, and in some cases it appeared to be even more intense. It was enough to keep them from walking on their own to Sick House, leaving frightened friends and roommates to call and ask what they should do. Scattered as they were throughout *Galahad*, it was up to these friends to get them in somehow, even if it meant carrying them.

Alexa had barely had time to breathe when the first patient staggered through the door, supported by a grim-faced friend.

* * *

In an instant, the voices pouring from Bon's mouth stopped, as if a power switch had been thrown. His eyes flickered, then clamped shut as another cry erupted from his mouth, this one louder and more agonizing. Still on his knees, he seemed to lose his balance and appeared ready to topple. Triana dropped down beside Bon and grabbed his shoulders, steadying him. She felt tremors running through his muscles, a shudder that seemed to come from deep inside him.

"It's okay," she said softly into his ear. "It's going to be all right." She had no idea if her voice registered with him or not.

How much time had elapsed since Titan had unleashed its power again? She had lost all perception of time. Were *Galahad*'s engines beginning their overload march again? Had Gap or Roc found a way to buy them some time before the inevitable explosion? All of these thoughts fought their way into her mind as she knelt in the dirt, her arms encircling Bon, propping him up, feeling the shivers of pain that coursed through his body. It took a moment for her to realize that she was crying.

Nine percent. Nine point five. Gap watched the meters and once again marveled at the power that the Cassini was able to command at this distance. Yet he himself was, at the moment, completely powerless. I'm just standing here, he thought, watching. Watching and waiting. Waiting for the end.

He felt Hannah's grip on his hand intensify. She looked into his face, her eyes shifting back and forth between his. Strong eyes, he realized. There was fear in there, sure. But strength, too, an inner strength that mesmerized him. The ends of her mouth curled up into a faint smile and, once again acting on impulse, he lowered his face and brushed her lips with a light kiss. When he pulled away, her eyes were closed, and she tilted her head to rest on his shoulder.

Although pretty sure he didn't want to know, he threw a quick glance at the power meter, afraid that the dreaded ten-percent mark had been breached.

The red digits spit out the news: ten point five.

37

Triana recognized that her contact with Bon might somehow do more harm than good, but she knew that on at least one level it was the right thing to do. This was the moment she had searched for, the time for her to step up and give Bon the support he needed. Regardless of her feelings over the past several months, regardless of the hurt and confusion between them . . . he needed her now. With her arms firmly around his chest, she placed her mouth against his ear again. "Please, stop," she said softly. "Thank you for your help, but please stop now. Please stop."

Would this help Bon communicate with the Cassini? Maybe, maybe not.

"Your touch is killing us," she whispered into Bon's ear. "Please, do not help us anymore. Please, stop now."

Her gaze skated down to his lips. The voices were silent, but Bon's lips were definitely moving. No sound came from his mouth, but his lips appeared to be carrying on a spirited conversation.

"We appreciate your help," she said softly, "we are thankful. But we cannot survive if you do not stop. To help us, please stop what you're doing."

Bon's lips continued to flutter, and now his eyelids slipped open a fraction of an inch, emitting the brilliant orange sheen.

Triana felt another shudder, and it took a moment to register with her that it wasn't coming from Bon. *Galahad* had trembled.

She heard the sound of sobs behind her, coming from Channy. From the corner of her eye she watched Lita climb to her feet and walk around to comfort their fellow Council member. Was there anyone with a better heart than Lita?

A memory of her dad suddenly burst into her mind, his smiling face, his gentle eyes. There was no sound with the memory; it was a silent montage, a jerky collection of images flipping past one another like a personal slide show. As usual, any recollection of her dad brought a tinge of sadness but a warmth that still permeated her soul. She felt her own muscles around Bon tighten. Her eyes closed again, and she breathed deeply, letting a sense of calm settle within her.

Again, she had no sensation of time. She had drifted away, her arms around Bon, the two of them leaning against each other, supporting each other. The sounds around her had melted away, merging into a blend of background white noise. At some point she finally became aware of a new sensation: a hand resting on one of hers. She slowly opened her eyes, with her head against the side of Bon's, and looked down where her hands were clasped in front of his chest.

It was one of Bon's hands. It took a minute for the image to make sense, for her mind to register that something was different. Then she heard his voice.

"Tree."

Her breath came out in a start. She pulled her head back and leaned to one side. Bon turned to look into her face. His eyes were almost back to their normal ice blue.

"Bon?" she said, a tentative shake in her voice. "Are you okay?"

His head tilted forward, his forehead coming to rest against hers. "Yeah," he said. "I'm okay."

Triana bit her lip. "What . . . what happened?"

"I don't know." He paused, then added, "I think it's over."

The casual way he said it startled her. She let go of him and fell into a sitting position in the dirt, staring up at him. "What? You mean . . . ?"

He shrugged. "Yeah."

Triana shot a look toward Lita and Channy, who were staring, wide-eyed, listening to the exchange. Channy finally broke the silence with a nervous giggle, her eyes gleaming with the residue of tears.

"So . . . that means we're okay?" she said, still holding on to Lita.

Bon said, "I think so."

Lita tilted her head back and laughed. She pulled Channy into a bear hug and let out a whoop of joy. "I can't believe it!"

Triana still sat in the dirt. Her feeling of disbelief lingered, and it was obviously apparent in her expression because Bon shrugged again, as if to say "Don't ask me." It finally dawned on her that there was an important call to make. She scrambled to her feet and sprinted out of the field, scattering plumes of dirt from her shoes.

She rushed into Bon's office and quickly punched the intercom, connecting with Engineering. "Gap," she called out. "Gap!"

The sounds that came back to her brought a wave of relief and joy and caused her to drop into Bon's chair. The screams that cascaded across the levels of *Galahad* could only be sheer happiness. A celebration was under way, and in her mind's eye she could see the hugs, the backslapping, the tears. She leaned back in the chair and brought her hands up to her face, wiping the tension out with a heavy stroke. The cheering was relentless, and she found herself in no hurry to interrupt.

She looked up to see Bon, Lita, and Channy standing across the desk from her, smiles on their faces. Did Bon's smile contain something more?

"Tree," came Gap's voice through the intercom. "I guess I don't have to tell you the news, do I? I'm assuming you can figure it out from—" Another roar blocked the rest of the sentence, and Triana grinned.

"You've told us everything we wanted to know," she yelled back, trying to cut through the noise. "Why don't we . . ." She waited for the cheering to subside, then decided upon an easier way to retrieve information. Smiling, she cut off the intercom and looked at the others. "Oh, let them celebrate. They've been on the front line through most of this." Lita and Channy nodded, smiles stitched across their own faces.

"Roc," Triana said. "I'm pretty sure you can give us the details."

"Do you want the good news or the bad news?" the computer said.

Triana repressed a laugh. "Whichever you prefer, Roc."

"Well, the good news is that the Cassini cut off its repair project after running up our ion drive system to about eleven percent above normal."

"Eleven?" Lita said. "Wow, we shouldn't even be here."

"And that's the bad news," Roc said. "My code rewriting not only bought us the extra time that saved our lives, but it allowed us to exceed all of the plateaus that the experts claimed was possible. That means I'm going to be expected to provide miracle after miracle the rest of this trip, and I just don't know if my poor circuits can keep it up. You're a very demanding group of humans, you know."

Triana chuckled and stood up to embrace Lita and Channy. "I love you both," she murmured in their ears. "Thank you for being here."

Lita's only response was a smile as she squeezed the Council Leader's shoulder. Channy wiped her eyes and exclaimed, "We need a party, and quickly." With that, she turned and trotted out of the office and down the path toward the lift.

Lita looked after her, and then turned to Triana. "You know, I couldn't adore that girl more than I do." With a quick glance at

Bon, she added, "Well, I guess I better get back to Sick House. Who knows what Alexa is having to deal with?"

She strolled out of the office, and Triana knew her friend well enough to know that Lita was giving her privacy with Bon.

Triana just didn't know if that was a good thing right now or not. In the past twenty-four hours her emotions had taken a wild ride, and at the moment she couldn't tell what she was feeling. Her instincts, however, told her that Bon had warmed again.

She decided to keep it all business for the moment. "Well, you did it."

"I couldn't have done it without you," he said, taking one step toward her. "Not that I didn't know what to say, but your encouragement back there really helped. I . . . I have to admit I was pretty scared."

"We all were."

"But not all of us were dialed in to the Cassini."

That stopped Triana cold. She had forgotten that Bon not only attempted to communicate with the alien force, but that it had enjoyed total access to his brain, a concept that made her skin crawl.

"I'm sorry," she said. "That must have been . . . pretty frightening."

He shrugged, a gesture that she recognized as one of his primary forms of conversation. It often seemed to mean that he was uncomfortable with the discussion.

"Why don't you go get some rest," she said, placing her hand on his forearm. "We'll all get together later. I think we have a lot to talk about."

He gazed at her green eyes. "Okay," he finally said, and she wondered if he had picked up on her sudden distance.

She squeezed his arm once, then let go before he could say more, and walked past him, out the door.

It was an exit strategy that she realized she had utilized far too often.

38

It had become one of his favorite spots. Gap stood against the window on the lower level, the one just down the corridor from the Spider bay. It was, he had decided, one of the quietest locations on the ship. Rarely would someone trek to the bay that housed the Spiders and the SAT33 pod, and it was slightly out of the way for anyone who wanted to visit the gym or Airboard track.

Just the secluded setting he was looking for. Hannah stood beside him, her eyes skimming across the brilliant star field before her. The scene usually transfixed Gap as well, but now he found that he couldn't take his eyes off Hannah.

What a change, he decided. A week earlier he hadn't been able to think of anything except Triana and Bon. Had his feelings been able to shift so suddenly? Did he really have feelings for this impressive girl from Alaska? And, more important, had his feelings for Triana dissolved completely? Was this a distraction, or was this new infatuation legitimate? And how did one know for sure?

He decided that, for now at least, it didn't matter. He felt a sense of happiness, and that was an emotion that was alien to him just days ago. Who knew where these feelings would lead? But that was the beauty of exploring them, wasn't it? Suddenly, all of the weight that had been resting on his shoulders—and his soul—evaporated. And, he concluded, he deserved to feel good for a while.

Without another thought, he put his arm around Hannah and pulled her close. She leaned her head against his shoulder and slowly laced her fingers through his.

I appreciate your honesty with the crew," Roc said. Triana sat alone at her desk, her journal open before her. The crisis had ended almost six hours earlier, and, although she had tried to sleep, she had tossed and turned until finally she conceded defeat. Sleep was not going to happen for a while.

"If you mean about how close we were to blowing up, there wasn't much choice," she said. "The word would have spread eventually."

"True, but you showed a lot of leadership in letting them know right up front."

"I just hope I wasn't overly dramatic. It almost feels unreal to say that we were seconds away from death."

"But it's a fact," Roc said. "If I'm correct—and I'm always correct, by the way—we were down to our last ten seconds."

Triana slowly shook her head. "It's too much to think about. I don't know how many more close calls we can have before our luck runs out. First the stowaway, now the Cassini. We always seem to skate right along the edge, don't we?"

"It's why I signed up for this job," Roc said. "Of course, it was either this assignment, or take that job measuring variables in water pressure in San Diego's sewer system. Very tough decision, obviously, but I broke down and chose you over San Diego's toilets."

Triana put a feigned expression of gratitude on her face. "Oh, Roc, that's the nicest thing you've ever said to me."

She picked up her pen and glanced at what she had contributed to her journal so far: a recap as the crisis unfolded at the end, along with the final gift that the Cassini had bestowed upon the crew of *Galahad*. That stubborn one percent of power increase held on after all was said and done, pushing the ship along its path that much more quickly. Roc would have to recalculate their course, but that was a challenge he enjoyed.

What had the Cassini left inside the dozen crew members it had linked with? What tweaking had stayed behind in their minds and bodies? Lita had already promised a long, arduous examination, and wouldn't be satisfied until she knew that all was well. Triana knew one crew member who would grumble throughout the testing.

She looked ahead to the upcoming Council meeting. As a leader, she recognized the importance of lessons learned from any conflict. What had they learned from their first contact with another life-form beyond Earth? How would it serve them should they encounter intelligent life among the planetary system at Eos?

In her own mind, the primary lesson had been one of assumption. She, along with all of the other members of the crew, had experienced what could only be described as the default emotion when faced with something new: fear. Their initial reaction to the power beam had been fear that an alien being was attempting to destroy them. But why? And how ashamed should they be that, all along, the Cassini had only been trying to help? In the end, it came down to communication. We should never forget, she resolved, that understanding one another should be the first step. We assumed an enemy. How long would it take that instinct to wash from the human program?

And during their darkest hours, she had been convinced that things always went wrong. Wasn't there a personal lesson in there for her, as well?

She reflected on her description of the final connection between Bon and the Cassini. She hadn't yet received all of the details from him, and so didn't know exactly how the exchange had played out. The Council meeting was scheduled in about an hour, and she would wait to get the story along with the others.

And isn't it ironic that, after desperately wanting to know the contents of his mind for so long, suddenly I'm not so sure. It seems to have taken another life-threatening jolt to shake me from my obsession. I still feel something for Bon. At least I think I do. But now it has become an element of my life, not the overriding fixation that it was for months. Of course, this is happening just as Bon seems to have decided to explore his feelings for me. That figures. Will we ever be on the same page at the same time?

She set down the pen, then quickly picked it back up and added one additional line.

I'm not giving up on us yet.

Triana stood, walked over to her bed, and fell onto it. Rolling onto her back, she threw an arm over her eyes and didn't move for a long time. The sleep that had eluded her began to creep in.

And her final thoughts before drifting away were natural for her.

What adventure awaited them at the mysterious edge of the solar system, the mystifying region known as the Kuiper Belt?

think a quick recap is in order right now. The ship narrowly averted disaster for the second time in four months, and the Council found a powerful helper in Hannah Ross. That's all good.

The whirlwind of romance has taken a couple of twists and turns that I just can't keep up with anymore, so I'm checking out of that scene for a while. Those crazy kids are just going to have to figure it all out for themselves. Or not.

Here's an interesting thought for you to chew on, however: If the translator truly provided an exchange of thoughts and feelings between Bon and the Cassini, wouldn't the powerful life force on Titan now be aware of the deadly assault on Earth by Bhaktul Disease? And isn't the Cassini all about helping? Hmm. Could that mean something down the road?

Galahad will soon be streaking out of the solar system. Knifing through the Kuiper Belt should be a fascinating experience, and since it is most likely the birthplace of Comet Bhaktul, I would expect some frayed emotions to rise. Let's just keep our fingers crossed that there's not another entity like the Cassini lingering out there in the cold vacuum of deep space. Or, if there is, couldn't they just ignore us as we shoot by?

I'll be busy over the next few days reprogramming the ion drive system and doing basic maintenance on the ship. Chores, really.

Although I pretty much saved the ship and everyone aboard yesterday—okay, with a little of their help—I still have my chores.

But I think I also need to keep a close watch on the crew. When it comes to getting along with one another, things have been very good. Much too good, if you think about it. How much longer can that last before something—or somebody—pushes the boundaries? Is it fair to expect that 251 teens will all agree on everything all the time?

I would say that's a no. And I expect that The Cassini Code will be just about the time that things get out of control, with the mystery of the Kuiper Belt as the backdrop.

Read on, my friend.

The warning siren blared through the halls, running through its customary sequence of three shorts bursts, a five-second delay, then one longer burst, followed by ten heavenly seconds of silence before starting all over again. There could be no doubt that each crew member aboard *Galahad* was aware—painfully aware—that there was a problem.

Gap Lee found it annoying.

He stood, hands on hips and a scowl etched across his face, staring at the digital readout before him. One of his assistants, Ramasha, waited at his side, glancing back and forth between the control panel and Gap.

"Please shut that alarm off again, will you?" he said to her. "Thanks."

Moments later a soft tone sounded from the intercom on the panel, followed by the voice of Lita Marques calling from *Galahad*'s clinic.

"Oh, Gap, darling." He sensed the laughter bubbling behind her words, and chose to ignore her for as long as possible.

"Gap, dear," she said. "We've looked everywhere for gloves and parkas, but just can't seem to turn any up. Know where we could find some?" This time he distinctly heard the pitter of laughter in the background.

"Are you ignoring me, Gap?" Lita said through the intercom. "Listen, it's about sixty-two degrees here in Sick House. If you're trying to give me the cold shoulder, it's too late." There was no hiding the laughs after this, and Gap was sure that it was Lita's assistant, Alexa, carrying most of the load.

"Yes, you're very funny," Gap said, nodding his head. "Listen, if you're finished with the jokes for now I'll get back to work."

This time it was definitely Alexa who called out from the background. "Okay. If it gets any colder we'll just open a window." Lita snickered across the speaker before Alexa continued. "Outside it's only a couple hundred degrees below zero. That might feel pretty good after this."

Gap could tell that the girls weren't finished with their teasing, so he reached over and clicked off the intercom. Then, turning to Ramasha, he found her suppressing her own laughter, the corners of her mouth twitching with the effort. Finally, she spread her hands and said, "Well, you have to admit, it *is* a little funny."

He ignored this and looked back at the control panel. What was wrong with this thing? Even though his better judgment warned him not to, he decided to bring the ship's computer into the discussion.

"Roc, what if we changed out the Balsom clips for the whole level? I know they show on the monitors as undamaged, but what have we got to lose?"

The very humanlike voice replied, "Time, for one thing. Besides, wouldn't you know it, the warranty on Balsom clips expires after only thirty days. Sorry, Gap, but I think you're grasping now. My recommendation stands: shut down the system for the entire level and let it reset."

Gap closed his eyes and sighed. Some days it just didn't pay to be the Head of Engineering on history's most incredible spacecraft. He opened his eyes again when he felt the presence of someone else standing beside him.

It was Triana Martell. At least *Galahad*'s Council Leader seemed relatively serious about the problem. "I don't suppose I need to tell you," she said calmly, "that it's getting a little frosty on Level Six."

"So I've heard," Gap said. "About a hundred times today, at least." He turned back to the panel. "Contrary to what some of your Council members think, I *am* working on it. Trying to, anyway."

Triana smiled. "*My* Council members? I'm just the Council Leader, Gap, not queen. Besides, you're on the team, too, remember?"

Gap muttered something under his breath, which caused Triana's smile to widen. She reached out and placed a hand on his shoulder. "You'll figure it out. Has Roc been any help?"

Her subtle touch was enough to jar him from his bleak mood. He felt the ghost of his old emotions flicker briefly, especially when their gazes met, his dark eyes connecting with her dazzling green. A year's worth of emotional turbulence replayed in his mind, from his early infatuation with Triana, to the heartache of discovering she had feelings for someone else, to his unexpected relationship with Hannah Ross.

Even now, months later, he had to admit that contact with Triana still caused old feelings to stir, feelings that seemed reluctant to disappear completely. Maybe they never would.

"Well?" Triana said. He realized that he had responded to her question with a blank stare.

"Oh. Uh, no. Well, yes and no."

Triana removed her hand from his shoulder and crossed her arms, a look Gap recognized as "please explain." He internally shook off the cobwebs and turned back to the panel.

"I'm thinking it might be the Balsom clips for Level Six. That would explain the on-again, off-again heating problems."

"But?"

"But Roc disagrees. He says he has run tests on every clip on Level Six, and they check out fine. He wants to shut down the system and restart."

Triana looked at the panel, then back to Gap. "And you don't want to try that?"

Gap shrugged. "I'm just a little nervous about shutting down the heating system for the whole ship when a section has been giving us problems. What happens if the malfunction spreads to the entire system?"

"Well, we would freeze to death, for one thing," Triana said.

"Yeah. So, maybe I'm being a little overly cautious, but I'd like to try everything else before we resort to that."

The intercom tone sounded softly, and then the unmistakable voice of Channy Oakland, another *Galahad* Council member, broke through the speaker. "Hey, Gap, did you know it's snowing up here on Level Six?"

Triana barely suppressed a laugh while Gap snapped off the intercom.

"I'll quit bothering you," she said, turning to leave. Over her shoulder she called out, "Check back in with me in about an hour. I'll be ice-skating in the Conference Room."

"Very funny," Gap said as she walked out the door. He looked over at Ramasha, who had remained silently standing a few feet away. A cautious grin was stitched across her face. "What are you laughing at?" he said with a scowl.

They were only chunks of ice and rock. But there were trillions of them, and they tumbled blindly through the outermost regions of the solar system, circling a sun that appeared only as one of the brighter stars, lost among the dazzling backdrop of the Milky Way. Named after the astronomer who had first predicted its existence, the Kuiper Belt was a virtual ring of debris, a minefield of rubble ranging from the size of grains of sand up to moon-sized behemoths, orbiting at a mind-numbing distance beyond even the gas giants of Jupiter, Saturn, Uranus, and Neptune.

Arguments had raged for decades over whether lonely Pluto should be considered a planet or a hefty member of the Kuiper Belt. And once larger Kuiper objects were detected and cataloged, similar debates began all over again. One thing, however, remained certain: The Kuiper Belt posed a challenge for the ship called *Galahad*.

Maneuvering through a region barely understood and woefully mapped, the shopping mall–sized spacecraft would be playing a game of dodgeball in the stream of galactic junk. Mission organizers could only manage a guess at how long it would take for the ship to scamper through the maze. Taking into account the blazing speed that *Galahad* now possessed—including a slight nudge from an unexpected encounter around Saturn—Roc told Triana to be on high alert for about sixty days.

Now, as they rocketed toward the initial fragments of the Kuiper Belt, both Roc and the ship's Council were consumed with solving the heating malfunction aboard the ship, unaware of the dark, mountainous boulders that were camouflaged against the jet-black background of space.

Boulders that were on a collision course with *Galahad*.

Tor Teen
Reader's Guide

About This Guide

The information, activities, and discussion questions that follow are intended to enhance your reading of *The Web of Titan*. Please feel free to adapt these materials to suit your needs and interests.

About the Author

Dom Testa grew up a world-traveling U.S. Air Force "brat" with a passion for radio. He got his first radio job at the age of sixteen. In 1993 he joined Colorado's MIX 100, where he now cohosts the award-winning "Dom and Jane Show." He is a frequent speaker at schools and libraries, and his passion for reading, writing, and education is profoundly evident in his Galahad books, as well as in his Big Brain Club, a website dedicated to encouraging young people to be proud of their intellectual accomplishments. He lives in Colorado.

Writing and Research Activities

I. Into the Great Unknown
  A. What does the word "unknown" mean to you? Write a definition, article, poem, or story or create a painting, model, or other visual artwork depicting your sense of the unknown. Go to the library or go online to find several definitions of "unknown" and related words, such as "uncertainty" and "knowledge." Compile your creative works and research into a collage or diorama presentation. If desired, make an illustrated list of famous quotations about the unknown.
  B. As a *Galahad* crew member, you have mixed feelings about capturing the Titan pod. Write an e-mail to Triana citing your reasons for or against capturing the pod and what you suspect it may hold. Or, with classmates or friends, role-play a conversation in which you and other crew members discuss your uncertainties and questions regarding the pod's capture and possible contents.
  C. After four months aboard *Galahad,* you have begun to have some routine in your life. Write at least three journal entries describing your daily activities, high points, challenges, your thoughts as you anticipate four-plus more years aboard the ship, and your deepest concerns about your unknown future. As you write your journal entries, consider whether having a routine makes dealing with the great unknowns in your life harder or easier.
  D. In the character of Lita, write a series of medical reports describing the headache ailment of the crew, your treatment choices, and your reaction to Bon's strange eyes and speech. As a medical professional, what do you make of this unknown "disease"?

E. On January 29, 1984, the following quotation from the late Librarian of Congress, author and scholar Daniel J. Boorstin, appeared in *The Washington Post*: "The greatest obstacle to discovery is not ignorance—it is the illusion of knowledge." Write a short essay explaining how this quote applies to Triana's reflections at the end of the novel, and to the greater ambitions of the *Galahad* project.

II. A Moon Called Titan

A. Go to the library or go online to learn more about Saturn and its moons, particularly Titan. Use your research to create an informative poster, including details on why Titan might be capable of supporting some type of extraterrestrial life.

B. Visit http://www.nasa.gov/mission_pages/cassini/main/index.html to learn more about the real Cassini-Huygens Mission to Saturn. Make a list of at least five important facts confirmed, or discoveries made, during this mission. Write an article for your school newspaper describing the Cassini-Huygens Mission and explaining why it is exciting and important. With friends or classmates, discuss the connections between your research facts and the plot and themes explored in *The Web of Titan*.

C. Learn more about the Titans of Greek mythology and their relationship to the Olympians, particularly the Twelve Olympians, during the War of the Titans. Write a short essay detailing your discoveries and relating them to your understanding of the novel. Conclude the essay with your thoughts on how the story of the Greek Titans might offer hints or insights into the events of the next installment of the Galahad story, *The Cassini Code*.

III. Reason and Romance

A. Can a computer feel? Go to the library or go online to learn more about cutting-edge research on artificial intelligence. Use your research to create an informative poster or pamphlet addressing this question. Include a short paragraph describing your understanding of Roc's "relationship" with the leaders of *Galahad*.

B. Had it not been for her relationship with Kelvin Pernice, Nina Volkov might have made it aboard the Titan pod, possibly dramatically changing the fate of *Galahad*. Write a prologue chapter to *The Web of Titan* in which you imagine the relationship between Nina and Kelvin and give more detailed reasons for her missing the pod launch.

C. With a friend or a classmate, role-play a conversation in which Gap decides to seek Channy's advice about his feelings for Hannah, Ariel, and Triana. Invite other pairs of friends or classmates to role-play the same situation. Afterward, compare and contrast the outcomes of each role-play.

D. Lita's song describes her complicated feelings about being a part of the *Galahad* mission. Think of a time when you had to make a choice or sacrifice in your life, considering what your "logical mind" felt was right versus what your heart told you. Write song lyrics describing the situation. If desired, compose music to accompany your lyrics or set them to the melody of a favorite song.

E. The *Galahad* crew begins to get a sense of the Cassini as a being with some sort of collective intelligence. In the character of the Cassini, describe yourself and your thoughts about *Galahad*, its crew, and your efforts to "improve" them.

F. Using colored pencils, modeling clay, or other craft materials, create an illustration or model of the Cassini.

Compare your creation with the works of friends or classmates. What colors, shapes, or other elements are common to some or all of the Cassini representations? Which representations are most unique and most satisfying?

G. In the character of Bon, write an extended journal entry describing the connection/relationship you had with the Cassini. What made it painful? Was there anything good about it? Why do you think your connection with the Cassini was the strongest among the *Galahad* crew? Do you hope or fear future connections? How has your connection to the Cassini affected your relationships with members of the *Galahad* crew?

Questions for Discussion

1. In the prologue to *The Web of Titan*, Roc cites "fear of the unknown" as a critical human trait. Describe the ways in which this fear plays out on different levels in the course of the novel. How does Roc provide a bridge between the unknown and the known for both the *Galahad* crew and the reader? What makes a computer the ideal character for this role in the story?

2. The opening paragraphs of chapter one describe a storm around Saturn and Titan. How does this visual description foreshadow the actual troubles that befall the crew and the discoveries they will make about Saturn's largest moon?

3. What relationship troubles in the novel's early chapters threaten to distract the crew from the critical job of capturing the pod? How does Gap respond to the attention he receives from Ariel and Hannah? Why does he react this way? Does his injured arm have any effect on his actions and choices? Explain.

4. How might you explain Triana's attraction to Bon? Is she ready for a real relationship, or is grief at the loss of her father still too powerful an emotion to make this possible? How has the death of Dr. Zimmer also affected Triana's emotional state?

5. Who discovers the beam focused on *Galahad*? What do the Council members make of this discovery? How does Roc help them deal with this challenge?

6. What do the crew members find aboard the pod? What, or who, is suspiciously absent from the vessel? Had you been aboard *Galahad,* what actions might you have suggested Triana take after opening the pod?

7. In chapter ten, Hannah begins to suspect that another life force is responsible for the energy beam. How does she react to this possibility? How do the other crew members react?

8. Throughout the novel, various crew members experience flashbacks and memories of loved ones on Earth. Are these experiences helpful or hurtful? How have four months in space begun to alter the teens' thoughts about the past and the future?

9. What, if any, relationships do you see between Lita's frustration with the headache patients in Sick House and Gap's difficulties with the ion drive power plants? How does their sense of powerlessness affect their actions and decisions? Compare the concerns for the well-being of the sick crew members to those for the safe operation of the ship.

10. What is important about Lita's friendship with Triana? In what ways do they support each other? Do you enjoy a friendship with anyone similar to that of Lita and Triana? Or do you think the pressure of the *Galahad* mission makes their friendship different from friendships in your life? Explain your answer.

11. In the beginning of chapter twenty-eight, Triana contemplates the evolution of life on Earth from dinosaurs to Homo sapiens. Do you agree with her that another life-form will succeed humans in an unbreakable cycle? Or are humans smart enough to find a way to carry on?

12. What is Lita's reaction to the headache patients' orange eyes and Bon's strange speech? Had you been a Council member aboard *Galahad*, do you think your reaction would have been similar or different? Would you have left Bon in Sick House or moved him to some sort of containment cell? Would you have tried more aggressive treatment for the headaches?

13. How does the crew finally learn about and find the translator? How does Bon make use of the device? Do you think he could have controlled it without Triana's support? Is Bon done with the Cassini now? What evidence suggests that the alien life-form's presence remains entangled with *Galahad*?

14. Do you think that *Galahad*, having endured the attack of a madman in *The Comet's Curse* and the encounter with the Cassini in *The Web of Titan*, stands a chance at completing its mission? Should the crew consider a return to Earth? Do they really have any choice but to continue? If you were aboard *Galahad*, what would be your hopes for the future at this point?

15. At the end of the novel, Triana writes in her journal, ". . . after desperately wanting to know the contents of [Bon's] mind for so long, suddenly I'm not so sure." Do the Cassini know the contents of Bon's mind? How might this mind link compare to or contrast with the connection Triana wants, or wanted, to make? Can *The Web of Titan* be read as an exploration of connections, intellectual and emotional, and their risks and rewards? Explain your answer.